# THE
# BLACKSMITH

"2019"

# THE
# BLACKSMITH

*a novel by*

**BRYAN A. SALISBURY**

# DEDICATION

*I would like to dedicate this book to my lovely and patient wife, Andrea, who I have always found a constant source of support. Her willingness to encourage me and all my endeavors has always been the rock on which I stand.*

*Also, to Mrs. Johnson, my high school English teacher, who made me promise to write a novel someday.*

# ACKNOWLEDGMENT

*To Sue Petrie, who has been an invaluable source of information and steady guidance through the publishing process. She is a skilled editor with the wherewithal to let an author's voice come through.*

# CHAPTER 1

**T**HINKING. That's what Blake Thorton did an awful lot of. Ever since leaving his family in New York, he had wandered and roamed to places that many men only dreamed of or read about in books. As his horse slowly walked down the dusty road, the rhythmic clopping of hooves helped to keep Blake's mind moving, recalling experiences that made him smile, frown, and downright angry. Most were just memories, neither good nor bad, but in their own way pieced together the chart of his life.

Blake's mind was somewhere in the South Pacific with warm ocean breezes, sandy beaches and crystal blue water when he noticed something different in his horse's gait.

"Ah, dammit Bull, what have you gone and done to yourself now?" Blake asked.

He was a big man, broad in the shoulders and narrow in the hips. He eased out of the saddle to examine what was going on with his horse. His horse was a Morgan, bred for endurance and the power needed for a hard day's work. Blake named him Buliwyf for a Viking king he had once read about, and, as was the custom of the times, shortened his name to Bull.

Bull was on the smallish side for a horse according to most westerners, but, from the first time he and Blake met, there was an immediate connection and both felt a kinship that could be difficult to explain to anybody who does not understand horses. He never let Blake down and Blake valued him far more than just about anything in his life. A lot of cowboys would laugh at this. They felt horses were a commodity, to be sold or traded, or worked until they were used up and discarded for another. But, the few who truly understood horses knew they were intelligent, loyal and many times the difference between life and death. Bull did seem to have developed a limp in his right front. Blake ran a firm but gentle hand down his shin, slightly massaging and feeling for warmth. He gently raised the hoof to discover that one of the shoes had worked its way loose and was hanging by just a couple of nails.

"Well, that's not good," Blake said with a sigh. "We are going to have to find a place to get this fixed." Normally Blake kept spare tools in his saddlebags to be able to fix this but, unfortunately, he had not been able to restock what he needed at the last town he was in. What he needed was a blacksmith, or a farm or ranch …. someplace that had the items he could make the repairs with. In the meantime, Blake took a knife from the sheath on his hip and worked the loose shoe off the rest of the way. Better no shoe than a loose one, he thought.

"Well, old son, I guess we're going to be walking for a while so let's see what's on up ahead." Bull, who had been with Blake for a long time, shook his head almost as if he agreed with him, and then rubbed his head against Blake in an effort to get rid of the flies and sweat. "Leave it to you to make me walk," Blake said. "You know how I hate to walk." Bull just blew and pricked his ears looking forward up the trail as if to say, "Well, let's get to it."

It was about mid-morning on the trail and there was not a cloud in the sky. Blake had drifted for some time and wasn't exactly sure where he was. He had crossed the Mississippi River a while ago, heading west. He was just following his nose to nowhere in particular and not in any rush. The trail was fairly wide and not too stony, so Blake took his time, trying to be careful not to bruise the bottom of Bull's foot because that could mean a great deal more walking for Blake. Scrub brush lined the trail on both sides with a few trees of good size that offered occasional shade, but the day was warm and pleasant. That "feel good" warmth that came after a hard winter was with the promise of milder more comfortable times ahead.

Blake had enjoyed a great deal of solitude of late. Not that he didn't care for people, it was just getting the chance to be able to get his head clear of some of his past. He had been born in upstate New York, brother to two older sisters and one older brother, with a set of twins, one boy and a girl, who came after him. His father owned a blacksmithing business which had always kept the family warm and fed. His mother was a task master, always keeping the children busy with work, her remedy for mischief. Though very tough, she could be equally as kind and loving. Blake always thought she was quicker to encourage with her hand than a kind word, but he never held that against her because he could be quite a handful sometimes.

Blake's father was thrilled whenever boys came along in the family because there would be help in the forge when they got old enough, and eventually, they could take over the business. Unfortunately for his father, Blake had little interest in blacksmithing, although he had a great talent for it and would use that talent to finish early with his tasks and sneak off on some young man's adventure. The more work his father had given him, the faster he finished and the better he got.

There was not a school where Blake grew up, but his mother held school at night after supper and taught all the children reading and writing, and his father taught them math. His father was known far and wide as a shrewd businessman and thought math was the most important skill to have so you didn't get cheated.

Blake was probably the best student among the children, and his mother always blamed his leaving on her teaching him to read. He was a voracious reader and read everything he could get his hands on. His favorites were sea stories, tales of adventure in faraway seas inhabited by pirates and warships in tropical settings. He knew he would go there someday, but would have to run away to do it. As he grew in size and strength, the pull of this high adventure became unbearable. The day after his sixteenth birthday, he left. He knew that it would hurt his mother and father but he felt deep inside him that he had to go. Being trapped in a forge, beating metal into submission was not ever going to satisfy his lust for faraway lands.

"Hopefully, we'll find something up ahead, boy," Blake said as he scratched behind Bull's ears. "You get to rest for a spell and I'll get a hot meal." They started up the trail and had gone about half a mile when a lone figure stepped out about a hundred feet away. Bull stopped and snorted softly. "I see him, boy," Blake said quietly. "What do you suppose he wants?"

As they stepped closer, Blake could see a short man wearing some of the worst rags he had ever seen. The man was dirty with a sour look on his face and squinty eyes. He had a long beard that probably held many different types of vermin including lice, ticks and maybe a mouse or two. His right hand rested on the butt of a Colt Walker tucked in the belt around his waist. The gun seemed to have a lot of rust and dirt on it, more than the man himself, and did not look like it had been fired in a very long time. At twenty feet away, Blake could tell by the man's odor that he hadn't even had a fleeting acquaintance with soap and water for a year.

"That there's far enough," the stranger growled. "This here is a stickup and I'll thank you kindly for keeping your hand away from that pistol!"

Amused by the man, Blake smiled at him. He always carried a Colt Peacemaker on his hip that was in immaculate condition but he felt no need to draw it at this time. "Yes, sir," Blake replied.

"We is going to make this simple," snarled the stranger. "You give over your pistol, money and anything else that's got value and I won't blow a hole through your middle."

"No," Blake said flatly.

Flabbergasted, the stranger was taken back by Blake's response.

"What in tarnation is so hard to understand, you idjut?" he roared. "Do what I told you!"

"No," Blake said calmly.

"Mister, you are wearin' on my last good nerve. Just do it!" he barked.

"Or?" Blake asked, smiling.

"I'll shoot you in your guts," exclaimed the stranger his hand tightening on the grip of his pistol.

"With what?'" Blake said.

"What do you think? With this here pistol, you peckerwood." No longer feeling he had control over the situation anymore, the stranger was trying to stand firm.

"You pull the trigger on that thing you will likely blow your fool hand off," Blake stated matter-of-factly.

"It shoots just fine, mister," the stranger replied slightly insulted.

"Then you might as well get to it then," Blake said trying to keep from laughing.

The stranger blew an exasperated breath. "Well now you done it, mister. You forced me to play my ace in the hole."

"And that is?" Blake asked.

"My friend is up in them bushes just spittin' distance away, with a fine Greener shotgun." Once again, the stranger seemed confident.

Blake hadn't expected that there might be two of them and took a quick glance around him to see if there was anyone around. The situation seemed ridiculous because if you're going to hold someone up, you would come right out with a decent firearm. He called out, "Is there someone up in those bushes?"

"Yup," a small voice said.

"Come out where I can see you." Blake's voice had a more commanding tone. "Now!"

A faint rustling came from the bushes and out came a second man looking equally disheveled, very sheepish and, as Blake expected, his hands held no shotgun. His beard was slightly longer and darker than the first and his clothes were in worse condition.

"What a fine pair of highwaymen," Blake chuckled. "Whose bright idea was this?"

"His," the second man said, keeping eyes on the dirt ten feet in front of him.

Irritated, the first man hissed, "Would have worked too if'n you could run a bluff, dummy. That's why I'm the leader of this here outfit."

"I told him it weren't gonna work," the second man hissed right back trying to stand up for himself.

"Do you two have names?" Blake asked.

"I'm Avery and this here is Hap," the first man stated. "We're kin, but our daddy said if'n we was to use our last name he would hunt us down and whup us for bringing so much shame to the family."

"Can't hardly blame him there," Blake said. "So Avery, you're the leader?"

"Hell, yeah," Avery stated proudly.

"Well, Avery, it has been my experience that the man with the most intelligence should be the man in charge, and seeing how he said your plan wasn't going to work, that's you, Hap." Hap picked up his head and looked around for a second with his eyes fixed on Blake. "And what's more, Hap, when Avery gets one of his hare-brained schemes, I want you to slap him on the back of his head to remind him of just who's in charge." Hap smiled broadly and stood up straighter. "Then Avery, I want you to say, I'm sorry, Hap, I'll never do that again." This made Hap smile even more through his crooked brown teeth and he gave a stern look at Avery.

"The hell you say, mister" shouted Avery.

Hap shot a glance at Blake and Blake looked at him as if to say, what are you waiting for? Hap struck Avery with enough force to knock Avery's mangy hat into the dirt.

"Ow, dammit, that hurt!" Avery yelled. He was not at all happy with the recent turn of events.

"What do you say?" Blake asked.

"No, goddammit, I won't!" Avery screamed. Hap struck him again. "Quit it, asshole."

"Hap is in charge now, so just simmer down and accept it," Blake said matter-of-factly.

Avery's range of emotions ran through him like a freight train. First anger, then disbelief, then he looked like he was going to cry. Finally, with a pouty look befitting a six-year-old, he said softly, "Sorry, Hap, I won't do that again."

"There you go," Blake said, pleased with the new hierarchy. Hap was pleased, too, but Blake had doubts the gang was in better hands.

# CHAPTER 2

**F**OR some reason, Blake liked these two. He didn't feel they were truly bad men, just down on their luck. He was in a quandary as to what to do with them so he stalled for time, thinking. He asked them, "Where's the closest town?"

Hap thought about it for a second and said, "MacIntyre is about two miles that away," throwing a thumb over his shoulder.

Blake said, "All right, I'm going to tell you two what we're going to do. Seeing as you two smell so bad, you're going to take me to that town. You're going to walk ahead of me and you're not going to try anything funny."

Avery had a worried look on his face and asked, "Are you going to take us to the sheriff and have us arrested?"

"I'm pondering on it some, but if you two can behave yourself, there's something I want to do. So, why don't you two turn and get going and I'll be upwind of you the whole time," Blake replied.

As they were walking, Blake considered turning them over to the sheriff but decided against it. Maybe these two just need a hand up. "What do you think, Bull?" Bull shook his head and Blake said, "Well, I'm going to try it anyway."

It was roughly two miles to town and Blake followed behind the two men, walking with Bull the whole way. As they crested over the rise of a small hill, Blake got his first look at MacIntyre. It was a simple little town with many false front buildings on the main street. Seemed like there were some nice houses with well-kept yards and, out in back of the main buildings, there were smaller houses that were not so well kept but still not ramshackle.

As they neared the town, Blake hollered out to Hap and Avery, "Hold up there, let me catch up." The two stopped with quizzical looks on their face and waited. When Blake got up to them he said, "You both pretty familiar with this town?" Whereas Hap replied, "We've been thrown out of that saloon a heap of times and spent some time in that jail yonder. Always for being drunk but not for robbing folks and such."

Blake asked, "You got a barber shop anywhere near here?"

Avery replied, "There's one next to the general mercantile. I know I smelled me some lilac water when I passed there."

"Do they have a bathtub?" Blake asked.

"Don't know," said Avery. "Ain't partial to them myself."

"Apparently," Blake said. "Let's go find out."

They walked down the street about a block and saw a sign for Dooley's Mercantile. Right after that was a red, white and blue barber pole. Blake said, "There it is. In you go, boys." He tied Bull to the hitching rail out front and scratched him behind the ears. "I'll be out in a few minutes." Bull hipshot his back leg and dropped his head slightly.

It was a typical barber shop. One chair. The barber was sitting in it reading the newspaper, not very busy. He was a well-kept man with pomade in his hair, a thin mustache and a neatly starched white shirt. When they entered the barbershop, he looked up in horror at the ghastly sight of Hap and Avery. He looked at Blake and said, "May I help you gentlemen?"

Blake, only slightly embarrassed by his company, asked the barber, "Would you happen to have bathtubs?"

"Why, yes, sir, we do. Two real nice ones. Shipped in from St. Louis last year, and only the price of five cents per bath."

Avery blustered, "Ain't taking no bath. Haven't had one in over a year. Ain't taking one now."

Blake looked at him firmly, "Would you rather have the sheriff smell you the way you are or fresh and clean?"

Hap said, "Well, umm, I could do with a bath. Are you thinking of taking us to the sheriff?"

Blake said, "No, I want to see how you clean up first, then I'll decide."

Avery said, in a low voice, "I suppose it wouldn't hurt no one, but I just want you to know I'm against it."

The barber said, "If you're intent on washing these two men, the charge will be ten cents because I'll have to change the water."

Blake said, smiling, "Fair enough, in you go, boys. I'll be back directly, don't you let these boys go anywhere when they're done. As a matter of fact, mister ahh…" And he looked at the barber and the barber said, "That would be Mr. Brady, Bill Brady."

"Alright, Mr. Brady, I'll be back directly. You take their clothes, hats, boots, everything and burn them. That ought to keep them here when they're done."

Hap and Avery stood there with their mouths open and they blustered, "Can't take our clothes. We be naked as jaybirds. Can't have the women folk seeing us like that."

"Let me worry about that," Blake stated. "Now, in you go."

Grumbling and muttering to themselves, they entered the back room where the tubs were and started to strip.

"Do the best you can with them, Mr. Brady, and when you're done, I want those beards gone and their hair short. Try to make them look respectable."

"Harrumph," said the barber. "Not much chance of that but I'll see what I can do. It may take quite some time."

"Well," Blake said thoughtfully, "A man died who was in a hurry once."

The barber shot him a puzzled look and shrugged his shoulders.

Speaking loud enough for Hap and Avery to hear him, Blake said, "You boys are going to get a haircut and shave and I don't want any trouble about it." In the back he could hear Avery muttering to himself, "Gotta' take a bath, gotta' take a haircut, gotta' take a shave. This dang fool is trying to make us into bankers." Blake was laughing to himself as he walked out the door and down the boardwalk to the general mercantile.

As Blake opened the door to the store, a small bell tinkled, announcing his arrival. A younger man looked up at him from in back of the counter and came around to greet him. He smiled and stuck out his hand and said, "Welcome. How may I help you, sir?" About the same size as Blake, he wore a pinstriped shirt with back elastic bands above the elbows. There was a pretty woman with long dark hair stocking some shelves nearby. Blake assumed she was his wife. A young girl, roughly about four years old in a gingham dress, came running over to see him. Smiling, Blake said, "Yes, I believe you can," and he shook the man's hand.

"Well sir, my name is Joshua Dooley and that is my wife, Terry, and my daughter Madeline. My son, Ethan, is over behind the counter sleeping. We just bought this store and we are trying to get the shelves stocked up. We're a little low on some things but we are expecting a shipment in any day now."

"Pleased to meet you and your family, Mr. Dooley. I need some clothes, boots and such. My name is Blake Thorton." He immediately liked them and touched the little girl on the head.

"Please call me Josh. Are the clothes for you?"

"No, for two other men," replied Blake.

"Those two I saw you taking into the barber shop? They looked like they sorely needed some fresh ones," Terry said.

"That would be them, ma'am. I'm having the barber burn the present ones."

"Probably for the best. They did look beyond repair," Terry replied. "I think I can guess what size they need, if I'm wrong we'll find some that fit."

"Obliged ma'am, I'm sure you'll do fine, and I'll need everything top to bottom including some sort of hats," Blake told her while he was looking around the store. Terry and Josh started putting together the piles of clothes and Blake began looking for some items he might need for himself. Madeline was following him when he turned and he almost knocked her over, "Whoops, sorry, little lady," said Blake catching her.

Terry came right over to see what happened and apologized to Blake, "Sorry, she can be awful curious sometimes."

"No harm done," smiled Blake.

"Would you buy me some candy, Mister?" Madeline cooed.

"Madeline!" Terry said sharply. "You leave the gentleman alone!"

Blake smiled warmly at the little girl and knelt on one knee in front of her. "Can you recite the alphabet? Because, with your mother's permission, I will buy a piece if you can. But you have to earn it."

Before her mother could say anything Madeline rattled off the alphabet without any hesitation.

Blake smiled. "How high can you count?" She got to about eighteen before she hesitated scrunching up her face. "Well, that's real good. Now ask your Mom because I think you earned a piece for your brother as well, when he wakes up."

Madeline quickly turned to her mother with pleading eyes. Terry looked at her with a disapproving eye, then she looked at Blake. He just winked at her to let her know it was alright with him.

Terry melted and said, "Just one, young lady," and she held the jar down with some bright red and white peppermint sticks in it. The young hand darted quickly in it and pulled out two sticks. "Madeline …" Terry warned, but Madeline cut her off and said, "One is for Ethan, Mommy."

"I'll take Ethan's later, missy. Now put one back." Obviously, Terry was onto her tricks. Madeline complied and put one back in the jar. She turned to Blake and said, "Thank you, Mister," and skipped off to enjoy her newly won treat.

"You're welcome, Miss," Blake called after her, but she was gone. "That is one smart little girl you got there ma'am. She's going to bear some watching."

"Don't I know it! She can be so precocious sometimes."

"Takes after her mother," Josh said teasing. "I believe I have everything for you, Mr. Thorton."

"If you're Josh, then I'm Blake."

"Alright, Blake, anything else? I mean you wanted just one set per man right?"

"That's my limit today, Josh. What do I owe you?"

"I figure ten dollars twenty five cents will cover it. I put in two belts to help the pants fit. The shoes are lace up, and freighter hats are good for general use."

"That's just fine. Say, when you mentioned that you were trying to set up, were you looking for help?" Blake asked as he took out the money and paid.

"Not really," Josh said "We're just getting started and I don't have enough money to pay anybody."

"I have an idea if you are agreeable." Blake proposed his plan and it was a little strange, but Josh agreed. Tipping his hat to Terry, Blake left the store.

* * * * * *

Blake walked back into the barbershop to check on the progress of his two miscreants. The barber came out looking somewhat frazzled. He looked at Blake and said, "Those two are something. When I tried to change the water on the one, he raised such a fuss about leaving, the other one got out of his tub and came over and cuffed him on the head. It was funny how quick he settled down and let me change the water. Anyways, they're almost done, but I still have the barbering to do."

Blake was trying not to laugh. He set the packages of clothes on a chair and took out five dollars. "Will this help?" The barber sighed and said, "It won't hurt."

"Good, now here's some clothes for them so they don't have to sit naked on your chair."

"I certainly appreciate that, I surely do," the barber said, nodding.

"Now is there a livery so I can put my horse up for the night?" Blake asked, still amused.

Pointing, Brady said, "Follow this street to the end and turn left, can't miss it." The barber was smiling now, getting the humor in the situation.

"I'll be back in a little while," and Blake left the shop. He walked over and got Bull. Walking down the street he noticed most of the people were friendly, some others eyed him with a degree of suspicion which is normal when a stranger is around. However, Blake was used to that and it didn't bother him. When he turned the corner, he found the livery just where Brady said it was. Right next to it was a building with "Blacksmith" painted across the top of the door. Great, he thought, now I can get his shoe fixed. As Blake approached the livery, a man came out pushing a wheelbarrow of horse droppings. He had been working hard due to the sweat staining his shirt. Blake waved at him and said, "Hello, is this your stable?"

"That's right, Mister. Joe Bergman is my name."

"Nice to meet you, Joe, I'm Blake Thorton. Do you have a place for my horse for tonight?"

"Sure do, just the horse or you, too?"

"Just the horse. Hopefully there's a hotel where I can stay."

"Sure is, you must have walked right by it. They are repainting the sign but I can tell you where it is," Joe said.

"That's great, I could use a soft bed tonight. I also need my horse reshod. He threw a shoe and I would like them all redone."

"That, sir, is a problem," Joe said pursing his lips. "See, the blacksmith shop is closed and I can't help you with my bad back."

"Well, if you lend me the tools I can do it then," said Blake.

"Wish I could, friend, but the bank has the keys to the shop, not that we have any shoes left. See, the blacksmith died some months back and we used them all up. This town's hurtin' for sure. Say, you ain't a blacksmith are you?"

"I've had some experience, and I can make my own shoes, but how can I get in the forge?" Once again Blake would need to use the skills his father taught him and, like so many times before, he would return to the forge.

"Just go over to the bank and talk to old, fat Weatherby and, if he's done pinching pennies for the day, he can help you," said Joe. Blake could tell Joe did not care much for the banker.

"Pretty tough, is he?" asked Blake.

"He's a carpetbagger from way back," Joe told him, "I suppose that he runs a good business, but not everyone can be one of the almighty MacIntyre's with more money than God. Some of us make a livin' two bits at a time. Not that I'm jealous, mind you, I do alright, but sometimes when times get lean, a man could use a little generosity. That would not be found in that bastard's heart."

Blake pursed his lips and said, "Well, I guess I'll go talk to him and see what I can do. You think you can take my horse, unsaddle him, rub him down good and give him a double order of oats?"

"Sure thing," replied Joe. "That'll be four bits for the rub down and oats and four bits for the night."

Blake took five dollars out of vest pocket and gave him the money along with Bull's reins. "Here you go, I don't know how long I'll be staying." He turned to walk away, but after a couple of steps, he stopped and turned back to Joe. "Say, do you work here all by yourself?"

"Yup, I do," Joe replied. "Sometimes I could use some help seeing as this damn back of mine has been givin' me fits, but I can't find someone I can get along with enough to hire 'em on permanent."

"I've got an idea that might just work out for the both us." Blake presented his plan to Joe who was very reluctant at first but said he'd try it with no promises. They shook hands and Blake headed back to the barbershop.

# CHAPTER 3

WHEN Blake got back to the shop he found Hap sitting in the waiting chair and the barber working on Avery's hair. Hap was sitting in his new clothes with his hat on his lap. Blake was awe struck on how getting a bath and a shave could change a man so. "I'll be damned," Blake said. "I wouldn't have believed it possible."

Hap looked up at him and said, "Feels kinda good. The barber put some of that lilac water in there and I smell like a meadow. Clothes fit good, too." He had on the green shirt and striped pants and probably the first pair of socks he'd seen in a long time. The boots were a worker style, just covering the ankle and with a low heel.

Avery did not seem to hold the same enchantment with the new duds. "They itch," he muttered. "And I smell like a girl." The barber stopped cutting his hair for a moment and rolled his eyes.

"Hell of lot better than when you first got here," Blake stated firmly.

"Amen," Brady chimed in. He stepped away from the chair to admire his work. "Well, Mr. Thorton, I believe you can make a silk purse out of a sow's ear." He removed the sheet from Avery and brushed him off as he stood.

"Well, you happy now?" a disgruntled Avery said. "You done made me look like a dandy." He ran his hand over his freshly shorn chin and short clean hair.

"Delighted," said Blake. "Now I can at least stand to be near you. Mr. Brady, thank you very much. You did a fine job."

"My pleasure, sir. Not often am I presented with quite such a challenge." Then he took out a broom and dustpan and started sweeping the ankle deep hair off the floor.

Blake opened the door and waved his hand to Hap and Avery. "Gentlemen, shall we go?" They both placed their new caps on their heads and went out the door onto the boardwalk. Blake followed and stood behind them.

"Are we fixin' to go down to the sheriff now?" Hap asked very quietly.

"Not just yet, boys. I'm hungry and could use a hot meal. I don't suppose you two could use some supper, could you? I'll pay."

"Hell yes!" Avery exclaimed his eyes lighting up. "Normally I won't accept no charity from no one, but ifn' you insist upon it, it wouldn't be polite to be sayin' no."

"Oh, I insist," Blake said flatly. "Is there a café around here?"

"Don't rightly know, usually we make our own grub, and it ain't all that good neither," said Hap, scratching his chin.

Blake saw an attractive woman coming toward them and stepped back to allow her to pass. "Excuse me ma'am, could you direct me to a place where we could find some dinner?"

"Yes sir, I would recommend Chrissy's." She smiled sweetly and pointed up the street. "She makes some of the best food in the territory at a reasonable price."

"Thank you ma'am, obliged," Blake said, tipping his hat. Then she continued on her way and said, "Gentlemen," and swayed easily past them. The three watched her go on her way and when she was out of earshot Avery giggled, "I think she's kinda' sweet on me."

"Yeah, right," Blake said as he pushed them both out into the street.

The three of them made their way down the street in the

direction the lady had pointed. The town was alive with people, but it wasn't crowded.

Several shops lined the boardwalk including a dressmaker, a leather store, and a bakery. Blake found the bank, but decided to wait until tomorrow to meet Mr. Weatherby. He saw a gunsmith and what he assumed to be the hotel because he had forgotten to ask Joe where it was. He could hear the tinkling of a piano toward the end of the street and saw the sign over the batwinged door calling it the Trail's End Saloon. Several horses were tied up in front and laughter and loud talk could be heard down the street. Suddenly Blake could smell the café, and it smelled delicious. His stomach growled and he realized that he hadn't had a good hot meal in over a week. His cooking on the trail wasn't bad, but couldn't compare to this. The next building down had a sign over the door announcing Chrissy's, and in smaller letters underneath, "All Welcome."

"I guess this is it, boys," and they entered the café. It was not a big place, but it could seat about thirty people with room for five at the counter. It was about half full of people of all sorts, business men, some cowboys and three drummers as near as Blake could tell by the valises sitting next to their chairs. Bright red and white checkered tablecloths were on each table with a small flower vase. It was clean and roomy with matching chairs. Obviously, the owner had a lot of pride in it. A woman came out of the rear door from the kitchen carrying plates of steaming hot food. When she saw the three of them, she said, "Sit anywhere you like, and I'll be right with you."

Blake was seldom taken back by a woman, although he could appreciate beauty. This woman was one of the prettiest he had ever seen in his life. She had long wavy blonde hair that fell past her shoulders and a flawless complexion. She was taller than most women, about five foot ten and a full figure that Venus herself would envy. Blake figured her to be about thirty or so, three or four years younger than himself. The one thing that detracted from her was a look of coldness in her eyes, something that told him that she was a no nonsense, up front, no bullshit woman who could take on anyone who got in her path. It was a quality that a beauty like her should not possess. What Blake didn't know was that Chrissy had lost her husband two years ago from a cholera outbreak in town. Life had been very hard for her since.

She set down the plates on the table near the door and came over to the three of them. "Just the three of you?" she asked curtly.

Blake hesitated for a moment and replied, "Ahh ... yes ma'am." She cocked an eyebrow at him and pointed to a table against the wall with four chairs. "Why don't you take a seat over there and I'll bring over a menu." Again her voice was not impolite but not friendly either.

"Fine," he said and they made their way over to the table and sat down, Hap and Avery on one side with Hap near the wall and Blake on the other side. Blake removed his hat and placed it on the chair next to him. He noticed Hap and Avery had not removed theirs and said, "Hats, gentlemen."

"What fer?" Avery grumbled. "My head might get cold."

"Because you're inside and about to have dinner," Blake said impatiently. They both reached up and removed their hats and Blake took them and placed them next to his.

The woman returned to the table with three menus and handed them out.

"This your place?" Blake asked with smile.

"Yup. The special today is chicken and dumplings with potatoes and carrots," she replied quickly. "You need a minute to look at the menus?"

Blake looked at Hap and Avery who shook their heads and said, "No ma'am three specials will be fine, and maybe some coffee." She grabbed the menus and headed back to the kitchen.

"I hope the food's hot, because it ain't gonna be for long ifn' she's carrin' it," Avery giggled.

"Behave," Blake warned. A minute or so passed when three cowboys strolled in. The one in the lead had an air of importance about him, like he owned the place and everything in it. The two behind him acted like they deserved respect just because they were with him. The first man had on clean clothes and a Stetson hat set on his head at a slight angle, his hands were soft and clean denoting he rarely did any real work. He wore a Colt Peacemaker on his right hip tied low and looked like he could use it. The other two men were a little dirtier but still looked like they really didn't work much either. They walked over to the table with the three drummers and just stood there, waiting. After a second or two one of the drummers noticed them and asked, "Help you, gents?"

"You're sitting at my table," said the leader.

"Sorry, sir, but this where the lady told us to sit," he replied not sure of what the problem was.

"Well, corset seller, this is my favorite table and I want you and your friends to leave." He sneered. The two behind him were doing their best to look menacing.

"See here, now," said the drummer impatiently. "We haven't finished our dinner."

The leader grabbed him by the back of his coat and stood him up growling in his ear. "You finished now?" The café got deadly quiet.

"Unhand me, sir," squeaked the drummer. Just then the lady came out of the kitchen holding a large coffee pot. She set the pot down hard on the counter and marched over to table. "Tom MacIntyre, what are you doing?" she yelled. "You will not come in here and treat my customers this way!"

"Aw, Chrissy, they were just leaving," the leader said with a big cocky grin, dropping the rumpled drummer back in his chair. "Weren't you, boys?"

A little shaken the salesman said, "I, I, suppose we were."

Chrissy never took her eyes off Tom and stated flatly, "Nonsense, sir, you haven't had dessert, and today, because of this misunderstanding, it will be on the house." Tom MacIntyre stared right back at Chrissy, his jaw set hard. "Wasn't that hungry anyway," he stated with a menacing tone. "But my father wouldn't like me to starve."

"Then perhaps he should teach you some manners, and that would be less of a problem," Chrissy said in a hard tone.

"Let's go over to the saloon, boys. The ladies are a lot more hospitable over there." Smiling, he tipped his hat toward Chrissy and strolled back out the door.

Slowly the people began to talk among themselves and started

eating again. Blake settled back down in his chair. He was starting to get up when the trouble began, but stopped when Chrissy
seemed to take charge. He wanted to see how things played out.

"Was you figurin' on takin' a hand in that?" Avery asked a
little nervous.

"Never know," Blake said quietly. "Just don't like it when people are getting pushed around."

Chrissy went over and got the coffee pot and started to top
off the customers' cups. She called toward the kitchen, "Bonnie,
three more cups please." A young girl appeared in the doorway
with the cups and Chrissy pointed at Blake's table. "Over there."
She was about sixteen years old, slim and with long brown hair
that hung down hiding most of her face. She moved quickly
and quietly to their table, set the cups down, and returned to
the kitchen without saying a word to anybody. She was obviously uncomfortable and did not want to attract any attention
to herself. As Chrissy made her way to the table Blake said to
her, "Those fellas give you much trouble?"

"Nothing I can't handle," she said sharply. "Best you mind
your own business."

"I mostly do," Blake said calmly. "Sometimes it is easier than
others." Chrissy cocked one eyebrow up and looked like she was
going to say something more but turned and went back to the
kitchen. A minute later she returned with three plates heaped
with food, one in each hand and the other balanced expertly
on one arm. When she placed the food in front of them they
wasted no time and started to dig in. The food was wonderful.
The chicken practically fell off the bone and the dumplings were
light and airy.

Blake watched Hap and Avery eat. It reminded him of wolves
attacking a buffalo carcass. He liked to watch men eat when
they were hungry, but liked it better when they were starved.
"Been awhile?" asked Blake.

"I reckon so," Hap answered around a mouthful of dumpling.

They both finished their meals before Blake was halfway
through his. Avery dropped his fork on his plate and belched
loudly. "Manners, boys," Blake said firmly. "You're not out on
the trail."

"Them was some right fine vittles, for sure," Avery said not the slightest bit embarrassed. When Blake finished his, Chrissy came over and started cleaning plates off the table. "Would you like some pie? We have apple today." Hap And Avery both nodded eagerly looking like two kids at Christmas and Blake said, "Yes ma'am, if you have enough to spare we will take a whole one. These boys seem like they could finish it off."

She went to the kitchen and returned with a whole pie, three plates and wedge of cheese. Blake cut a generous portion for himself, and then he slid it across the table. Hap cut the remainder in half and slid on to his plate while Avery just ate right out of the pan. When they were finished with that, Blake divided up the cheese and they devoured that, too.

As Hap and Avery sat back rubbing their stomachs with contented smiles on their faces, Chrissy saw they were done and was clearing the plates and asked, "Was everything all right?"

"The only thing sweeter than that pie would be a little kiss from you," said Avery with a silly grin on his face. Chrissy's eyes flashed and she drew in air to unleash her wrath. Hap slapped Avery on the back of his head.

"Ow! What was that fer?" he said loudly. "I didn' mean nuttin.'" Hap shot him a very firm look and then looked at Chrissy and then back to him. Avery looked down at table and said quietly, "Sorry, ma'am, I won't do that again." Blake leaned back and smiled. Chrissy, not knowing what do, said, "Well…I, I…guess," though still beside herself she continued. "That will be two dollars.

Blake stood and took four silver dollars out his pocket and handed them to her. "Two for the lunch, two for my companion's rudeness." He placed his Stetson on his head and gave Hap and Avery theirs. Touching the brim of his hat he said, "Ma'am," and started walking for the door. Hap and Avery both touched the brims of their hats and followed close behind. Chrissy stood there watching Blake until he was gone. She cocked her eyebrow once more, dropped the money in her apron and went about her business.

\* \* \* \* \* \*

They stepped onto the boardwalk and felt the air. It was cooler now and the shadows were getting longer. Blake checked his pocket watch. It was about four o'clock. He wondered if the barber would still be open so he could get cleaned up himself. Avery said, "A little snort sure would be tasten' good about now."

"I will give you fifty cents each, to go over to the saloon. You can't get into too much trouble with that. You boys are set up to sleep in the loft of the livery tonight. Mr. Bergman said he would lend you some blankets and such. I'm going to go and get cleaned up and turn in myself. Meet me here at dawn for some breakfast because you're going to have a long day tomorrow."

"Livery!" Avery griped. "Where you fixin' to bed down?"

"In the hotel," Blake said.

"Why can't we stay there?" Avery whined.

"Because you have no money, and I don't imagine you even have a blanket to sleep under. If that doesn't meet your needs, I hear the jail cots are real comfortable." Blake had a cold look on his face that said the conversation was over.

"A beer and soft hay to sleep on sounds right good to me. Thank you, Mr. Thorton," Hap spoke up. He looked like he was going to cuff Avery again. Blake looked at Avery and said, "Well?"

"Bettern' jail, I figure," Avery grumbled.

Blake handed Hap a dollar. "See you in the morning then." Blake turned down the street and headed for the barbershop. He could hear Avery trying to get the dollar from Hap and Hap not relenting. They bickered until they were out of earshot. "Hope this works," Blake said to himself. He figured he had about a fifty/fifty chance. Blake entered the barbershop just as Brady was finishing with a customer. "Got time for one more?" he asked. The barber smiled. "Yes sir, Mr. Thorton. The wife doesn't serve dinner till six o'clock."

"Bath, too?"

"No problem, I still have some water on the stove. You head in and I will be right with you."

Blake wished he had gotten some clean clothes from his saddlebags but he could change when he got to the hotel. The bath felt great, Blake always enjoyed being clean. It was something his mother had insisted on in his younger days. When he was done he got dressed and went out and sat in the chair. Bill went to work trimming his hair. "Those two you brought in here earlier," Bill asked. "What was that all about?"

"Had a little trouble with them on the road into town today. I guess I figured they were lost souls who needed a hand up. I think a man acts more respectable if he looks more respectable."

Bill leaned the chair back and placed a warm towel on Blake's face to soften his beard while he started working up the lather in his shaving mug. He removed the towel and lathered up Blake's chin. As he started to shave him he said, "I hear what you're saying about looking respectable, but I know a few neat, clean men who haven't got a respectable bone in their body."

"As do I, Mr. Brady. Just thought I'd give it a shot."

"That's very Christian of you. I wish you luck." Bill was finished and removed the sheet from Blake. Blake stood up and Bill brushed off the remaining clippings.

"What do I owe you?" Blake asked reaching in his pocket.

Bill held his hand up and said, "For what you paid me this morning, and what you're doing for those two fellas, we're square."

"Appreciate it." Blake shook his hand and left the shop. He walked over to the livery and picked his saddlebags and rifle. After he checked on Bull, he made his way to the hotel. It wasn't real fancy but it was clean. Strolling up to the desk he saw the clerk, a small skinny man with a face that reminded Blake of a weasel. The man seemed irritated that Blake had interrupted the life-and-death task that he was working on. "Yes, sir," the weasel said in a huffy voice.

Blake could abide some rudeness in people but this man jangled his nerves. He threw his dirty saddlebags on the counter creating a dust cloud, causing the little man to cough. "Got any rooms?" Blake said shortly.

"A hotel full of them," the man replied, obviously bothered.

"I will be needing one for the night, facing the street. How much?" Blake leaned in close to the little man.

"Five dollars a night, sir," he answered not giving Blake an inch.

"A little steep, isn't it? Is it clean?" Blake was toying with him now.

"I assure you, sir, all our rooms are extremely clean," then looking at Blake and his saddlebags. They should exceed your expectations."

"I hope so, I have very high standards."

"Room 208 then. Please sign the register." He spun the book around for Blake to sign. Blake signed with an illegible scrawl and set twenty dollars on the counter.

"I'll get your change, sir," the clerk replied.

"Keep it," Blake said with a slight growl in his voice. "I've enjoyed our conversation so much I may stay a bit longer."

"As you wish, sir." The clerk replied in a snippy tone and handed Blake the key. Blake took the key firmly and grabbed his saddlebags off the counter. He picked up his rifle and headed for the staircase.

"If you wish to dine in our dining room," the weasel called, "we insist on clean attire."

"I'll just bet you do," Blake said flatly without turning around. He found the room with no trouble and went in. "Damn," Blake thought, "it is nice." It was spacious and neat. It had a large bed with a comfortable quilt and a dresser with a porcelain wash basin. Two clean white towels sat next to the basin and several framed pictures hung on the walls. Blake opened the windows to allow fresh air in and took off his dirty clothes. Lying down on the bed he took a nap. It had been a long day. A couple hours later, he woke. It was dark now and lights from the street filled his room with a warm glow. Blake lit the small lamp next to the bed and dug his pocket watch out of his vest. Nine o'clock. He felt a little restless, like a shot of whiskey or maybe brandy might be just the thing to settle him down. Finding his clean clothes in his saddlebags, he put them on, strapped on his gun belt and headed downstairs. The weasel was still behind the counter and said in a snotty tone, "Is your room satisfactory?"

"Tolerable," Blake said flatly and kept walking out the front door.

\* \* \* \* \* \*

Blake strolled down the boardwalk toward The Trail's End saloon. He stopped at the batwing door and took a look around. Some places this far west could be pretty rough, a place for thugs and cutthroats, while others could be quite posh. Blake tried to avoid dives because he rarely was hunting trouble and the really nice places he just couldn't settle into. As luck would have it, this was a nicer place with a mahogany bar and a shiny brass foot rail. A large mirror hung in back of the bar. It had a clean looking bartender wiping down some beer mugs. About a half dozen men were leaning against the bar talking and laughing, some were occupied with a few of the girls in bright dresses showing as much of their fair skinned bodies as they could. There was a small man playing the piano on the far wall. He wasn't very good. An enormous man sat at the end of the bar in a high chair. He was very tough looking with a permanent scowl on his face. He wore a heavy beard with long hair, Blake guessed he was about six foot eight or nine and weighed about three hundred fifty pounds. He was definitely a bruiser.

The place had six tables and half of them were occupied; most all of them had a card game going. Blake was a fair hand at cards, but shied away if the game took a serious turn. Low stakes and just for fun, that's what he liked. He made his way in and settled at the end of the bar. As he looked around at the tables, he noticed Tom MacIntyre and the two men from the café earlier. Tom had his hat pushed back and was studying his cards. One of the other men took notice of Blake and tapped Tom's sleeve, nodding in Blake's direction. Tom glanced up quickly and looked back at the other man shrugging his shoulders.

"What'll it be, mister?" the bartender asked in a friendly voice.

"Shot of your best whiskey and beer," Blake replied.

"The good stuff is a dollar a shot, if that's alright, sir."

"That's fine," Blake said, and threw a five on the bar. The bartender smiled and reached under the bar and pulled an ornate bottle and poured the shot. Blake took a sip and marveled at the smooth taste and character of the whiskey. He had had the rotgut that most cowmen drink and decided if he couldn't afford the good stuff then he would have none at all. Savoring the warmth of the whiskey, his eyes scanned the bar until they met the eyes of a very well dressed man looking back at him. The man smiled, picked up his drink and sauntered over to Blake. He wore immaculate clothes, black pants and coat with a starched white shirt and a string tie. His boots were highly polished and a flat crowned Stetson sat on his head at a slight angle. He was a handsome man, the type women swoon over. Blake did not see a gun but would bet he had one hidden somewhere.

"Good evening, sir," he said in a smooth voice. "New in town?"

"Just got in today," Blake said politely.

"I noticed you ordered the better whiskey. You are a man with tastes for the finer things. My name is Daniel LaClare, Dan to my friends," he held out his hand for Blake to shake it.

Blake shook it and smiled, the man had hands as smooth as his demeanor, friendly tone and a disarming smile. A gambler Blake guessed. "Pleased to meet you. Blake Thorton."

"Perhaps you would care to indulge in a friendly game of cards?" Dan asked, smiling. He had the look of the cat about ready to pounce on a mouse.

"Maybe later. I think I will just enjoy my drink and relax for a while."

"Alas, I don't think I will tarry much longer, it seems difficult to get a table together and I grow weary," Dan said in a disappointed voice. Then he took a cheroot from his breast pocket and lit it.

"Yup, but the night is young and if you let me have one of your cigars, we can enjoy a drink together."

Dan smiled and reached in his pocket and gave Blake a cigar. Blake lit and inhaled deeply. He really enjoyed a good smoke with whiskey. "Two more, please," he called to the bartender

"Right away, sir," the bartender called back. After the bartender left the drinks, Dan picked his up and took a sip. "Nectar of the Gods, thank you. Now what would you like to talk about?"

"How long you been in town, Dan?" Blake asked casually.

"Oh, about a month, but I am considering moving on. There is not much excitement in this town, with little hope of replenishing my purse."

"What do you know about Tom MacIntyre?" Blake asked in a low voice.

"He would be the reason to move on. Bad sort, Blake, bad sort. He likes to play cards but does not care to lose. If he has a failing night at cards he will take a nasty turn and accuse everyone at the table of cheating. Mind you, sir, I do not cheat. My profession is gambling. I do not have to cheat." Dan told him in an equally low voice. "A few nights ago, Lady Luck was smiling upon me. I was forced to leave the table with just a few dollars because Mr. MacIntyre accused me of impropriety. I have not been able to get a decent table together since."

"That's too bad," Blake said. "Sometimes you win and sometimes you don't. What does the sheriff think about what he did?"

"Ah, there's the rub, my friend, Tom's father owns the biggest ranch in the territory and has amassed a great amount of wealth. In a small town such as this it would be unwise to … piss him off." Dan smiled. Blake got his full meaning.

"Living on Daddy's coat tails and is a spoiled piss-ant," Blake said flatly.

"I believe you have the gist of it, sir, but make no mistake, he's a dangerous piss-ant," Dan warned.

"Hmm," Blake said and finished his beer. "Well, Dan, it has been a pleasure. I'm going to turn in." Blake stood and shook his hand.

Dan smiled, "Staying at the hotel?"

"Yup."

"Pleasant little snake at the desk over there, isn't he?"

"He reminded me more of a weasel," Blake replied. They both laughed and Blake left.

# CHAPTER 4

**B**LAKE slept peacefully that night and woke early as the sun was causing the night sky to turn gray with streaks of yellow. It promised to be another fine warm day. He rose and went over to the basin. After washing the sleep out his eyes, he dressed, buckled on his gun belt and headed downstairs. The air was cool and refreshing. Blake yawned and started over for Chrissy's. People were starting to come out and go about their day. Josh Dooley was sweeping off the boardwalk in front of his store and gave Blake a wave, "Morning," he called out. Blake waved and called back, "Morning, Josh."

He was just about to the café and was wondering if Hap and Avery were going to show, when the two of them rounded the corner from the livery. Blake had serious doubts if they would come or if they had took off for the tall and uncut. "Morning, boys," he said as they got closer. "How'd you sleep?"

"Weren't no featherbed like the hotel, but I'm guessin' it were alright," Avery grumbled.

"You shore snored enough for it bein' jest alright," Hap chimed in. "Dreamt I was bein' et by a bear."

Blake smiled and said, "How about some breakfast?"

29

"Can't speak for ol' sourpuss here, but I'd be obliged," Hap said grinning.

"Suppose vittles won't hurt none," Avery grumbled some more.

"All right, then," Blake said and they went in the diner.

Chrissy was there looking fresh and prettier than ever. She gave Blake a slight smile which made her more attractive. "Sit where you like, boys. Coffee?" she asked.

"Please," Blake said and they took the same seats they had yesterday.

"Three coffees, Bonnie," she called out. The same young woman came out quickly with the cups and a large pot. Again she would not look at them. Blake got a slightly better glance at her this time. Through the long hair he could see blue eyes and a thin tight mouth. What he noticed this time was a thin scar that ran down the side of her face from the corner of her eye almost to her lip. He felt something bad had happened, he didn't know what, but it didn't look like an accident.

"Thank you," Blake said as she poured.

"Welcome," she replied in a whisper and hurried back to the kitchen.

"What can I get you?" Chrissy asked in her usual curt tone. "The special this morning is hotcakes with eggs and bacon."

"That sounds fine." Blake had a big smile on. He was trying to get Chrissy to cock her eyebrow at him. He didn't know why but it amused him.

It worked. She strutted back into the kitchen and returned with plates piled high with scrambled eggs, hotcakes and bacon, all piping hot and smelling delicious. The three of them dug into the food and, again, Hap and Avery ate like they had been starving for weeks.

"I could get used to this," Avery said around a mouthful of eggs.

"Umm hmm," Hap agreed.

"Well, gentlemen, that brings me to why I asked you here. I don't think you two are bad men, I think you got on the wrong trail because of some bad ideas," Blake said, looking directly at Avery. "I arranged for work for both of you. What you have is a chance to make something of yourselves. Either that or we can go down to the jail and talk to the sheriff. It's your choice." They both stopped eating and looked at each other.

"Jobs," Avery said almost choking. "I ain't never really had no payin' job before. I ain't so sure I cotton to it all that much."

"At the rate you two were going, you were going to end up in jail or worse. I'm giving you a chance. Take it or leave it," Blake said matter-of-factly.

"Mr. Thorton, I'll be takin' you up on it. I'm clean and fed for the first time in a long while. I plumb forgot how good that felt," Hap said firmly. "I don' got no idea why you're doin' this but I ain't gonna look a gift horse in the mouth. I'm in and ifn' my dimwit brother had the sense God give a goose, he would, too."

"Damn, Hap, work?" Avery looked like he had been gut shot.

"Hell yeah," Hap stated.

"How long does we have to do this?" Hap asked, still unsure.

"You're set up for one month. Come to work sober every day, and no stealing," Blake said. "If you work hard and keep your noses clean, maybe they will hire you on permanent. No promises. After that you're on your own. What'll it be?"

"I'll not bring you any shame. I'm in," Hap said. "Well, Avery, what you thinkin'?"

"Well seen' as you're the leader now," Avery said in a mocking tone, "I guess I can do it for a month."

"It's settled then," Blake said. "I will set you up with a tab at Chrissy's so you can use your money to find a better place to stay and get yourself some more clothes. Just don't get too fat eating her cooking," Blake said with a chuckle in his voice.

"Boy, howdy, ain't that the truth," Hap said smiling.

After they finished breakfast, they got up to leave. "Wait for me outside," Blake said. He made his way over to the counter where Chrissy was refilling coffee for some other customers. "Need a minute of your time, ma'am," Blake said politely.

"What can I do for you?" Chrissy asked with the same terse tone she always seemed to have.

There was something about this woman that intrigued Blake. He wondered if this was just her makeup or if she wore an attitude like a shield. "Have I done something to offend you? Because normally someone needs to know me better before I piss them off so bad," Blake said smiling. One of the cowboys at the counter choked on his coffee and laughed.

"No sir, she's always pissed off," he said laughing.

Chrissy's face turned a bright red and her eyes flashed with anger. "Perhaps," she said with a slight growl in her voice that quelled any laughter. "If you would take that smart-aleck smirk off your face, you could see that I am very busy and I have no time for shenanigans or flirtations."

"Damn, I like her," Blake thought. The look in her eyes and color in her cheeks made her all the more appealing. "Well then, I will try to be more serious, ma'am," Blake said. He was still smiling a little but he couldn't help it. "I have a business proposition for you."

"And that would be...?" she growled back.

"Those two men I have brought in here a couple times, I would like to run a tab for their meals. Or I can pay up front, whatever you want."

"Tabs are not the way I like to do business, people can get forgetful and I suffer. Seeing as how I just met you and don't know if you are trustworthy, I think I would prefer payment up front." She had a good point, Blake thought.

"But how can I be sure I can trust you?" Blake asked still with a devilish smile.

"Because you approached me," she said not wavering.

"Fair enough. How much?"

"How long?" she shot back.

"One month."

"They seem to have hearty appetites, I'll probably lose money," she said. "Sixty dollars."

"Fifty," Blake said. "They might not eat every meal here."

"Then I will keep track of each meal until that money runs out. Sixty," she said firmly.

"Seeing as you are willing to go to the trouble to do that, I'm agreeable," Blake said taking out three twenty dollar gold pieces and gave them to her. "It has certainly been a pleasure doing business with you." Once again Blake smiled, the smile that got under her skin, and he tipped his hat and headed for the door. When he reached the door he turned to look at her once more. She was looking back at him with her eyebrow cocked. He laughed to himself and joined up with Hap and Avery.

\* \* \* \* \* \*

Blake's plan was to set up Hap to work at the mercantile with Josh Dooley and his family, and Avery over at the livery. He thought by splitting them up they might do better. He wasn't sure and still thought his odds were about fifty/fifty that they might find a better way to live. He knew that it could be a difficult thing to change but these two had hit rock bottom with no prospects. Maybe this would help, maybe not. It was up to them now; Blake had done all he could. He didn't know why he did things like this, maybe he was atoning for some of his own past sins, or maybe it was the fact he had hit rock bottom himself and knew what it was to be hungry, dirty and cold. He remembered how lonely that was. How he felt shame. Most of all, how hard it had been to pull himself up and be a man. He had accepted the kindness of strangers before and knew that to honor what they had done for him could only be repaid by passing the same kindness to others.

Hap seemed to be a good fit for the store. He was humble and polite with the Dooley's and set right to work. Madeline took charge and led him by the hand to show him where everything was in the store. He was kind and gentle with her and seemed to like children. Avery waited outside while Blake introduced him to the family. "Are we all set then?" Blake asked Josh.

"Yessir," Josh replied. "We can't thank you enough."

What Hap and Avery didn't know is that Blake had fronted Josh and the livery man a month's wages for the two, with the understanding that it was for one month. No strings attached. If either of the two men didn't work out then they could let them go and keep the money for the wages. All he asked was for them to be given a chance.

When Blake left to take Avery down to the livery, Avery asked, "Where you takin' me then?"

"To the livery to work for Joe Bergman," Blake said.

Avery seemed annoyed. "Why does I have to shovel horseshit while Hap gets a clean store?"

"Because you and Joe seem to be better suited for each other. Plus I didn't think you would care for being around kids that much," Blake said flatly.

"Maybe you got yourself a point there. Hap never cared for my cussin' around youngers," Avery said scratching his chin.

Joe Bergman was less enthusiastic about taking Avery on, but he needed the help and showed Avery what he wanted him to do. They disappeared into the stable both grumbling under their breath. Blake turned to leave and suddenly heard Joe burst out laughing and said, "Good one, Avery," then they were both laughing.

"Maybe this might work," Blake said to himself.

Blake rounded the corner up the main street. He checked his pocket watch and saw it was about eight o'clock. "Well, let's go see if the bank is open," he said to himself.

As Blake was walking up the main street to the bank he heard a strange clacking noise coming from an alley between two buildings. What he saw next was a mystery to him, because it appeared to be a young man hitting a dog with a rock, except the dog didn't appear to be hurt or mind in any way. The dog just sat patiently waiting for the boy to finish. His curiosity getting the better of him, Blake moved closer to get a better look at what going on. As he got within a few feet, the boy suddenly realized he was there and jumped back startled. "Whatcha doing there, son?" Blake asked.

The boy appeared to be sixteen or maybe seventeen with very dirty blond hair that hung down in his eyes. His clothes were ratty and too small for him. He looked like he hadn't had a decent meal in quite some time. His fingers were raw from beating two stones together trying to separate a piece of rope that was tied around the dog's neck. "T-t-t-t-rying t-t-t-o b-b-b-break," the boy stammered. Obviously the boy had a stuttering problem.

Blake had heard of this before, and he didn't want to try to finish his sentence for him, so he asked, "Would you like to borrow a knife?" The boy nodded his head up and down quickly. Blake always carried a smaller knife on his belt on his left hip in front because he found it very useful for quick cutting jobs such as this. Removing the blade with his left hand, he held it out handle first to the boy. "Careful now, it's pretty sharp," Blake warned.

The boy gently took the knife and carefully cut the rope off the dog, who promptly started licking his face. He started to rub the dog's neck examining where the rope had rubbed a sore on it. He started to hand Blake back the knife, but held it a little longer to admire it. "Th-th-th-thanks," he said sheepishly.

As Blake took the knife back and returned it in its sheath, he continued to study the boy. Although he wasn't much to look at, he seemed polite enough and liked animals, so he couldn't be all bad. "What's your name?" Blake asked with a little smile.

Still not wanting to look Blake in the eyes the boy held his head low and stammered, "C-c-c-c-aleb."

"Fine name, son," Blake said holding out his hand for the boy to shake. With a suspicious look on his face Caleb shook his hand, but it was very timid and weak. Blake smiled, "When you shake a man's hand let him know you're there. Don't be shy about it and look him in the eye." Caleb grasped his hand a little firmer and briefly looked at Blake. "Well, it's a start," Blake mused.

Then a thought struck Blake. "Don't you own a knife?" The boy shook his head and stared at the ground. "A man should have a knife," Blake stated. "Never know when the need will arise." Blake knelt down on the ground and pulled up his pant leg over his boot. He pulled out a knife in a sheath almost exactly like the one he wore except it had a metal clip to hold it in place. He held it out to Caleb. "Here, you can have my spare," he said.

Caleb didn't raise his hand to take it but kept his head down and said quietly, "C-c-c-ccan't p-p-p-pay."

"I didn't ask for money, boy. It's a gift. You did a good turn for that dog and now I'm gonna do one for you." Blake held out the knife and just when he thought Caleb wasn't going to take it, Caleb slowly raised his hand and gently accepted the gift.

"W-w-w-what's y-y-yy-your n-n-name M-m-m-mister?" Caleb stammered.

"Blake Thorton," Blake replied, grinning broadly now.

"T-t-t-thanks," Caleb said and held out his hand to shake Blake's. Blake grinned and took his hand. The grip was much firmer this time and Caleb looked him straight in the eye.

"Well, I best be on my way," Blake said. "Take care now." The boy turned and ran down the alley with the dog right on his heels.

* * * * * *

The bank seemed to be opened because Blake saw people entering and leaving as he approached it. He made his way up the short steps when the door opened and out stepped Tom MacIntyre with the two same men who seemed to follow him around like puppies. Blake and Tom met face to face and just stared at each other.

"Going in the bank, mister?" Tom asked with a sneer to his voice.

"Seems like," Blake said.

"And what business do you have in there?" challenged Tom.

"My own," Blake replied. Blake knew when he was being pushed and felt his anger rise.

"Now what would a drifter want in our fine bank?" Tom sneered. "You planning on robbing it, are you?"

"Now that thought never occurred to me," Blake said. Then he smiled slightly, "But if I was, I sure hope you would be the first one to try to stop me."

Tom was taken back a little, but recovered quickly. "I've seen you around town. We're just trying to keep out troublemakers."

"I bet. It seems as though this town has all the troublemakers it needs."

"I don't think I like you," growled Tom.

"And I damn sure don't care. Now are you going to let me pass, or should we go see the sheriff and find out why you are being an asshole?"

They stared at each other for a few seconds. Blake knew he had embarrassed Tom in front of his men and Tom knew there was no backup in Blake. Tom gave Blake an evil grin and slowly stepped aside saying, "I'll be watching you, boy," with the emphasis on 'boy.'

"I'm ten years your elder, boy," Blake replied, putting the same tone on 'boy.' "You might want to keep that in mind." Blake gave all three men a hard look and walked by them into the bank. As he went in and had his back to them he listened close to make sure they left. The three of them seemed like the type to jump a man from behind. Blake tried to shake off the anger; he knew Tom MacIntyre and his kind. His type was always strutting around like they were kings. Intimidation was their weapon, and most people cowed to it. He could be dangerous if cornered, because if a man actually stood up to him, he would try to do something to save face. Usually, something stupid.

Blake eased the look on his face and studied the bank. There were three teller windows, all with bars. Two of them had a man dressed in a pinstriped shirt helping customers. One guard sat in the corner with a shotgun on his lap. He looked like an older gent and appeared to be taking a nap. A large, fat man sat behind a huge desk with stacks of papers on either side. As he scribbled in a ledger book Blake could see his jowls shake over his tie. He was practically bald and wore thick, wire rimmed glasses. Guessing that he must be Weatherby, Blake walked over to his desk.

"May I help you?" the man asked, looking over his glasses.

"Hopefully you can. My name is Blake Thorton." Blake held out his hand. "Would you be Mr. Weatherby?"

"I am," he said and gave Blake a sweaty, limp handshake.

"I understand you hold the keys to the blacksmith shop."

"I do," he said. "Are you answering the advertisement I sent out for opening up the shop we have in town? We surely need one here."

"No I'm not, I was just passing through and my horse needs to be reshod. Seeing as no one can help me, I was wondering if I could have use of the forge."

"Damn," Weatherby said throwing his pen on the desk, "I put out that notice six months ago and not even a nibble. Well, the rental fee is five dollars day."

"Kind of steep, isn't it? I only need it for a couple hours," Blake said back.

"You will have use of the tools and materials in there and mind you I have complete inventory of all that is in there so don't get light fingers," Weatherby said, using a very business-like tone. "And, the fee is what it is to try to recoup back taxes."

Blake was amused by the fact Weatherby knew what was in there. He doubted if he knew the difference between a fullering hammer and chainlink tongs. Well, no matter, he needed the forge and he had the money. "Fine," Blake said and gave him five dollars. Weatherby slid out the drawer in front of his enormous belly, got the keys and handed them to Blake.

"Have you ever run a forge?" he asked as Blake got up.

"Born and raised in one," Blake replied smiling.

"Are you sure you don't want to open for business? The town is desperate for a good blacksmith," he asked.

"Nope," Blake said and left the bank.

# CHAPTER 5

T HE condition of the blacksmith shop was deplorable. Tools and scrap metal were thrown haphazardly inside the door. If anyone else had rented it, they didn't take much care in putting things back. The lock was on the side door where Blake entered and a big sliding door was barred from the inside. Blake made his way over to the big door. After lifting the bar off, he slid the big door open. The wheels squeaked and groaned from lack of use. Light filled the large building and showed years of neglect. Two pigeons made a hasty retreat out of a bucket-sized hole in the roof. The roof itself was sagging in the middle where one of the support beams had broken. Dust and grime covered the anvils, benches and just about everything in the forge that wasn't covered by pigeon crap.

Blake knew that a forge was not a clean place to work, coal dust and smoke can collect everywhere and the slag from working metal was always covering the floor. Blake's father had always insisted that at the end of every day all the tools be returned to their proper place and the benches and floors were swept. If his forge was not kept orderly there would be hell to pay ... a lesson Blake was taught more than once.

There was a big shop anvil placed on a wooden block in the middle of the building. A smaller one was near the door. The smaller anvil was mounted on a stump that could be taken outside to shoe horses or do light jobs. A small forge with a crank style blower was sitting next it. Blake gave the crank a spin. Dust and coal ash flew up from the tuyere. A least that works, Blake thought, because without good airflow a forge is useless.

Blake took off his hat and vest and hung them on a hook near the door. He found a leather apron hanging close by and put that on. Rolling up his sleeves, he looked around for the tools he needed, most of which he found on the floor. One set of tongs was rusted and would not open. "I can fix that," Blake said to himself. He picked up the smaller anvil and set it outside and then carried the small forge out and placed it near the anvil. Picking some of the clinker out of the forge, he made a small well above the grate for the air exhaust. Then he placed some paper and kindling wood in the center. Reaching in his shirt pocket he took out a Lucifer, struck it and lit the paper. As the fire grew, he began moving the drier pieces of coal onto the fire while gently turning the blower. Soon the fire began to build and smoke quite a bit. But that was normal until the fire gets hot enough to eat the smoke. Blake recognized that smell, it was a smell from his childhood, from the ship he sailed on, the rear lines of battles from the War Between the States and the many places he used his skills in between.

Blake's father had been right, he said, "A skill like this will always provide for you. Smithing is always in demand." Blake had turned away from blacksmithing, not because he didn't like the work, he just wanted to see what the world had to offer. As fate would have it, he always seemed to end up back in a forge. It was home to him, familiar and comforting.

Once the fire seemed to be going strong he added green coal to the outside. The fire was burning bright and strong now and about ready to start heating metal. He placed the tongs that were frozen shut in the fire. They turned a dull cherry red and Blake pulled them out and started working the jaws open and closed. Every time he moved them it got easier until they moved freely. "That'll work," he said.

Blake had made hundreds of horseshoes in his life, for all sizes and shapes of horses. He had found the appropriate bar stock for Bull's shoes and placed a long length in the fire. Placing a hot cutter in the hardy hole of the anvil he placed the bright orange heated metal and cut pieces into the appropriate lengths. That was when he noticed he was drawing a crowd. In every small town or big city, the ringing of an anvil can be heard. Blacksmiths did not just shoe horses; they manufactured everything from forks and knives to parts for farm equipment. Blake had made hinges, chains, latches for doors, he had fixed wagons and plows and made just about every tool there was. MacIntyre had been lacking that sound for a long time. When people heard the ring of the anvil it was like a church bell to them. They wondered if a blacksmith had decided to reopen the shop and if they could have their things repaired or made.

"Are you the new smith?" a rather large woman asked excitedly. "I need some pot hooks repaired."

"I've got some busted shovel heads that could use some fixin,'" piped up a short man with a derby hat.

Another man called out, "We ain't had a horse shod for two months. When can you get to 'em?"

"Whoa, whoa, whoa, people," Blake said holding up his hand, "I'll just have the shop for the day. My horse needed shoeing and then I'm going to move on."

The mood in the crowd deflated like a balloon. "Damn," the man in the bowler said. "Say, would you be willin' to shoe just a couple of them? I'll pay for it."

A few people stood there with expectant eyes and Blake hated to let them down. He said, "Sorry, if I do it for you, I would have to help everybody."

"Dammit to hell, we sure could have used you," he turned and walked away kicking at a clod of dirt.

"Ain't your responsibility," Joe Bergman said. He had been standing behind Blake since the crowd showed up.

Blake turned a little startled. "Didn't see you there, Joe."

Then he said, "I grew up a blacksmith, and I know there is a powerful need for one in a town like this."

"You're right about that. I'm sure one will come along. You want me bring out your horse?"

"I'd be obliged."

Joe turned and called into the livery, "Avery, fetch Mr. Thorton's horse out here, will ya?"

Blake could hear grumbling inside, "Too lazy to get his own damn fool horse, I'm guessin'."

Blake smiled and asked, "How's he working out?"

"Just like the man who jumped off a ten story building in Chicago," Joe laughed. "Every time he passed a window he said, 'so far, so good.'"

Blake and Joe had a good laugh over that. "Well, I appreciate you taking him on," Blake said.

"He works alright, and his grousin' reminds me of my granpappy. Makes me laugh, it does," Joe said shaking his head. Then he returned to the livery.

Blake finished putting the shoes on Bull. Scratching him behind the ears he asked, "That better, old son? They treating you all right?" Bull shook his head up and down and nibbled in Blake's hand. "I swear you understand me sometimes." Blake had been thinking that with all this spare time left he could make another knife to replace the one he gave Caleb. He tied Bull up to the hitch rail and went into the forge to see if he could find some tool steel to make another knife. When he returned with a suitable piece he noticed a can of peaches sitting on the anvil. "Now where did they come from?" he muttered to himself, picking up the can. "Strange," he said. "Do you know who left these?" he asked Bull. Bull looked at him and blew. "You know, I'm getting tired of you not answering me," Blake chuckled. "Well I do love peaches." Setting the can on the anvil he opened it with his knife. Popping half a peach into his mouth, he savored the sweetness. He was sitting on the anvil when Hap came around the corner. He had a white apron on, looking very much like a store clerk. He approached Blake with a strange look on his face.

"Excuse me, Mr. Thorton, you seen a young scalawag runnin' thro' here?"

"No I haven't. What's the problem?"

"First day on the job, an' I gets stole from. Mr. Dooley tol' me not to fret, but figgered I could catch him. Chased him awhile but I went and lost him comin' this way."

"What did he steal?" Blake asked.

"Can of them peaches," Hap said pointing at Blake's can.

With that, a tremendous racket came from the livery. "What the hell! Come back here!" Avery was yelling at someone and, by the sounds of it, tipping over everything in the livery. Caleb came running out of the barn as fast as his legs would carry, with Avery close behind.

"That's him!" Hap shouted and jumped in front of the boy. Caleb tried to jump to his right but Avery tackled him around the legs. All three went down in a heap. Blake got off the anvil and started to untangle the bodies.

"All right, simmer down," he said as he picked Caleb out of the pile. He tried to wiggle out of Blake's hand but Blake had too good of a grip.

"That's the boy who done took the peaches!" Hap yelled pointing at Caleb.

"Near scared ten years off my life. He was hiding behind some grain sacks. He seen me an' lit out," Avery added.

Blake marched Caleb over to the anvil with the peach can on it. "Did you steal these peaches and leave them here for me?" Blake asked in a no nonsense voice. Caleb just looked at him for a second and then hung his head and shook it. "Why?" Blake asked.

"F-f-f-for kn-kn-knife," stammered Caleb.

"Don't matter," Hap said. "You is comin' with me to talk with my boss."

"Hold on," Blake said. "How much are the peaches, Hap?"

"Nickel a can, I think."

"Here's two bits. Pay Josh for the can and keep the rest for catching him. You did a good job."

"But I was the one who catched him!" Avery blustered.

Blake shook his head, "Yes, you did. Maybe Hap will buy you a beer later."

"Risked my life for a lousy beer. I'll let him do the catchin' next time," grumbled Avery.

"We is pards, I'll buy you two," Hap said.

"Now you is talkin'," said Avery vindicated.

* * * * * *

Hap and Avery went their separate ways and left Blake with his tight grip on Caleb. Blake sat him down on the water trough and stepped back. He had no idea what to do next. "You know what you did was wrong, don't you?" Caleb shrugged his shoulders and stared at the ground. "When a man talks to you, look him in the eye," Blake growled. Caleb raised his head slowly, trying not to let the tears show. Blake swallowed hard, he felt for the kid but he had to make him accountable. "When you steal and give it to someone else, it's still wrong and you make that person a thief, too."

"S-s-sorry," choked Caleb.

"Do you have a Ma or Pa?"

Caleb shook his head no.

"A place to stay?"

Caleb pointed out in back of the livery.

"Well the fire is out now and I don't feel much like starting it again. You stay right there till I get back," Blake said. He took off the apron, put on his hat and vest and walked Bull back in the livery. He saw Avery and asked him to saddle Bull. He went back outside to get Caleb. "Show me where you live." Caleb got up with his head low and led Blake to a row of shacks out behind the saloon. When he got to one that looked like no more than a chicken coop he stopped and pointed. Blake went in and couldn't believe how run down it was. Just a threadbare blanket on the floor and some broken furniture. There was no glass in any of the windows and no stove for heat or cooking. The mangy dog Caleb rescued was lying in the corner chewing on an old cow femur. He looked up at Blake and cocked his head. "Jesus Christ," Blake said, shaking his head. He needed time to think. He couldn't leave the boy like this and the boy couldn't make it on his own.

Blake walked back outside and closed the door. He looked at Caleb and drew a deep breath. He started walking back to the forge. "C'mon," he said to Caleb. The boy followed close behind keeping his head down. When they got back to the forge he instructed Caleb to sit by the door. "Make sure nobody steals anything. I'll be back in a while," Blake said. Bull was standing by the door of the forge saddled and ready to go. Blake threw his leg over him and trotted up the street and out of town.

Blake put Bull into a slow canter for a couple miles, then down to a walk. After an hour or so Blake found himself on top of a grassy knoll overlooking the town. He stopped and let Bull blow and relax. He was weighing things out in his mind.

First Caleb, he felt bad about the kid's condition, but Caleb wasn't his responsibility. Sure, Blake had helped Hap and Avery, but they were grown men and could make their way. He doubted Caleb could. He liked the town alright and thought maybe he could settle down for a while, but Tom MacIntyre was going to be a thorn in his side. Blake would like to get know Chrissy better, but you never know about women. At best it was hard to know what the hell went through a woman's mind.

Damn, this was hard to figure; he could ride on and drift or get involved up to his neck here. "What do you think, old son? We can just keep riding and forget this mess or go down and try and be a big hero," Blake said in an agitated voice. Bull turned his head around to Blake and blinked at him. "Come on boy, I leave it up to you. That way I have someone to blame if it goes wrong, either way." Bull reached back a little farther and bit Blake's pant leg. "Oh, hell, let's just get out of here," Blake said and tried to turn Bull away from town. Bull would not budge. "You, horse, are a pain in my ass. I will blame you anyway, you know." Bull shook his head and snorted.

\* \* \* \* \* \*

When Blake turned Bull toward town he went freely. He kept Bull at a walk. Sorting things out in his mind he thought that he could do the same thing for Caleb that he had done for Hap and Avery, but Caleb was different. He had that stutter which most people would not be tolerant of. Probably he would be branded the village idiot and never be given a fair chance. Maybe Blake could find somebody to take him but he would be little use until he got a skill.

Then it hit Blake like a thunderbolt. Blacksmithing. The town needed one badly and they could forgive a stutterer if they wanted something made or repaired. But, it could take several years to become even a decent smith and Blake wondered if Caleb had the brains and if he would be dedicated to learning. "I guess there is one way to find out," Blake said to himself.

He had reached the town now and rode up the street slowly, really taking it in now. If he committed to this, he would be here for a couple years at least. "Well, old son, you want to call this home for spell?" Bull pricked up his ears and quickened his pace. "Alright, but if this goes south, I'll blame you," Blake laughed and turned the corner to the livery.

Caleb was still sitting on the water trough when Blake rode by. Blake stopped and got off Bull and led him in the stable. He met Joe and told him of his plans. When Joe finished laughing and shaking his head he took Bull in and started taking his saddle off. "You think I'm crazy?" Blake asked.

"Crazy? No," Joe chuckled. "Your heart is in the right place, but your head is so far up your ass, it's right next to it." They both laughed at that.

"You may be right," Blake said still laughing and left the stable. He walked over to Caleb and said, "Here's how I see it, boy. I paid for those peaches and now you owe me that money. You are going to work it off by working for me until I say we are square. Understand?" Caleb kept his head down and nodded. "Not good enough, look at me and say it, clear?"

Caleb looked up through his stringy hair and said, "Y-yes."

"Fine," Blake stated. "Now give me a hand putting these tools back in the forge." When that was done Blake barred and locked the door. He dropped the keys in his pocket and sat Caleb back on the trough.

"The first thing is you stink and you need a bath. I won't have someone who smells like you working for me. I'll get you cleaned up and some proper clothes. Let's go." Caleb jumped up and followed Blake over to the mercantile. As they entered the store Terry came over to greet them. "Ma'am, this is the thief who stole the peaches this morning."

Terry looked at Caleb and her heart sank. "No harm done, Mr. Thorton, you p..." Blake gave her a quick look and shook his head slightly. "Oh, I see," she said.

"Apologize," Blake told Caleb firmly.

"I-I-I'm s-s-sorry," he said softly looking at her through teary eyes.

"Accepted," Terry replied, smiling sweetly.

"Now," Blake spoke up, "this young man is going to be working for me. He is going to need two complete sets of clothes, boots, hat and some work gloves. Would you be so kind as to have Hap bring them over to the barbershop?"

"Certainly," she said.

"Also I would like to start an account, if I could. I will be staying in town for a while."

"Absolutely," Terry said. Blake turned to leave, and she gently took his sleeve and turned to him, "You're a good man, Mr. Thorton."

Blake gave her a little smile, "Thank you, ma'am." He turned back to Caleb and pointed to the door. "Let's go," and he pushed Caleb out the door. When they entered the barbershop, Bill Brady was sitting in his chair reading the paper again. He looked up and shook his head. "What do you do? Look under every rock out there and drag whatever crawls out in here to get cleaned up?"

"It would appear I have a knack for it," Blake said. He flipped him a silver dollar.

"Good, Lord," he said ushering Caleb in the back, "I take it I am burning these clothes, too."

"Unless you want them," Blake said smiling. "New ones are on the way. I'll be over at the saloon. When he's done, send him over to me, please."

"Sure thing," Brady called back.

\* \* \* \* \* \*

Blake stopped by his hotel to get cleaned up and change his shirt, and then made his way to The Trails End. Business was slow and Blake stood at the end of the bar sipping a beer. The bartender named Clyde came down to him with a jar of pickled eggs. "Feel free to help yourself."

Blake fished one out and took a bite. "Do you know anything about a kid named Caleb?" he asked.

"The one who lives out back of here?"

"Yup, that's him."

"About sixteen or so, with blond hair?" Blake nodded and finished his egg. "His ma used to work here as a dove, nice enough, always a smile. His pa was probably a customer who was gone before she knew she was pregnant." He was done wiping glasses and stood there cleaning the bar.

"Anyhow, about two years ago she caught the clap and got real sick. Doc said if he found it earlier he might of helped but she was too far gone. She had the boy a while back and lived in the shack behind here, she tried to provide for him but times got real hard. She wanted Caleb to go to the school but that hawk-faced biddy of a schoolmarm thought he was retarded because of his stutter and wouldn't let him in. The old bat wasn't about to have a whore's child in her school, anyway. Della, that was his ma's name, tried to teach him but she didn't have much schoolin' herself. He lives out there in his ma's shack with that scruffy cur dog now. I tried to hire him on to do chores around here but once the cowpokes found he stuttered, they made such fun of him he ran off. I see him from time to time but he always runs away before I can talk to him. Why you asking about him anyway?"

"I met him today," Blake said. "Thought maybe I can help him."

"He's a lost cause I think. Hate to say it but the cards have always been stacked against him." The bartender walked away to refill a mug.

Blake continued to sip his beer when he felt a tap on his shoulder. He turned and saw Caleb. He could scarcely believe his eyes. He was thin to be sure and looked as nervous as a long-tailed cat in a room full of rocking chairs but, damn, he was handsome. He had piercing blue eyes and strong jaw. With his blond hair cut and combed he was sure to turn a lady's head. The bartender saw a new customer and came over to him.

"What can I get you?"

"Would you like anything, Caleb?" Blake asked.

"N-No."

"That can't be Caleb!" his mouth hanging open, the bartender was shocked.

"In the flesh," Blake smiled. "You hungry?"

Caleb nodded his head.

"Let's go down to the café."

"I will be truly damned and go to hell," muttered Clyde as he watched them leave.

# CHAPTER 6

**B**LAKE and Caleb entered the café and took a seat. Chrissy came out of the kitchen carrying food and left it at a table near them. Coming over to them with her usual hard expression she said, "The special today is beef stew and biscuits."

Blake was growing tired of cold receptions, so mimicking her tone, said, "Good afternoon ma'am, it's lovely to see you, too. Beef stew and biscuits sound delightful. May we please have two orders?"

Chrissy's face turned a bright shade of pink. Trying to figure out if she was going to light into Blake for his smart ass attitude or just ignore it, her eyes fixed on Caleb. "Do I know you?"

"Y-y-yes, m-m-ma'am."

Chrissy's face changed to disbelief. "Caleb?"

"Y-y-es, m-m-ma'am."

She stared at Caleb a second longer, then she closed her mouth and turned her gaze to Blake.

"This young man stole something earlier today and needs to repay me for it. I have decided to turn him from his life of crime and teach him a skill. I'll be staying in MacIntyre and will teach him the art of blacksmithing."

"Why?" was only thing she could find to say with a puzzled look on her face.

"Because," Blake said flatly.

She was taken back, totally at a loss for words. She opened and closed her mouth, like a carp on dry land. Finally she said, "I'll be right out with your dinners."

Blake turned to Caleb and caught the amazement on his face. "Speak your mind, boy." He tried but could not get any words out. Blake held up his hand, "Look, the town needs a black-smith and I need someone to help me. Because you owe me money, you're it. Once you have paid your debt, you'll be free to go. If you're not careful you might learn a trade that you can use the rest of your life. Make no mistake; the work is going to be hot, smelly and hard. But I think you will come to like it. You are big enough, strong enough, and smart enough."

That was the statement that shook Caleb, tears welled in his eyes, "S-s-s-stup-p-pid."

"A stutter doesn't make you stupid. I don't see stupid in you." Chrissy arrived with their food. She hesitated when she saw the look on Caleb's face. Blake continued. "I won't do this without you, son. Are you game to give it a try?" Blake held out his hand.

There comes a point in every man's life when he hits a cross-road. One way is more comfortable and familiar; the other scares him to death. One aspect of bravery is to plunge headlong into the unknown. The hardest step is the first. Caleb screwed up his face, it was a lot to take in. Suddenly he looked Blake straight in the eye, grabbed hold of his hand shaking it and said, "Hell, yes."

They agreed to meet at the café for breakfast the next morn-ing. Blake had made arrangements with Joe to stay in the loft with Hap and Avery. Afterwards, they had breakfast that was served by an almost pleasant Chrissy. Blake thought she smiled at one point but he couldn't be sure.

They headed over to the forge. Taking the keys from his pocket, he unlocked the door and opened the big door in front. "All right Caleb, the first thing we have to do is get this pig sty cleaned up. Take everything you can lift and put it outside. Try to keep the tools that look the same together. Put smaller things in boxes and be careful, some of it may be pretty sharp."

Caleb nodded and went right to work. After Blake thought he had a good start Blake left for the bank.

Mr. Weatherby was sitting at his desk working in a ledger. As Blake approached him he held out his hand without looking up. Blake sat in the chair across from him. "I would like to talk, please."

"About?"

"Purchasing the blacksmith shop."

Weatherby's eyes brightened a little. "Had a change of heart, have you?"

"You might say that. My circumstance has changed." Blake's voice had a very businesslike quality.

"Good, good. Well the price for the lot, building and its contents is one thousand dollars," Weatherby said sitting back in his chair.

Blake snorted, "I take it you haven't seen the lot, building and its contents lately."

"It may have fallen into a minor state of disrepair."

"The main header for the roof is broken, pigeons have been using it for an outhouse for what looks like a year and the access hole in the roof they have been using is big enough to throw a cat through … which, incidentally, has allowed many of the tools to rust and rot."

"Perhaps I can negotiate the price down a little. When, and if, I can secure a loan for you, I'm sure we can come to manageable figure."

"I will not need a loan. I wish to know your bottom price right now," Blake pressed.

Weatherby was flustered. "Perhaps seven hundred fifty."

Blake smiled now. "I have no idea what was owed on the building before and I do not care. I do know, however, that when the bank owns it, the bank is responsible for back taxes; I do not care how much that is either. What I do know is the town needs a blacksmith, and it would be better for you to get this building off your books. I will offer four hundred."

Weatherby took a handkerchief out and mopped his forehead. "Seven," he said.

"Five."

"Six and I will go no lower," Weatherby huffed.

"Five-fifty it is," Blake stood and held out his hand.

"Fine, five-fifty, then," Weatherby looked like he had been in a prize fight. He stood and shook Blake's hand. "I'll get the deed."

When he returned Blake reached in his shirt pocket and pulled out an enormous wad of bills. He counted off six hundred dollars and handed to the banker. Weatherby reached in his desk for the change and Blake took it. He signed over the deed and handed to Blake. "Now to the next bit of business," Blake sat back down.

"Lord, what now?" sighed Weatherby.

"I'll need a place to live. Do you have any reasonably priced houses?" Blake liked toying with him.

The banker pursed his lips. "I do have a modest house at the end of the street. It was owned by a Confederate officer who lived out his final days there. I know the house is in decent shape because it is two doors up from my own. A Negro woman has been living there; she was his servant and stayed on after he died. But I can have her out by day's end if you wish."

"And where will she go?" Blake asked.

"That is not my concern."

What a heartless bastard, Blake thought. "I would like to see it."

"I can take you over now but it will have to be quick, as I have other appointments this morning."

"Let's go," said Blake, as he stood up.

\* \* \* \* \* \*

They left the bank and turned right up the street. As Blake passed the street where his new shop stood he could hear the clanking of metal and knew Caleb was hard at work. Blake really did not think Weatherby was going to last by all the huffing and wheezing he was doing. He sounded like a steam engine about to explode. Finally the banker turned and opened a gate to a small white house with black shutters. It had two stories with a small porch on the first floor. Mopping his brow again he marched up the stairs and went in.

"No knock?" Blake asked and stood on the porch outside.

"The bank owns it," Weatherby puffed.

Just when Blake was about to give him a lesson in manners a small black woman appeared in the hall. She marched straight at them with fire in her eyes. Only about five foot tall, she was just as wide wearing a flour-coated apron and she was carrying a rolling pin. She pointed at them and yelled, "Who is you to come bustin' into my house like that?"

Weatherby stood his ground, "It's the bank's house, Sadie, and this gentleman is looking to buy it."

"I don't care. Knockin' is what decent folk do," she said with hands on her hips.

Blake took off his hat and stepped through the door. "Ma'am, my name is Blake Thorton, and I apologize for not knocking, if it would be no trouble I would like to look around some."

"Well, I knows the day would come," Sadie said relaxing a little. Then she shot the banker a dirty look. "I gots no say, do what you want," and stomped back to the kitchen.

Blake looked at the rest of the house while Weatherby rested on the porch. It had three bedrooms upstairs and a sitting room downstairs along with a kitchen and a small room on the side that was where Sadie obviously stayed. Adjacent to the kitchen was a room with a bathtub and dresser. There was a small back yard with a garden and some neatly pruned rose bushes. He went back to the kitchen where Sadie was baking some wonderful smelling bread. "You have done a fine job with this house, ma'am."

"Don't know where I is going now," she grumbled.

"Well if I buy the house, I would like you to stay on and work for me."

"Doin' what?" she said suspiciously.

"Well, cooking, cleaning and such."

"Nutttin' else?"

"Like what?"

She turned to Blake with her hands on her hips and a hard look on her face. "Major Crawford wanted all sorts of 'other' things, not that he could do 'em mind you, but he tried."

Blake smiled and looked down. "No ma'am, nothing else."

"I don't be needin' your charity, mister," she said looking straight at him. "But seen' as you be needin' help, I s'pose I could."

"How does twenty dollars a month sound?"

"Like you is funnin' an old lady," disbelief covered her face. Then thinking she asked, "How much for my room and meals?"

"I'll throw those in, but you have to do the cooking," Blake said smiling.

A strange look came over Sadie's face, and then she let out with a high pitched laugh. "You and me is goin' to get along fine, we is. An' fo' twenty dollars a month, there will be hot vittles and clean sheets for you, Mr. Thorton." Then her face got a very hard look. "If'n you try any foolishness I'll dent yo' head with this here rollin' pin."

"Deal," Blake said holding up his hand. "I may have a young man staying here that I just hired on. Will that be a problem?"

"No suh, tha'd be fine, but I'll need to go shoppn'. Ain't gots enough food here now."

Blake reached in his pocket and gave her forty dollars. "Twenty to stock the shelves and a month's pay in advance."

"Thank you and bless yo' heart, Mr. Thorton."

"If it would be no trouble, could you bring some sandwiches and something to drink over to the forge around noon?"

"Yes, suh, I'd be happy to," Sadie said taking the money. "Lord, two men to care fo', I'd best get movin'."

Blake smiled and turned to the door. As he went out he was greeted by an agitated Weatherby.

"Well, is it suitable, Mr. Thorton?"

"Yup, it'll do. Do you have a price in mind?"

"I think seven hundred is a very reasonable price," he stated.

"I think five is more reasonable."

"Five with no furnishings, then."

Blake thought for a moment and scratched his chin. "Six with the furnishings."

"Then the price is seven hundred," the banker said firmly.

"Then I will look elsewhere," Blake put his hat on and started for the gate.

Weatherby waddled to catch up, wheezing he said, "Six will do, six will do. Deal?" holding out a sweaty hand.

"Deal," Blake said shaking his hand then wiped it on his pant leg. "I need to go to the hotel and gather my things. I'll meet you at the bank to get the deed."

"It will be ready," puffed Weatherby.

Blake crossed the street and headed for the hotel. He went up to his room and removed his shirt which was hiding a money belt. Then he emptied his saddlebags and took four one-pound gold bars from a hidden compartment in the bottom. He counted the bills in the belt. There was about nine thousand dollars. He counted out six hundred and placed it in his shirt pocket. He repacked the saddlebags and placed the gold and money on top. Gathering the rest of his belongings he headed downstairs. The weasel greeted him with his usual sour look. With his usual snotty tone asked, "Checking out, sir?"

Blake tossed the key on the counter, "Yup."

"I will settle your bill in just one minute, sir."

Blake had enough of his rudeness. He leaned on the counter staring at the little man. "Why don't you keep the rest and go over to Dooley's Mercantile. Maybe he has a new personality for you, because your shitty one irritates me."

"Well, I never," huffed the clerk as Blake strolled out the door.

Back in the bank Weatherby was behind his desk waiting for him. "Everything is in order, Mr. Thorton," he said as Blake sat down.

"Here is your money," Blake said and gave him the money from his pocket.

"And here is the deed." Weatherby handed him the papers. "I will have the Negro woman out at once."

"There will be no need for that. I hired her on to take care of the house," Blake replied examining the deed.

"But you just purchased the property!" the banker said loudly.

"I was confident we would reach an agreement. Now on to other business."

"Good Lord, what now?" Weatherby slumped in his chair.

"I need to open an account," he said reaching in his saddlebag.

"How much will you be depositing?" Weatherby's eyes brightened a little and he sat up.

Blake set the gold bars on the desk and started counting out the money. "These gold bars and nine thousand dollars."

Weatherby's mouth hung open and said with an exasperated voice, "You could have easily paid my asking price for the properties."

"It was business, Mr. Weatherby, I did not want to be taken advantage of, plus I am certain you took no loss in the transactions." Blake set the money on the desk and leaned back in his chair.

"Forgive me, Mr. Thorton; you do not have the appearance of a man who has wealth. How did you come by this small fortune?"

Blake's eyes became very cold and hard. He spoke in a very controlled, calm voice, "I do not dress to put on airs. I dress for comfort and function. Secondly, how I came by my fortune is no one's business but my own. Are we clear?"

Weatherby swallowed hard, "Yes, sir."

"Good. Now I want you to set up a transfer from the Commercial National Bank in St. Louis in the amount of ten thousand dollars to be deposited into my account here." Weatherby was just staring at Blake with his mouth open. Blake smiled, "Don't you think you should be doing some paperwork?"

"Yes, oh my, yes," said the now-excited banker as he started to pull forms from his drawer and scribbled furiously.

"Take your time, Mr. Weatherby, a man died who was in a hurry once," Blake drawled.

When his business was concluded, Blake stood and gathered his things and made to leave. "Thank you, Mr. Weatherby. It's been a pleasure. It would cause me great displeasure to have our transactions broadcast around town or anywhere else for that matter."

"Property deals are a matter of public record here but, rest assured, personal accounts are strictly confidential," Weatherby stated firmly. Then he stood and shook Blake's hand.

"Fair enough."

* * * * * *

Blake returned to his new home to find Sadie had gone shopping. He put his gear in the larger upstairs bedroom and started taking a more leisurely walk around the house. Many of the Major's possessions were left; he would have Sadie box them up. He poked his head into Sadie's room and saw that it was little more than a woodshed. Daylight poked through several boards and there was a water stain on the ceiling. No parlor stove could be found and the bed was rickety with a few missing slats. Blake checked his pocket watch and saw it about noon. He headed back to the forge to check on Caleb. Turning the corner he saw Caleb sitting on the small anvil munching on a thick roast beef sandwich and drinking lemonade. Sadie was holding a basket standing nearby. "How's that sandwich?" he asked. Caleb had so much in his mouth he couldn't speak so he just nodded.

"When was the last time that boy et?" Sadie asked with suspicious look on her face.

"This morning," Blake said smiling.

"Good Lawd," she replied handing Blake a sandwich. "I gots to keep that in mind 'round dinner time."

Blake took a bite of his sandwich. The beef was tender and the bread was soft. "Fine sandwich, Sadie. I was wondering if you knew of a good carpenter," he said taking another bite.

"My nephew Sam does himself a fair job. Works at the lumber yard yonder," she said pointing with her chin.

"Have him come see me, please. I have some work for him, if he wants it. And move your things into one of the upstairs rooms."

"I'll send my nephew sho' enough but it ain't proper for me to be sleepin' up there."

Blake took a long pull of his lemonade. "Just until I can get your room fixed up, then you can have it back."

"My room's jest fine," she objected.

"For a chicken coop I suppose," Blake said with a wide grin. "Now don't give me any trouble or I'll throw you out in the street."

"Yous can try, but seein' as it's your house, I guess it's maybe alright."

"See how easy that is? Dinner at six?"

"Sho nuff," she said as she walked back to the house.

After they finished their lunch, Blake went in the forge to take a look at Caleb's work. Caleb had removed all the tools and was working on removing the piles of steel that were used to make various items. Everything had been sorted as Blake had asked and he took a mental inventory of what was there. He was pleased to find almost everything he would need, it was not as complete as his father's shop had been but they had a good start.

He and Caleb worked together cleaning out the rest and Blake started explaining the different metals and sizes to him. Blake noticed something about Caleb's face when he took a measuring guide and told him to measure a piece of stock that he was holding, he looked completely lost. "Do you know math and fractions and such?" he asked.

"N-no, not much," Caleb said quietly.

"Well, that stuff is pretty important to this work," Blake said, smiling. Caleb looked down, obviously troubled. "Not to worry, son, we'll get you there," and patted him on the shoulder. Blake checked his watch and pursed his lips. "I have an idea. You finish up here and I'll be back soon." Caleb nodded his head and picked up another handful of steel stock.

Blake took a walk over to the café. It was about mid-afternoon and he hoped it wasn't busy. Luck was on his side when there was only one couple sitting at a table. He sat at the counter and waited for Chrissy. She came out from the kitchen looking lovely as ever. Every time he saw her his heart seemed to skip a beat. She smiled a little when she saw him and came over.

"Mr. Thorton," she said a little warmer than usual, "would you care for some coffee?"

"Yes, ma'am. I was wondering if you could help me with a small problem."

Pouring him a cup she cocked an eyebrow, "Oh, and what would that be?"

"Caleb and I are opening the blacksmith shop as you know but the problem is he has never had much schooling. I have heard that the teacher wouldn't let him in school because of his mother and his stuttering problem. I could teach him what he needs, but I need to run the forge and we'll both be tuckered out at night. Would you happen to know of someone who could help us out? I would be willing to pay them."

"Hmmm," she thought and her eyes glanced toward the kitchen. "I may know someone," she said biting her lip. "Bonnie who works here for me was an A student when she went to school but after her 'incident' she has been very withdrawn."

"Incident?" Blake asked.

"About a year ago she went for a buggy ride with Tom MacIntyre. Supposedly there was an accident and she was hurt very badly. Her father thought there was more to it and accused Tom of mistreating her. No one could prove anything so the matter was dropped. Bonnie's father made it his mission to find out the truth but, before he could, he and his wife were killed when their house caught fire. Her parents and I were friends, so when she was well enough I took her in." She refilled Blake's cup and thought for a second. "Maybe this could bring her back to more of her old self. I know Caleb. He's nice boy. And I know she has sneaked food out to him on occasion. Maybe, just maybe…"

"Do you think she would help?"

"Let me talk to her." She cut Blake a piece of pie and started back to the kitchen.

"Was Tom MacIntyre hurt?" Blake asked.

"Not a scratch," she said coldly.

About five minutes later Chrissy came out with Bonnie in tow. "Bonnie, this is Mr. Thorton. He is the man who hired Caleb to work with him."

Holding out his hand Blake said, "Pleased to meet you, Miss." She gave him a quick glance but would not take his hand. Realizing his mistake Blake dropped his hand to his leg and continued, "It sure would be a big help if you could teach Caleb math and some reading and writing. I promise he'll work real hard." No answer was forthcoming so Blake looked helplessly at Chrissy.

Taking his cue she said, "You could teach him here at the café. Slow time is from two to four so it should be quiet for you. How does that sound?" Still no answer. Chrissy gently placed her hand under Bonnie's chin and raised it until their eyes met. "I'll be right here the whole time."

Courage is not a thing limited to men. Women have crossroads, too, and in some ways the paths are harder to choose. Bonnie was at one now. Her eyes darted back and forth searching for an answer. Perhaps it was Chrissy's strength or her motherly way but, for whatever reason, Bonnie took a bold step.

"I would like to help," she said quietly with a small smile.

"Excellent," Blake said. "You two ladies have been a tremendous help. Can we start tomorrow?"

"Tomorrow is Saturday," Chrissy said. "Perhaps they could start Monday afternoon."

"You bet. If that's all right with you, Miss." Bonnie nodded her head in agreement. "You can go over to Dooley's and get whatever you need, just put it on my account." Blake got up to leave, as he headed for the door he turned and said, "Two o'clock sharp, Monday afternoon."

Chrissy gave Bonnie a light nudge with her elbow and looked at Blake. Bonnie perked up and said, "Thank you."

"I'm the one who should be thanking you." Placing his hat on his head he touched the brim and said, "Ladies."

# CHAPTER 7

**B**LAKE made his way back over to the forge to find Caleb just about done. He told him about his arrangement with Bonnie. Caleb seemed to brighten up at the prospect of working with her. "You mind your manners around her, boy," Blake warned. "You are just going there to learn. Got it?"

"Y-yes s-sir, B-bonnie is a-a r-eal nice girl. S-sometimes she g-gives me an' S-Satan f-food."

"You and who?" Blake thought he heard him say Satan but that couldn't be right.

"S-s-Satan."

"Who the heck is Satan?" a totally confused Blake asked.

"Th-that's what A-a-avery n-named m-my dog."

"Why would he name him that?"

"I'll tell why," yelled Avery stomping over to Blake. "You tol' Joe to let him sleep in the loft wit' me an' Hap. We didn' mind till he brought that consarned mongrel wit' him. I tol' him I wasn' sleepin' with no dog, and he farted somethin' fierce."

"Caleb?" Blake asked.

"No, dammit, that there fool dog," Avery blustered. "God almighty, I never smelt such a foul thing. We runned for our lives.

I swear Hap puked and Joe come out of his office to see which horse died. Took quite a spell for tha' smell to clear. I says to m'self, only the devil can conjure a smell like that. So I done named him Satan."

Blake was laughing now, "Come on, it can't be that bad."

Caleb's eyes bugged out. "D-does it when h-he g-gets m-m-mad. It's r-r-rank."

"Caleb can stay with me tonight, so you won't have that problem again." Blake was still chuckling.

"Well Hap has been fixin' us up a room over at the store. So we's stayin' there now," Avery said. "Jest don' lettin' him bring that dog wit' him. You been warn't." Avery said as he headed back to the livery shaking his finger.

"Go gather your things, we'll get you settled in," Blake said. "And I think it would be best to leave Satan outside. I don't think Sadie will approve."

"I-I'll t-try, b-but h-h-e g-goes where h-he w-wants," Caleb said heading for the loft.

The dinner was everything they could have hoped for and more. Roast chicken and mashed potatoes with gravy. There were green beans and some of the best biscuits Blake had ever tasted. Sadie had made a fine peach cobbler for dessert. He and Caleb ate heartily and the only thing left were the dirty dishes. As Sadie was clearing the table she smiled at Blake. "I can't rightly remember when I see'd a boy eat like that; does an old lady's heart some good fo' shu'."

"Well, that was a fine meal, Sadie," Blake said. "I think I'll take a bath and shave."

"You jest be leaving your dirty clothes fo' me. I does a fine boiled wash."

"Appreciate it, ma'am. Caleb has only two sets, I'll see about getting some more."

"D-do I-I have t-to t-take a b-b-bath t-too?" a very concerned Caleb asked.

"Yes, you do, and get used to it," Blake said firmly. "Now help Sadie with the water while I get some clean clothes." Blake got up from the table and gave Sadie a wink. "You have my permission to scrub him good if he gives you any trouble."

Caleb's eyes shot up and looked back and forth between Blake and Sadie. There was genuine terror in his eyes.

Sadie winked back at Blake. "He'll be as pink as a newbor' shoat he will."

The bath felt great and the shave even better. Feeling like a new man, Blake went out and sat on the porch to take in the cool night air. He smiled to himself, thinking of the turns his life had taken the past few days. It had been a long time since he had any real purpose. A man never knows if his actions will come of any good but he sure felt he had taken a good trail now. Sadie came out on the porch with a box in her hands. "Don' know ifn' you smoke, but the major left these fine ceegars, thought maybe you'd be likin' one."

"After a fine meal like that, it would be a pleasure, thank you." Blake took one and fished a match out of his pocket, lighting it he sat back in his chair.

"Why is you helpin' that boy?" Sadie asked.

Blowing smoke out towards the yard Blake asked, "What do you mean?"

"He done tol' me about what you is doin'. Givin' him work and schoolin' an' all. Yo' don' seem like a man wantin' to put down no roots. So why you doin' it?"

"I was just trying figure that out, Sadie. The only answer I have is the boy needed help and I could do it. It just seems right."

"You is a good man, sho' nuff, a strange one, but good." Not completely satisfied, Sadie went back in the house.

Blake smiled and flicked some ashes from the cigar. "It's been said of me."

Caleb came out onto the porch when he was done with his bath. They both enjoyed the cool night air while Sadie busied herself in the kitchen cleaning up. She was singing to herself an old song that Blake had never heard before. He felt the peace of settling down and sprouting roots. Life on the trail had benefits to it but it lacked the good feeling of home cooking and a warm bed.

"You ever play chess or checkers, Caleb?" He shook his head no and Blake got up to see if there was a set in the house. Sadie helped him find a very expensive set that contained both games. Apparently the major had loved playing and had purchased a fine set carved from ivory with a mahogany and walnut board. Blake set up a game of checkers on a table in the parlor and called Caleb in. "Checkers is an easier game to get the hang of to start. When you get better, I'll teach you chess."

Caleb was a quick learner and they played several games. Each time his skill improved. Blake held back a little to give him confidence until Caleb won.

"I-I w-won!" he shouted, when the game was over. He was beaming from ear to ear.

"You sure enough did, son," Blake said smiling. "I guess I'm rusty, but you played a good game, congratulations." Blake stood and shook his hand, then he checked his watch. "I guess we should turn in. We're going to be busy tomorrow."

"C-c-an I-I t-tell S-sadie?" Caleb asked, still grinning.

"Sure you can, but then up to bed with you," Blake said putting the pieces away.

Caleb ran to the kitchen and told Sadie about his triumph and she told him he must be smart because she never had a head for those games. Caleb promised to teach her if she wanted. He told her good night and ran up the stairs. Sadie leaned out of the kitchen door and smiled at Blake. Blake smiled back and said, "Good night, Sadie."

\* \* \* \* \* \*

The next morning Blake woke to the smell of coffee and frying ham. He got up and washed up in the basin on the dresser. After putting on some fresh clothes he went into the hall to see both of the other bedroom doors open. He followed the aroma downstairs and found Caleb already eating and Sadie pouring more batter on the grill. "Must have slept late," he said reaching for the coffee.

"I gets up wit' the chickens, I do," Sadie said. "That boy smelt my cookin' and came runnin'."

"I can't blame him there," Blake said sitting down. "How is it, Caleb?"

"Mmmmffff," was about all Caleb could say around the hot-cakes in his mouth.

Sadie set some ham and hotcakes in front of Blake. "I'm going to get fat eating like this every day," he said while putting syrup on his hotcakes.

"Won' be a problem ifn' you is late every mornin'. That boy will have it all et'," Sadie said laughing.

Blake was about halfway through his breakfast when Sadie startled him by yelling, "Scat!" and clapping her hands.

Both he a Caleb turned to see Satan sitting at the screen door of the kitchen wagging his tail. She picked up a broom and headed for the door.

"Sadie, don't!" Blake yelled as she opened the door. Satan ran between her legs and over to Caleb. He put both front feet on his chest and started licking syrup on his face.

She started after the dog with the broom when Blake held up his hands and said, "I wouldn't do that."

"Get yo' filthy dog ass out my kitchen," she yelled and brought the broom firmly down on his back. Satan jumped down and hid underneath the table.

"D-d-don't m-m-ake him m-m-mad," Caleb stammered.

"Huh?" she said.

That's when Satan did what Satan does best. As the smell crept its way from under the table and up to the nostrils of his victims, the realization hit all of their faces simultaneously.

Sadie clapped her hand over her nose and turned to run for the back door. Unfortunately all three of them had the same idea and almost got stuck in the doorway. Finally they freed themselves and were standing in the backyard gasping for air.

All Sadie kept saying was, "Lawd, Lawd, Lawd."

Blake's stomach was doing flips like riding the high seas in a hurricane. Caleb was using his shirttail wiping his tearing eyes. Blake drew in a lung full of fresh air and blew it out. "Sadie I would like to introduce Satan."

She looked through the screen door and could see the dog munching happily on a piece of ham he had pulled from the table; she looked back at Blake and said, "Who?"

"That's Caleb's dog, Satan."

She looked at Caleb with a very confused stare, "Yo' named yo' dog Satan?"

"N-no m-ma'm. A-avery did."

"It's not a good idea to make him mad," Blake chimed in.

"Lawd, that ain't a natural thin' comin' out of him, fo' shu'. Worse than any polecat I's ever smelt," replied Sadie waving her hand in front of her face.

"Best you get in the house and open the windows, Caleb, before that smell starts sticking to things," Blake said. Caleb gave him a worried look. "Well it's your dog, and I'm not doing it. Now git."

Caleb pulled his shirt up around his nose, took a deep breath and ran into the house. Throwing windows up as fast as he could he ran out the front door, gasping for air.

"Upstairs, too!" Blake yelled from the back of the house.

They heard him running up the stairs and into each room opening windows. Then back down to the yard. Satan barked at him when he passed by.

"What's we gonna do 'bout him?" Sadie asked Blake.

"Caleb?"

"No! That fool dog."

"I guess we don't make him mad."

"How's I gonna knows wha' makes him mad?"

"I think that's pretty clear," Blake said smiling.

Once the house was safe to enter, Blake and Caleb left for the forge with Satan trotting close behind carrying a ham bone that Sadie had given him as a peace offering. Blake unlocked the door and had Caleb open the main door and all the windows. Examining the structure damage Blake took a piece of paper from his pocket and started making notes on what he would need to repair it. He tried to explain everything to Caleb in detail. Caleb, never having done anything like this before, listened attentively and asked good questions. The main beam of the shop had cracked and was sagging because it was undersized and could not take a heavy load of snow. Blake figured that the first heavy snowfall would finish it off and the whole building would collapse. Finding a measuring tape, he started taking measurements for the materials he would need. Blake started to tell Caleb the complicated method on how he intended to fix it when a tall muscular black man entered the forge.

"Excuse me, suh'," he said. "Mah name is Sam, an mah aunt says you was wantin' to talk with me."

"Yes, I do Sam. Pleased to meet you," Blake said extending his hand. "I'm Blake Thorton and this here is Caleb."

Sam very hesitantly shook his hand and did the same for Caleb. "Mah aunt was sayin' yo' might be havin' some work fo' me."

"Are you a decent carpenter?"

"Ah reckon I is, never had no house I built fall down, an no roof leaked, neither," Sam said proudly.

Blake smiled. "Sounds good. Let me show you something to see what you think." Blake showed Sam the cracked beam and how the roof was sagging. "How would you fix this?"

Sam looked at the whole thing scratching his head, and then he climbed up on one of the benches to check closer to the roof. Jumping down he wiped his hands on his pants. Still looking up at the beam he said, "Ah would build me a brand new beam next ta' the old one. Th' trick is jackin' up the roof till she's right. Then puts a support on the new one."

"What size beam do you think I should use?" Blake asked.

"Th' old one looks to be a six by six, but this being a forge an you be hangin' stuff from there, ah would use twelve by twelve oak fo' shu'."

Blake was impressed; Sam seemed to have a good grasp on the work and how to go about it. "I've made a list of the wood I'll need. Do you have this on hand at the mill?"

"Yes suh," Sam said looking at the list. "All but the oak. Boss'll have to cut the logs to size. Maybe take a day or two."

"That's fine," Blake said. "Give him the list and I'll come over and square up with him later."

"Is this what yo' want me workin' on? Cause ah works at the yard all day."

"I might need some help if you're willing at night, but I really want you to fix up your aunt's room at my house. It needs new siding outside and the roof fixed, also the walls plastered inside and a parlor stove put in. I want everything painted, too." Blake said. "I'll pay you fifty dollars and I'll buy the materials. You can work in your spare time."

"Them's white man wages, suh," Sam said very sheepishly.

"The color of a man's skin doesn't concern me," Blake said firmly. "What I care about is the type of job he does. Are you a family man?"

"Yes suh, gots me a wife, Marie, and two little ones, Rachel and Lil' Sam."

"Then take it for them and make them proud. How does that suit you?"

Sam smiled broadly, grabbed Blake's hand and shook it vigorously, "Rights down to th' ground, suh, rights down to th' ground."

"When can you start?"

"When's I gets done at th' mill tonight."

"Great," Blake said reaching in his pocket. "Here's fifty dollars, twenty five for materials, and twenty five for you to get started. When you need more, come see me."

"Yes suh, an' thank yo', suh. Ah's got to be getting' back now." Sam pocketed the money and ran out of the forge.

\* \* \* \* \* \*

Blake and Caleb spent a few hours cleaning the forge and preparing to replace the beams. Blake found a couple of wagon jacks that might work to lift he roof but they were short and he might have to do it in multiple stages. They found several block and pulley sets that would come in handy, along with the tools to cut the wood. Sadie brought some sandwiches and lemonade for lunch and Blake told her about meeting her nephew. "Seems like a nice man," he said.

"He's got hisself a big heart, he does. Works real hard, too," she said proudly.

After lunch Blake had Caleb show him where the lumber yard was. As they walked up to a building where the office sign hung Blake noticed an enormous pile of machinery parts and tools that needed repair. Blake pointed at it and told Caleb, "There's some work for us."

They entered the door under the office sign and saw a tough looking man covered in sawdust drinking coffee and eating a sandwich. "This your mill?" Blake asked.

"Yup," the man said putting the rest of the sandwich in his mouth.

"Name's Blake Thorton. I had your man Sam bring you a list of wood I'll be needing."

The man gave Blake a sour look, "Yeah, I got it, might take a while for them beams, though."

Blake looked out a window in the back and saw a pile of oak logs that would work fine. "Why's that?" he asked.

The man stood and wiped his hands on his shirt. "Because I ain't in no particular hurry for a man who pays a nigger a white man's wages," he stated crossing his arms.

"He seems like a good man to me," Blake said stiffening.

"He is. It's just I know white men who could use the work."

"He came recommended," Blake said firmly.

"I bet he did. He works hard, never late, never drunk, has yet to piss me off," he said taking out a plug of tobacco and biting a chunk off. "But friend, he's black. That means he gets niggers wages, pure and simple."

"So you pay more to a man who is late, drunk, and pisses you off?"

"When I can get those son-of-a-bitches to show up," he grumbled and spit a stream into the cuspidor near his desk.

"Well I guess that makes sense somewhere," Blake said. "Did Sam tell you what I wanted the lumber for?"

"Nope."

"I'm opening the blacksmith shop but I need to fix the building first."

"Really," he said lightening his tone. "We sure can use you."

"Yup," said Blake as he now crossed his arms. "And looking at that heap of broken tools out there we may be doing some business. I'll keep that in mind after I see how long it takes for you to get me my lumber."

"Well, horseshit," he said sitting on the corner of his desk. "I'll have it to you Monday afternoon, Tuesday morning at the latest." He stood and held out his hand, "Al Conner is the name."

Blake shook his hand. "Pleasure."

\* \* \* \* \* \*

Blake spent the rest of the day teaching Caleb about the forge. They moved the small forge outside with the anvil. Blake showed him the different types of coal and how to start a fire in the pot. Caleb learned quickly, but what was more, he wanted to learn. He wanted to know the name of every tool and how to use it. The only time he frowned was when Blake would tell him that a tool was advanced and he needed to learn the basics first. Blake had him turning the blower for the forge and he seemed bored until he made a mistake and burned off a piece of metal because it was too hot. "A smith is only as good as his fire," Blake told him. "There is a real knack to getting a fire just right and keeping it there. The fire is alive, a living breathing thing that needs care and constant watching."

When he got better at tending the fire, Blake had him start forging nails. "This is how everybody starts, must of made a thousand nails for my father before he let me move on to other things." Blake taught him how to draw out metal to a point, how to cut it off using the hardy, and how to put a proper head on the nail.

"T-there's a-a lot t-to l-l-learn," said Caleb as he quenched a nail.

"Yup, there is and it's going to be like today, everyday for a long time. You still want to do this?"

"Hell, yes," Caleb said smiling.

Blake checked his watch. "Getting pretty close to suppertime. Why don't we let the forge cool and clean everything up. We don't want Sadie mad because we're late." When they were done and headed home Satan appeared in back of them following close behind.

"That stupid dog is going to get himself shot," Blake laughed.

"S-she w-wouldn't," a genuinely scared Caleb said.

"She might."

As they came around the back of the house they found Sam hard at work removing clapboards on Sadie's room. Satan started barking furiously at him and he stopped.

"Call Satan off," Blake told Caleb, who promptly whistled and tapped his leg. "How's it going, Sam? Join us for supper?"

"No suh, ah's need the light to work, if'n you don' mind none,"

Sam said. Then pointing his hammer at Satan. "Is that there th' cur dog Aunt Sadie was tellin' me 'bout?"

"That sho' is," Sadie piped up from behind the screen door. Satan barked once at her and wagged his tail. She came out and handed Blake and Caleb towels. "You two get cleaned up over at the pump. I'll get yo' supper on the table. Yo' dog, can eat outside."

They took the towels and headed for the pump, unbuttoning their shirts. Blake removed his and heard Caleb whistle and say, "W-what t-the hell."

Blake had forgotten about his tattoo, which covered a vast majority of his upper body. It started just above his elbows, went over his shoulders covering his chest and back all the way down to just above his knees. It was a great swirling pattern with lines and dots that accentuated his muscles and physique. He looked at Caleb's bugging eyes and said, "What's the matter? Never seen a tattoo before?" he asked, pumping the handle as water poured into the bucket. Splashing some on his face and arms he looked back at Caleb who just stood there and stared. "Best get cleaned up, son." He flicked some water in face to bring him around.

Caleb blinked his eyes and stammered, "Y-y-yes sir."

Sadie came to the back door, "Come and get....." her voice trailed off when she saw Blake, "Good Lawd, Almighty," she said coming out the door towards Blake. Her eyes were wide as she approached him. Blake started to put his shirt on but she stopped him. "Sammy comes here," she called over her shoulder. "Lawd, I never..." whispering to herself as she traced a line on Blake's arm with her finger.

"Yes, ma'am," Sam said when he got near her.

"Yo' see these here marks?" Sam nodded. "Yo' Granpappy tol' me 'bout men with these here marks over in Africa where he was from. Only th' greatest warriors get them. I knowed yo' was sumptin different, but this here places yo' high above most men, fo' shu'."

Blake shrugged on his shirt, "No ma'am, I'm like everybody else."

"Oh shu' yo' is," Sadie laughed.

"Let's eat," he said rolling his eyes.

**CHAPTER 8**

**D**INNER was meatloaf with mashed potatoes and gravy. Fresh baked bread and collard greens with apple pie for dessert. When they sat down Caleb kept asking Blake to tell the story of the tattoo. Finally relenting, Blake started. He had left home the day after his sixteenth birthday. He had been born in Duanesburgh, which was in upstate New York. He followed the Schoharie Creek to the Mohawk River. From there he made it to the Hudson River down to New York City. The journey had taken much longer than he thought and he was almost out of money and starving. He slept in alleys near the docks and stole food where he could until he heard two drunken sailors talking about a merchant ship bound for China around Cape Horn. Blake knew that they would be heading through the South Pacific and that was his dream. He found the ship and tried to get hired on but the first mate had him thrown off because he had no sailing experience. Not daunted, he stowed away on it but was soon discovered after leaving port. When he was presented to the captain he took pity on him and let him stay aboard. At first he was treated harshly but soon proved his worth and became a fair seaman. Several months later found him rounding Cape Horn in some of the worst seas imaginable. The ship's blacksmith along with many others were washed overboard while cutting away torn sails. The ship had been badly damaged and was in need of repairs. Blake took on the duties of blacksmith because of his experience. After limping the ship into a port on the coast of South America the crew spent months repairing and refitting the ship so it could continue on. Blake was becoming a respected member of the crew, despite his age, almost nineteen. He could handle himself as well as any man on board.

Once again he was bound for China. Three months after leaving South America his ship was set upon by pirates. Blake was working in the forge when the ship was attacked. It was a bloody battle and many of Blake's shipmates were killed. They were no match for the vicious pirates and the remainder were taken prisoner. When the captain of the pirates saw the leather apron on Blake he ordered Blake to be brought aboard his ship. Once again being a blacksmith would save his life. All his tools were brought aboard and he was forced to make repairs to the ship and their weapons. He was treated badly, kept in chains when he wasn't working and fed small amounts of food, barely enough to keep him alive.

For roughly a year he endured life aboard the pirate's vessel. He longed for home and the peace that came with it. His fortune came in the form of a typhoon. The ship was not in great condition and could not withstand the pummeling of the hurricane force winds. The captain spotted an island and prayed for a safe cove to take shelter in but the ship collided with a reef and was torn apart. Blake somehow managed to float ashore on a piece of wreckage and awoke to bright sun shining on his face. Straining to open his salt crusted eyes he could see the island. Getting to his very shaky knees he could see shapes moving in the trees above the shoreline. Just when he started to stand a stone tipped spear stuck in the sand at his feet. Exhaustion overtook him and he passed out.

He woke sometime later inside a wood and grass structure, a bitter tasting liquid was being poured into his mouth by a beautiful native woman. She had long black hair and golden suntanned skin. Naked from the waist up, she was a sight to behold. Blake tried to rise but she held him back gently and smiled. There were leaf wrapped poultices on his wrists and ankles where the chains had chaffed him. His clothes were gone, an animal hide loincloth was all he had on. He fell back into a peaceful sleep and awoke the next day. Feeling much stronger he stood and went outside. There seemed to be an argument among the men, most of who were a fierce looking bunch, many of them tattooed heavily with bones decorating their ears and hair. The arguing stopped when they saw him. A large older man with a large bone necklace approached him. It took all of Blake's nerve not to run but he stood his ground. The man's eyes were piercing and the look in them was not at all friendly. He gestured toward the beach and grunted. Blake was unsure of what he wanted and headed for the beach followed by several of the warriors. When he got there the captain of the pirate ship was tied to a cross in the sand along with one other of the pirates. The captain was in rough condition but perked up when he saw Blake.

"Boy," he said in a raspy voice, "cut me loose and we'll send all these devils to hell."

The large warrior with a bone necklace walked past Blake and picked a large piece of wreckage with a chain hanging from it. On the end of the chain was a shackle that was used to secure Blake when he was not working. Then he took the shackle and placed it on Blake's wrist and grunted. Blake nodded his head and said, "Yes." The warrior seemed to understand, and then he knelt down and placed it on his ankle and grunted. Again Blake said, "Yes."

He stood and pointed at the captain, grunting again and then placing the shackle back on Blake's wrist. Blake knew that he figured out that he had been a prisoner. Blake hardened his jaw and looked him squarely in the eyes. "Yes."

The big warrior turned to the others and spoke loudly and clearly, when he was finished the others talked among themselves and then started to chant. The big warrior turned to Blake and handed him his spear. Blake took it and turned to the captain, and, as he slowly walked toward him, he saw the fear in his eyes.

"Now don't be hasty lad. We can get clear of this we can," he pleaded.

"Yeah, yeah c'mon boy we can take 'em," the other pirate said.

Blake turned back to the warrior chief, looking straight at him he raised the spear up and stuck it in the ground. The chanting stopped immediately. The chief's eyes burned at Blake. Blake turned and faced the pirates.

"There's a good lad, now cut me loose."

Blake reached down and drew the captain's heavy cutlass from his belt.

"Burn in hell, you bastard." Then he raised the sword up and brought it down deep into his neck. Horrified, the other pirate started screaming and Blake brought it down squarely on his forehead. Blood sprayed in great fountains from their wounds and Blake watched as the life left their eyes. Blake was covered with blood spray and the sword dripped with gore. He felt no remorse, he felt only that these men needed to die and he escorted them to hell. Turning back to the chief he walked back slowly and knelt in front of him and presented the sword in both hands. The chief took the sword from him and raised it high above his head. He turned to the rest of the tribe and screamed loudly. The rest joined in and led Blake back to the village.

* * * * * *

Blake's strength returned rapidly. He was fed regularly and, when he was ready, they taught him to hunt and fish to help carry his weight with the tribe. A high cliff ran along one side of the cove where he washed up after the wreck. He went hunting up there and looked down in the water. He could see an outline of a ship submerged about a hundred feet from the base of the cliff. It appeared to be only ten feet below the surface. It had to be the pirate's ship he was on, and he would make it a point to see if he could salvage anything from it.

Blake started to make his way back to the village when he spotted black flecks far out in the ocean. He watched for a while and as they got closer he could see they were actually six out-rigger canoes with ten men in each one. Blake ran as fast as he could to tell the men in the village of the boats. He had learned only a few words of their language and managed get through to one of the warriors what he saw. The warrior started yelling and suddenly the village exploded into chaos. Women grabbed children and ran for the jungle. Any man that was able took up weapons and ran for the beach. There were forty or fifty in all, carrying knives, clubs, axes and spears all made from stone. The only metal weapon was the sword Blake had given the chief. As the boats drew nearer Blake could see a human skull mounted on the bow of each canoe, with angry looking warriors paddling with all their strength.

Fourteen tattooed warriors came to the front line on the beach all holding a spear and screaming war cries. When the boats got close enough a big savage stood in the canoe threw a spear. It fell short and stuck in the sand in front of the war-rior's line. A few seconds later the men on the beach started throwing spears with deadly accuracy, wiping out ten or twelve of the attackers. The attackers pressed on, now claiming casu-alties on the island side. Suddenly, the beach was awash with men fighting and screaming in furious hand to hand combat. Blake clubbed one of the attackers crushing his skull, picked up his spear and skewered another. He could see the chief cut-ting a swath through them with the cutlass swinging back and forth, taking limbs and heads as he went. Blake suffered a blow to his back and found himself in a death struggle with one of the attackers. The warrior was on top of him with the shaft of his spear across his throat. Blake was using every ounce of strength to hold him off but the lack of air was taking its toll and he started to lose consciousness. He could see his death in the man's eyes when suddenly his head disappeared and he rolled off. The bloody, gore-covered chief stood above him holding the cutlass. Smiling, he helped Blake to his feet and ran back into the melee. Gasping for air Blake could see maybe ten of the attackers swimming for their boats and scrambling to make their escape. Blake's tribe had suffered heavy losses but managed to turn them back. Several warriors hurled spears at them but they were soon out of range. The surf was red with blood, men were helping the wounded and others were killing any wounded attackers.

Weeks after the attack, Blake took a small canoe and the woman who nursed him back to health when he got to the island out to where the ship had sunk. Diving in the crystal clear water he searched the wreckage for more weapons. He found one small knife and one short sword. Then he saw something that made him smile, a hammer from his forge. Could it be possible that more of his tools survived the wreck? Time after time he dove, bringing up tongs and other hammers. Blake grew more and more excited as he kept finding tools until he saw the anvil.

Practically leaping into the boat, the two of them went back to it as fast as they could paddle. He ran to the chief and tried to make him understand what he had found. Finally leading him down to the boat he showed him the tools. The skeptical chief was not impressed until Blake pointed to the cutlass. He had learned a couple words in their language; one of them was 'more'. The chief grinned broadly. For the next week, with the help of the tribe, Blake retrieved the anvil, more tools and pieces of metal from the wreck. While the tribe kept bringing more of the wreckage ashore, Blake built a fire pit for the forge and fashioned bellows from animal hides. He showed women how to make charcoal for the fuel and when all was assembled, he started making weapons. He made them from chains and shackles, from mast bands and even from broken hinges.

Soon he had knives and swords for every warrior in the tribe. He also used small pieces to make arrowheads. Blake showed them how to make bows and arrows and then how to use them. His status rose quickly in the tribe and soon everyone was helping him.

A year or so later they were attacked again. This time they were outnumbered three to one. Blake stood on the beach with the other warriors armed with the weapons he made. The battle was much shorter this time. His tribe lost one warrior and two were wounded. There were no escapes by the attackers. Unfortunately, Blake was one of the wounded. He suffered a blow to the head and was unconscious for a long time. When he awoke one week later, his body burned as if it was on fire. The same woman who nursed him before was there and was rubbing a salve over his body. She helped him to his feet and that's when Blake realized he was tattooed with the same markings as the warriors in the tribe. Grimacing in pain he stepped out of the hut and was cheered by the entire tribe. Several weeks went by and he was married to the woman who had nursed him to health, who was also the chief's daughter. They lived happy and content for a year, producing a son.

One day while cradling his son outside the hut a very excited boy ran into the village talking about a big canoe in the water. Blake ran to the beach with the rest of the warriors and saw a large ship anchored past the reef with a small rowboat coming ashore. Blake told the chief not to attack until he could see what they wanted. He agreed and let Blake meet the boat. It was an American Merchant ship investigating the island for fresh water and food. A short portly man who was in charge saw Blake and was taken back for a moment. His words sounded strange to Blake. "And who might you be?" he said. "Do you speak English?"

Blake smiled broadly, "Not for quite some time, sir."

Blake told the man his long story.

"That's quite a tale, sir, quite a tale," laughed the portly man. "I'm sure the captain will be wanting to hear it himself."

Returning to the ship he came back with the captain and several crewmen who were treated to a feast as Blake's guests. The captain offered Blake passage back to New York but regrettably not his wife and son, citing that being the only woman on the ship would cause too much trouble. It was the hardest decision of his life. Blake yearned to return home and see his family, he needed to apologize to his parents for leaving, but more so to tell his father that he was right about blacksmithing and how it saved his life several times.

Heartbroken, he explained to his wife about the torment of leaving her. She told him that a warrior must follow his own path and he would never be gone from her as long as his son lived. The next morning he stood on the beach hugging his wife and son as three heavy chests of his were loaded on the rowboat.

"What the hell is in these chests, mate?" grunted one of the seamen.

"My tools and anvil. Never know when they might be of some use," Blake said smiling. He shook the hand of the chief who looked solemn. "Be well, chief, and may your necklace protect you." The chief grunted and smiled. The boat pulled away from shore and Blake watched his family shrink. He could barely make out the anvil sitting on the stump and the solid gold necklace around the chief's neck glittered in the sun.

"My Lawd, that was one tale to remember," Sadie said.

The night had grown late and Blake was tired. He stood and stretched, "I'll think I'll turn in. What do you say, Caleb?"

"T-that w-was r- really s-s-somethin'," he said shaking his head, walking up the stairs. "R-really s-somethin'."

Blake followed him up the stairs, went into his own room and closed the door. He smiled to himself because he left part of the story out. When the natives were bringing him all the metal from the ship, not knowing the difference, they bought him all the pirates' treasure. When they brought him empty chests Blake got an idea. He removed the jewels and melted down all the gold into bars. Then he packed them all into the three chests, taking some leftover and making a huge necklace for the chief instead of the bones. He left the tools for the tribe. When the ship docked in New York he deposited all of it into four separate banks. It all totaled well in excess of a million dollars.

# CHAPTER 9

THE next morning found them eating breakfast in the kitchen. As Sadie cleared the dishes, she spoke while wiping her hands on her apron. "It bein' Sunday an' all, I's thought I's would go to the church for service, if'n you don' mind none."

"I don't mind, Sadie," Blake said. "I plumb forgot. Have a nice time."

"You is more than welcome ta' come. There be only the one church and they welcome everyone. Real nice preacher, too."

Blake pursed his lips and thought. "Haven't been to church in a long time," he said. "I reckon I'll pass."

"I-I w-would like t-to g-go, p-please," Caleb asked, looking hopefully at Blake. "I-I n-never b-been."

"You don't need my permission to go, son," Blake smiled. "We can take the day off. Sundays are a day of rest anyway, right Sadie?"

"Sho nuff," she said. "He can sits with me, I'll teach him right."

"C-could I-I g-go f-fishin' after?" he was grinning ear to ear now.

"If'n you bring a passel a catfish home, I'll be makin' ma granny's recipe fo' supper, wit' some right fine cornbread."

Blake stood up and put on his hat. "It's settled then. I'll see you two for supper." He strolled down to the livery and found Bull in the back paddock happily munching on some hay. When Bull saw him his ears pricked and he trotted over to Blake. "Did you miss me, old son," Blake said scratching his ears. "What do you say we go work out some of the knots in our backs?"

He led Bull into the barn and saddled him. While cinching the saddle girth, Joe came out of his office. "Going somewhere?" he asked.

"Seems like a fine day for a ride, and I could use some fresh air."

Yawning and scratching his belly Joe said, "It is a fine day sure enough. There's some real pretty country west of here. Just follow the road past the church and turn right at the fork, that'll take you out near the MacIntyre spread. He sure picked a nice place for a ranch."

Blake put his foot in the stirrup and threw his leg over Bull, waving to Joe, said, "Thanks, maybe I'll do that."

Blake rode out of the livery and turned left up the street, most of the townsfolk were making their way to the church. He saw old fat Weatherby with whom Blake assumed was his wife because she was equally large and sour looking. Josh Dooley and his family were on their way, with Madeline holding firmly onto Hap's finger, practically dragging him. "Morning, folks," Blake said tipping his hat. "Hang on tight there Miss Madeline, don't let him get away."

"She kinda insisted. Hope the roof don't go fallin' in," Hap grumbled.

Josh and Terry laughed and Josh said, "I think our daughter is the new Episcopal missionary." Terry just rolled her eyes.

"Well, I haven't seen any lightning so you might be all right," Blake teased. "Enjoy the day." Farther up he passed Chrissy and Bonnie. "Good morning ladies," he said as he caught up with them.

"Good morning, Mr. Thorton, will you be joining us for service?" Chrissy asked.

"No ma'am. Haven't been in a church for a long time. I figure Jesus has his hands full enough without worrying about me."

"The Lord has time for us all," Chrissy stated firmly.

"Maybe so. But Bull here insisted that I take him for a ride and wouldn't take no for an answer."

"I see," she said cocking her trademark eyebrow. "Perhaps he will wish to rest next Sunday."

Smiling, Blake said, "Perhaps, but he is a mighty strong willed horse. Good day, ladies." Blake touched the brim of his hat and kicked Bull up into a trot.

"I'd hate to live on the difference which is more strong willed, him or that horse," muttered Chrissy watching him leave.

"Him," Bonnie said quietly. Chrissy looked in surprise at her and they both started giggling.

Blake kept Bull at a trot until they were clear of town, then he eased him up to a moderate canter. He always marveled at his strength and his endurance. Small in stature, sturdy in structure Blake thought. He may never win a race, but he can pound the ground all day long and look for more the next day. Bull seemed like he was enjoying the run and was pushing on his bit a little so Blake said, "If you're feeling ambitious," then in a louder voice, "knock on it!"

Blake let him have his head and could feel Bull draw his hind legs underneath him and take off. They were in a trail-eating gallop moving as fast as they could. Blake leaned forward over his neck to cut down on wind resistance and let him fly. The perfect rhythm of Bull's feet and his breath made him sound like a freight train on a runaway course. Blake saw the trail to the MacIntyre ranch to the right but they were moving too fast to make the turn. Sitting back up in the saddle he began to slow Bull's pace and, after about a mile, had him back down to a fast walk. Bull was still fired up and had a prance in his walk. Blake rubbed his neck. "How'd that feel, boy? Pretty good? You can still move with the best of them."

He turned Bull back around and headed for the turn to the ranch. He rode up the turnoff until they came over a small rise. It was one of the most spectacular views Blake had ever seen. There was a huge valley with high hills on either side. There was lush green pasture with several hundred beeves roaming around grazing. In the center with a large stream winding its way in back of a large white house with a wraparound porch and two large barns. Blake could see the smokehouse, bunkhouse, corrals and several other buildings that comprised the MacIntyre ranch. Men were hard at work breaking horses, herding cattle and doing chores.

Behind him Blake heard riders approaching. He turned Bull to meet them when a team of horses pulling a buggy and three riders approached. The driver of the buggy stopped when they were a few feet away. A large, heavily muscled man with a shock of red hair under a broad brimmed Stetson hat eyed him from under bushy eyebrows, "An' who might you be?" he asked in a thick Scottish brogue.

Blake tipped his hat and smiled. "My name's Blake Thorton. I hope I'm not intruding. I was told that this was the prettiest piece of land in the territory and had to see for myself." Blake assumed he was the patriarch because one of the riders was Tom MacIntyre giving him a sour look.

"An' what is it you're thinkin'?"

"I traveled some sir, and I have never seen prettier."

"'Tis true, laddie, an' it would be all mine, Ian MacIntyre is m' name," he said holding out his hand.

"Pleasure to meet you," Blake responded, giving him a firm handshake.

"These two bonnie lasses are my daughters, Mary and Katherine," waving his hand to twin girls who were seated behind him. They were very pretty and about fourteen years old. "An' this is my son, Thomas."

"Pleased to meet you ladies," Blake said tipping his hat. "Tom and I have met."

"Oh?" the older MacIntyre said, looking at Tom.

"He's a drifter Pa, seen him hanging around town," Tom said with a slight sneer in his voice.

"Begging you pardon, Tom," Blake said using a smooth sarcastic tone, "I am reopening the blacksmith shop." Then with a broad smile, "I'll be staying a while."

Ian turned back to Blake genuinely pleased, "Are you now? Tis bonnie news for us all. M' smith tries to help the town, but his duties keep him very busy on m' ranch. Are you a skilled smith, lad?"

"I can hold my own." Blake eyes were burning into Tom's and Tom smiled back at him.

Ian MacIntyre could never have built a ranch such as this by not being cunning, smart and perceptive. He sensed the tension in the air. "I would be sure Thomas meant no harm, Mr. Thorton. I am wishing you luck and prosperity. Perhaps I will be testing your skills with a wee bit of work my smith canna handle himself."

Blake turned back to him and smiled. "I am at your service, Mr. MacIntyre. Good day, sir."

"Good day, Mr. Thorton." And slapping the reins on his horses, they left.

Blake turned Bull in the opposite direction and trotted away. "I've got a feeling this is going to be real interesting," he said.

Bull snorted and shook his head.

\* \* \* \* \* \*

Blake enjoyed the rest of the afternoon riding around the surrounding area. The land was green and growing, the sun was warm, and the air smelled of wildflowers beginning to bloom. He and Bull arrived in town around supper time. Blake spent a good half hour brushing down Bull only to turn him out in the back paddock and watch him find a sandy spot and roll until he was completely covered with dirt again. Bull stood and shook, glancing back at Blake as if to say, aren't you glad you wasted your time?

"Jerk horse," Blake muttered and started for home.

The smell of frying catfish greeted him at the door and Sadie was in the kitchen singing again. "How was church?" he asked, leaning over the pan breathing in the rich aroma.

"Fine, fine, that preacher sho' do give a powerful sermon, he does," replied Sadie.

"I see Caleb had some luck."

"Fo' sho' he did, got us some right fine catfish. Now get cleaned up 'cause we is almost ready to eat."

Blake did as he was told and enjoyed the meal almost as much as Caleb's recounting of the great battle fought against the biggest catfish west of the Mississippi. Sadie rolled her eyes several times and she and Blake shared some hidden smiles. Caleb sure was proud and deserved his time in the sun. Blake seemed to think the boy hadn't had much of that in his life.

When supper was over and the dishes washed it was dark. They were all sitting on the porch when Blake rose and stretched and said, "Think I'll head down to the saloon for a nightcap."

"Caleb perked up, "C-can I-I c-c-ome t-t-too?"

"Don't see why not."

"Yo' come home drunk and I's will lock th' door an' ya'll can sleep in th' yard with that fool dog," warned Sadie.

Blake smiled. "We'll behave mother, promise," he teased and kissed her on top of the head."

"Scat!" she yelled swatting him with a nearby broom.

Making a hasty retreat off the porch Blake and Caleb headed up the street.

The Trail's End wasn't crowded so they headed for the bar. Three of the tables were occupied by men playing cards and the piano player had not gotten any better.

"What'll it be gents?" Clyde the bartender said walking up to them.

"I'll have a beer and shot of your good whiskey," Blake said. "What do you want Caleb?"

He stood to full height and said, "S-same."

Blake turned to him with one elbow on the bar. "Really now. If you're sure."

"Y-yup."

"Set them up, barkeep," Blake said turning back.

When the drinks arrived Blake held up his beer mug to Caleb. "Here's to your health." They clinked their mugs together and took a swallow. Caleb's face scrunched up like he didn't care for it much and he set the mug down. "Don't care for it son? Ever had whiskey?" Caleb shook his head no. "Well try just a sip, and don't spill any."

Caleb took a tentative sip. To the casual observer they would have thought he tried kerosene.

Blake smiled. "No harm in not liking alcohol. It's expensive and can lead to trouble." Blake turned back to an amused bartender. "Got any sarsaparilla hiding back there?"

"Sure do, I'll fetch you some."

When Caleb tried it he liked it just fine. They were talking and enjoying their drinks when Blake felt a silky arm slip though his. Turning he was face to face with a pretty redheaded woman. Her dress was very low cut revealing her large creamy breasts. Her red hair was pulled back in curls with a large feather sticking out. "Hi there," she said seductively, "where have you been hiding?"

"I had to sail all the way from China to get here, sorry I'm late," Blake said flirting back. "And what's your name, darlin'?"

Pulling his arm tighter to her chest and batting her large green eyes, "Michelle to my friends. What's yours, honey?"

"Blake," he said. Caleb cleared his throat and Blake came out of her trance. "And this is Caleb, ma'am."

"Pleased to meet you, Caleb," Michelle said smiling sweetly.

Caleb turned bright red and looked down at the bar. "Ma'am," he said.

"You handsome boys want to buy a lady a drink?"

Blake summoned over the bartender who poured her a drink from a bottle under the bar. Blake knew it was probably just tea but he was enjoying the company so he didn't mind. The three of them talked for a while. Blake knew she was a prostitute but he found her intoxicating. It had been some time since he shared a bed with a woman and she was really making him consider taking her upstairs. She pressed hard against him with his arm now completely between her breasts and whispered in his ear, "Why don't we go up to my room? I'll show you a real good time."

Fate was a funny thing. Blake was in a tough spot because he didn't want to leave Caleb there alone, and thoughts of Chrissy flashed in his mind and yet he had no real ties to her. Then there was Michelle who was ready, willing and more than able to satisfy his primal needs. He was just about to apologize to Michelle and decline her offer when a huge hairy hand grabbed her shoulder and spun her away from him.

"There's other customers that need tending," he growled. It was the huge man Blake saw before sitting in the corner. Up close he was even more intimidating; he had hands the size of hams, and forearms the size of Blake's thighs. He stood a full head taller than Blake with long hair and a great bushy beard that almost concealed his black beady eyes.

Apparently, Michelle did not care for being interrupted while conducting business. Her green eyes flashed with anger as she slapped him on his broad chest. "Back off, you big lummox!" she snapped. "I'll see to the others when I am done here."

He brushed her aside roughly. "You've wasted enough time on this one, now git."

Blake was not one to see any woman manhandled so he stepped in between them. "Maybe she has, or maybe she hasn't. I believe the choice is hers."

The huge man looked down on Blake, his voice sounding like distant thunder, "I say she's done here."

Blake turned to Caleb smiling. "See the problem with men like this is no one will ever take them head on. Because he is so big he thinks he can push people around and there's nothing they can do. The first thing you do is get them down to your size." With that, Blake brought up his foot and sent it crashing into the big man's knee. Howling in pain he dropped to his other knee, then he grabbed the bar rail and started to stand back up. Blake punched him hard in the middle of his chest causing he man to gasp for breath. "See now we are the same size," Blake said calmly. "May I borrow your tap hammer?" he said to the barkeep. The bartender brought a large wooden mallet up from beneath the bar and handed it to Blake. "You see Caleb it's not how hard you hit, it's where you hit," as he brought the hammer down squarely between the gasping man's eyes. The human buffalo dropped to the floor like a pole axed steer. "You see how easy that can be?" Blake handed the hammer back to its owner.

Caleb just stood there with his mouth hanging open as was most of the bar. Dan LaClare strolled up to Blake and looked down at the heap of man on the floor. "I do believe he is going to be very upset with you when he wakes," he drawled. "May I recommend you be elsewhere when he does."

"Perhaps that would be best," Blake said imitating him. He turned to Michelle, took her hand and kissed it. "Maybe, another time, ma'am?"

Still staring at the man on the floor she said, "Looking forward to it."

Blake turned Caleb around and ushered him out the door.

Halfway down the street Caleb glanced back at the saloon and said, "H-h-how'd you d-do t-that?" looking at Blake in amazement.

"Remember that Merchant ship that brought me back? I had some fights and a little Chinese fellow took pity on me and taught me some things he learned in a Shaolin temple. Kind of comes in handy sometimes, don't you think?"

Caleb shook his head yes and sputtered, "Yeah."

\* \* \* \* \* \*

Early the next morning Blake woke up, washed, shaved and put on some clean clothes. Coming down the stairs he could tell breakfast was cooking because the whole house smelled of bacon and fresh bread. Smiling he strolled into the kitchen and poured himself a cup of coffee.

"Good morning, Sadie. Breakfast smells great."

"Well sits yo'self down an' I'll fix yo' a plate. I's saved some 'for the boy eats it all," Sadie said grinning.

Caleb looked up from his plate; his cheeks were stuffed like a squirrel gathering nuts.

Blake leaned back in his chair laughing. "You know son, nobody is going to steal that, so you can take your time and chew."

Caleb took a big swallow, "I-It's a-a-awful g-good." Then took another huge forkful of eggs and shoveled them into his mouth.

Blake shook his head in amazement. "I'm going to go broke feeding this kid," he muttered. Sadie set his food down and he looked up at her, "Thank you. How is Sam coming on the back room?"

"Jest fine, got the outside done, and the roof ain't leakin' no more. He tol' me to ask yo' 'bout the stove."

"I'm going to get Caleb making horseshoes this morning and I'll go get the stove and pipe from Dooley's store," he said as he dug into his breakfast.

"Appreciate it, I do, gets a might chilly sometimes."

A small bark came from the back door. Satan was sitting there wagging his tail.

"Yo' jest wait there, Mr. Dog, I is comin'," Sadie said picking up a plate of table scraps. She opened the screen door and set the plate on the steps. Satan gobbled up the food and was done practically before she closed the door.

"You two are friends now?" Blake asked.

"He done killed a rabbit in th' garden and a fat rat from somewhere yesterday. He be all right wit' me, long as he don't let no wind in the house. Lawd, that was awful."

Blake and Caleb laughed and got their hats off the hook by the door. Satan was very excited to see Caleb and ran around barking. He followed them all the way to the forge. Blake had Caleb get the firepot started while he found the steel for horseshoes. He showed Caleb how to make a shoe by bending, shaping and punching the holes. Caleb's first attempt was terrible but Blake was patient and after a half dozen tries, Caleb made a good one. "Now do that same thing fifty times," Blake laughed as he patted him on the back. Blake took off his apron. "I've got to go to the mercantile and get Sadie's stove. Be back in a while."

The bell over the door rang when Blake entered, which brought Madeline running. "Good day, sir. May I help you?" she said boldly.

"I need you to pick up that stove over by the wall and carry it to my house, please," Blake said politely.

She turned quickly and ran to the small pot belly stove. Then she turned to Blake and said, "I can't lift that, you silly, I'll get Daddy," and thundered off to find her father.

Terry came out of the back room carrying Ethan on her hip. "Good morning Mr. Thorton. How are you today?"

"Please, ma'am, call me Blake. Who is this handsome little spud?"

"This is Ethan," she said bouncing him on her hip. "Josh will be right with you. I am finishing up with another customer."

With that Chrissy came out of the back carrying a bolt of fabric. "I'll take two yards of this and some thread," she told Terry. Her eyes caught Blake's and she smiled a little. "Good morning," she said.

"Ma'am," Blake said touching the brim of his hat.

"Here," she said holding out her arms to Ethan, "I'll take him so you can cut the cloth."

Terry handed her Ethan and Chrissy smiled down at him cooing softly.

Blake wandered over to her and tickled Ethan on the cheek. "How come you don't smile at me like that?" he asked Chrissy.

"Maybe because he hasn't developed a smart attitude yet," she said never taking her eyes off Ethan.

"Certain women bring that out in a man," Blake said grinning.

"Hmmm," she muttered, cocking her eyebrow.

Josh appeared from the side door. "Hello Blake, what can I do for you?" They shook hands and Blake gave him a list and made arrangements for the stove to be delivered while Chrissy and Terry finished their business. Blake kept stealing glances their way admiring how good Chrissy looked holding a baby.

"I said, is there anything else?" Josh teased a distracted Blake.

"Huh?" Blake asked, and then realizing he had been caught gawking at Chrissy said, "no that's it."

Their business concluded, Chrissy turned to leave. "I'll see Caleb promptly at two then, Mr. Thorton."

"Damn, I forgot," Blake said. "Give me one of those dollar Ingersoll watches, please." Josh took one out of the case and handed it to him. "If you would indulge me, ma'am, I would like to talk to you."

"I need to get back, but if you can be brief," she said.

The truth was Blake had no idea why he said that he wanted to talk with her and he felt like a schoolboy on the playground. He took money out of his pocket and gave it to Josh.

"There's a hundred dollars here," Josh said.

"Really?" Blake said, watching Chrissy leave. "Well put it toward my account." He was trying to catch up with her and bumped into a cracker barrel.

"Hey, Blake," Josh called with a big grin.

"What?"

"Oh, nothing."

Blake could see he was being teased and growled back, "Shut up." He opened the door and left.

Josh walked over to Terry. "I would have thought it gets easier when you're older."

"Apparently not," she replied, watching Blake run by the window.

\* \* \* \* \* \*

Blake hurried to catch Chrissy just as she reached the edge of the store. "Excuse me, ma'am," she turned to look at him. "It occurred to me that I don't know your last name."

"O'Bryan, Christine O'Bryan. Is that why you wanted to talk to me?"

"Well, that's one of the reasons," he said. "I wanted to know if...." Blake was stopped by a grizzly-like roar coming from the alley between the buildings. When he turned toward the noise, he saw a huge form lumbering straight at him, gathering speed. Blake recognized the big man from the saloon barreling toward him. Left with not much time to think, Blake grabbed Chrissy's arms to get her out of way of the charging beast. When she was safely back around the corner he plucked an axe handle out of a barrel and, swinging it low, caught the big man's shin, causing him to stumble. The big man pin-wheeled his arms trying to regain his balance and ran headfirst into a passing wagon. As his head hit the two-by-twelve board on the side of the wagon, the board cracked and the wagon rocked, almost tipping over. The startled driver pulled back on the reins yelling, "What the hell hit me!!??"

Blake got back to his feet dusting himself off and walked over to the heap of man on the ground.

"Good Lord," the driver said jumping down, "I though a full grown bull rammed me."

"Just about," Blake said.

"Damn fool broke my wagon side board," the driver sputtered, "and I can't move my wagon without running him over."

The big man hit dead center on the wagon and fell out cold and face up between the wheels. Blake tossed the driver a five dollar coin and said, "Here you can use that to fix your wagon, if you help me drag him out of there."

"Sure thing, Mister," he said, pocketing the coin. They both grabbed a foot and dragged him back into the alley. "He sure is one heavy son-of-a-buck, ain't he?" he puffed wiping his sleeve across his forehead.

"That he is," Blake replied shaking his head. Stepping over the big man's legs they left the alley.

Chrissy peeked around the corner as Blake stepped out. "What on earth was that all about?"

"I have no idea, but he seemed right angry with that wagon," Blake said shrugging his shoulders.

She cocked her eyebrow at him. "The wagon, really? Are you sure he wasn't after you?" she said, not believing him.

"Couldn't have been me," Blake said innocently, "I hardly know him." Chrissy continued to stare at Blake pursing her lips. "So, does Bonnie have everything she needs for teaching Caleb?"

"Yes, I believe so."

"Good, then he'll be there on time," said Blake tipping his hat. "Good day Mrs. O'Bryan."

She watched him walking back toward the forge and drew a deep breath. Exhaling loudly she shook her head and smiled.

Back at the forge Caleb had made good progress on the shoes. He was dirty and sweating but he grinned from ear to ear. Blake examined the shoes and pointed out some things he could do better but all in all he was pleased. He handed Caleb the pocket watch he bought earlier and Caleb was stunned. Blake had assumed that Caleb could tell time but quickly realized that he couldn't. Blake taught him how to wind it and explained the basics of reading a watch. "It's you're responsibility to be over at the café for school on time," he said. "I'll help you for a while, but it's up to you."

Caleb held the watch to his ear and smiled at the ticking sound, "I-I w-will, t-thanks."

Joe Bergman strolled out of the livery, eating an apple.

"Hey, Joe," Blake called to him, "got any horses in need of shoes?"

"Several," Joe said.

"If you want, we're ready to put some on."

"Hell, yes," he said. "Be right back."

He went in the livery and came out leading a mare. "She's a good one to learn on, stands quiet."

"Thanks," Blake said taking the mare. "Fetch the shoeing box over there, Caleb, and we'll try out some of those shoes you made."

Blake taught Caleb how to trim, reshape and nail the shoes on. Blake did a front and back shoe and had Caleb try the other side. The mare stood patiently for Blake but fussed a little when Caleb tried. Just when Blake was going to step in to help, Caleb stopped and stood up and talked to the horse.

"Whoa there, girl," he said. "This is my first time, so take it easy now."

He stroked her head gently and the mare nuzzled his hand. Running his hand gently down her neck and down her leg he gently picked up her hoof and went back to work.

"I'll be damned," Blake whispered to himself.

When he was done Caleb stroked her neck softly. "Good girl," he said.

Blake came over to inspect his work. "Good job, son," he said rubbing the withers on the horse.

"T-t-thanks," Caleb smiled.

"How come you don't stutter around horses?" Blake asked gently.

Caleb shrugged his shoulders. "N-n-not a-afraid of th-them."

Blake placed his hand on his shoulder. "You keep going like you are, and you will be a fine man. I see it in you. There's nobody in the world that you should hang your head to, just remember that." Caleb nodded. "Now take the mare back to Joe and see if he has another one to shoe."

Caleb took the lead rope and walked her back in the livery. A few minutes later he walked out with a gelding. Smiling he gave Blake a silver dollar. "F-from J-Joe."

"That's yours, son. You earned it. Soon you'll have a whole pocketful of them," Blake said smiling. Caleb put the shoes on two more horses with Blake's guidance and was getting more confident with each one. That was all the shoes Caleb had made. He took the watch out of his pocket and checked it. He held it out to Blake, who looked and said, "Twelve o'clock, Sadie should be bringing lunch soon." With that she came around the corner carrying a basket. Caleb ran up to her and showed her the watch and money he made. They sat in the shade of a nearby tree to get out of the sun and enjoy their meal. When they finished Caleb rebuilt the fire and started making shoes again. He checked his watch constantly holding out for Blake to read. Each time Blake told him the time and how much longer before he had to go.

At a quarter to two Blake told Caleb to get cleaned up and head to the café. He continued to make shoes for the rest of the afternoon. It had been a long time since he had done any serious blacksmithing and he could feel the fatigue creep into his muscles. There a peace that comes from blacksmithing; it is difficult to describe because it looks like dirty, hard, sweaty work. Perhaps right in the center of it all, the violent pounding on the anvil, the intense heat of the forge and the steaming hiss of the metal in the water of the slack tub, it is like the eye of a hurricane. Blake liked it there and felt completely at peace.

\* \* \* \* \* \*

It was about quarter past four when a very excited Caleb ran around the corner carrying some books. There was a scared look on his face and when he got to Blake all he could do was point back up the street. Caleb could not get out any words and was becoming more and more agitated.

"What's the matter son?" Blake said calmly. Caleb's jaw worked frantically but still there were no words. "Stop!" Blake yelled firmly and grabbed his shoulders. That seemed to settle him down a little. "Now, tell me what's going on, slowly."

Caleb drew a deep breath and concentrated on every word. "Th-th-the b-bb-big m-man is p-p-pissed," he said pointing up the street.

Blake didn't have to wonder who he was talking about because the big lummox was making his presence known. "Where is that yellow bellied coward?!" roared the big man from around the corner.

Blake pursed his lips and asked Caleb, "The big guy from the saloon?" Caleb nodded affirmatively. Blake reached behind him and picked up a large set of tongs. "Well, shit, this has got to stop," he muttered.

The big man turned the corner being followed by several of the townsfolk. The area around his eyes was turning purple from being hit on the head twice and the welt on his forehead gave him a ferocious appearance. Both ham sized fists were clenched as he stomped toward Blake. "I've come to settle accounts," he snarled.

"You, sir, are a hard man to keep down," Blake said smiling.

He was directly in front of Blake when he stopped and stood glaring at him. "Damn right I am." Blake could feel his hot breath on top of his head.

"Didn't I already whup you twice?" Blake asked.

"Yeah, and you cheated both times, but now you ain't got nowhere to hide," he growled.

"You really don't expect me to fight you fair, do you? You're too big for that, you'd tear me apart."

"Just like I'm gonna do now."

"I have a better idea."

Taken a little off guard the big man said, "What?"

"I don't want to be mangled by you, and you don't want any more knots on your head. So why don't we call it a draw and become friends?"

"Don't need no friends, an' what makes you think you can beat me again?" the big man said angrily.

"Because I did twice without breaking a sweat," Blake said smiling. He could see the wheels turning in the big man's head. The anger slowly left his eyes as he thought about what Blake said.

"You ain't never gonna fight me fair are ya?" he asked.

"Nope."

"Well, I ain't never had me a friend before, and you proved you can whup me, I'm guessin' I can give it try."

"Good," Blake sighed in relief. "Put it there," and held out his hand.

The big man took Blake's hand and shook it. Blake's hand nearly disappeared in his.

"What's your name?" Blake asked.

"Percival Feathers," he said. Someone in the crowd in back of him snickered. Percival turned slowly and gave them a hard look. "It was my Pappy's name and he was right proud of it."

Blake tried to keep from smirking. "How about I call you Big Man, it seems to suit you better."

"Kinda like that," he smiled. "Ya think I could talk to you about somethin' for a minute?"

"You bet, Big Man."

Big Man turned to the crowd of onlookers and growled, "The rest of you can piss off." Without a moment's hesitation they found better places to be. He and Blake talked for about five minutes, then they shook hands again and Big Man lumbered off.

Joe was leaning on a hitching rail nearby laughing and shaking his head. Blake strolled over to him, "What's up, Joe?"

"I was just wonderin' why you don't sound like a church bell when you walk, with those big brass balls you got swinging," he said chuckling.

"Jesus, I almost soiled my pants when I saw him coming," Blake laughed.

"What'd he want to talk about?" Joe said wiping a tear from his eye.

"I had to promise him something."

"I'd keep it."

"I intend to," said Blake. "I intend to."

# CHAPTER 10

Tʜᴇ next morning found Blake and Caleb waiting in the forge for their lumber to be delivered. When they got home the previous night, Sam was already working on Sadie's room and told them he would be by with the lumber first thing in the morning. Sadie was very happy with her room and talked all through supper how she couldn't wait to have a warm place to sleep this winter. She asked Blake if it would all right if Sam's wife and two children could stop by and see it. Blake suggested that if the weather was good they should all have dinner together tomorrow because he would like to meet them. She was hesitant at first because usually colored and white folks don't eat together but when Blake explained that he would damn well eat with whoever he pleased, she relented and promised a special meal.

At the blacksmith shop they only waited a few minutes when Sam showed up driving a wagonload of lumber.

"Morning, Sam," Blake said shaking his hand. "That looks like some fine wood you got there."

"Yes suh," he said. "You wants it right here?"

"Yup, that's fine," Blake said putting on his gloves. The three of them unloaded and separated the lumber into different stacks according what it was used for. "So are you bringing the family over for supper tonight?" Blake asked.

"Sho' nuff, the Mrs. was cookin' up a storm before I left. I has me a fiddle ifn' yo' want me to bring it. Womenfolk likes my playin'."

"Sounds real good. We'll see you tonight then."

"Sho nuff," Sam said, touching the brim of his hat. He slapped the reins and was gone.

Blake and Caleb set to work getting the main beam ready. Blake measured and re-measured all the cuts so there were no mistakes and they drilled and, using oak pins, put the main support together on the ground inside the forge. Caleb tried to pick up the 'U' support to see how heavy it was. "H-how w-we going t-to lift t  this?" he asked.

"The same way you lift a five-hundred-pound yardarm up a fifty-foot mast," Blake said as he laid out the ropes and pulleys. He secured them on various points on the walls and took the slack out of the ropes. Caleb looked doubtful as they began pulling on the ropes until it started to rise and fell solidly into place. Then they took off all the ropes and secured them across the building to the opposite walls. Blake explained that when the main beam in the roof broke the roof sagged and pushed the walls out a little. "This will keep the whole thing from crashing down on us when we jack up the roof, hopefully," he said. Once again Caleb had a doubtful look in his eyes.

Sadie brought lunch but didn't stay because she had a lot of work to do to get ready for supper. As she was leaving Blake asked, "You're not going to too much trouble are you?"

"Lets me be worryin' 'bout that," she chided. "Ah said ah was makin' somethin' special and I is."

"Yes, Ma'am," Blake said biting into his sandwich.

Blake and Caleb worked on bracing for the roof until it was time for Caleb to go to the café for school. Blake spent the rest of the time calculating how much the roof would have to be jacked up to make it straight again. Unfortunately, none of the jacks would do it in one shot, so he would have to jack it up in stages.

Blake was deep in thought when Caleb returned. "H-how are y-you going t-to do this?" he asked Blake.

Blake wrinkled his brow and scratched his head, "Like my father always said, I'm going to have to cogitate on it some."

"W-what's c-c-cogitate?" Caleb asked confused.

"It means think on it, it's going to be tricky but I think it's doable," Blake said smiling. "Why don't we head home and get cleaned up for supper. Maybe it will be clearer in the morning."

When they arrived at their house, Sadie had already set up a table in the backyard and brought out chairs. Sam's family was there and she introduced Marie and the children to them. Marie was very pretty; she had long black hair pulled back in a ponytail, large soft brown eyes and a charming smile. Her daughter, Rachel, was about four years old and Blake could tell that she would equal her mother's beauty when she got older. Little Sam was two, and had a stocky build; he, too, was going to be handsome and strong.

The aroma wafting from the house was incredible, fried chicken and a heap of golden biscuits with three different vegetables. There were fresh cut flowers on the table, with what Blake assumed was the Major's good china dishes. Caleb's dog, Satan, came trotting into the yard and the kids immediately took to him, chasing him around and giggling as he licked their faces.

The whole scene made Blake smile and gave him a long forgotten feeling of family and peace. He and Caleb went into the house to wash and change their clothes. When they came back outside, Sam had arrived carrying his fiddle. The kids ran up to him and hugged his legs, begging him to play them a tune. He obliged with a lively song that made them dance and laugh. When he finished, they sat down and joined hands. Blake asked Sadie to say grace because it was her family. Blake watched Caleb, it was apparent that this was all new to him and he was unsure how to act. Blake caught his eye and gave him a wink relaxing him a little. As soon as prayers were over they all dug in, enjoying the feast, laughing and telling stories the whole time. Just when Blake figured he couldn't eat another bite, Sadie and Marie brought out a bubbling peach cobbler and a chocolate cake. Even Caleb, who never seemed to get enough to eat, was slowing down but managed to finish off large pieces of both desserts. The women started clearing the table and Sam picked up his fiddle and played some more, he even knew a sea chantey that Blake recognized from when he was on board ships. When Sam played a waltz, Blake asked Sadie to dance while Marie coaxed a clumsy Caleb into trying.

Marie finished dancing with him, sat down at the table near Blake and watched Sadie take a turn dancing with Caleb. The two children were fascinated with Blake and crawled up on his lap. "You have yourself a fine family, Marie," he said.

"Thank you, suh. I try hard, but they are troublesome. Rachel bears constant watching, and Lil' Sam gets into everything."

"That would be their job," Blake smiled as he tickled Rachel, making her giggle. "You should be right proud of Sam, too. He's doing a fine job on his aunt's room."

"Oh, he is," she replied giving Sam and the children a loving look. "I's can't tell you how much the money you is givin' Sam helps. Times is hard, but he always keeps food on the table. He helps with our babies, too."

"I can tell," Blake smiled. "Children this fine don't get that way by accident. But it has been my experience that manners are taught by the mother. You should be proud of yourself."

"Thank you, and bless your heart, Mr. Thorton, suh." Marie smiled and reached over and tickled Lil' Sam on the cheek.

As the sun was setting and the night began to cool down, Sam and Marie said their good-byes and each took a sleeping child off Blake's lap. Blake stood and stretched and made his way to the rocking chair on the front porch with a cigar.

"I wants to thanks you for havin' my family fo' supper," Sadie said sitting in the other chair, "you is a blessin' fo' shu'."

"It was my pleasure. You have a real nice family and I can't remember when I've had a better time," Blake said blowing smoke into the yard. "What's Caleb up to?"

"He's workin' on somethin' Miss Bonnie tol' him to do. Practicin' letters an' numbers an' such. Yo' is changin' his life fo' sho'."

Flicking an ash over the rail Blake said, "He's worth it."

"Well I is plumb tuckered out, I'll think I is going to turn in," she said. "If'n yo' don't need me no mo'."

"No ma'am, good night, and that was the best fried chicken I ever ate."

"Learned how from a Creole woman on the plantation, Lawd she was some cook, sho' nuff'," Sadie replied going in the house, "Good night, suh."

Blake leaned back and closed his eyes listening to the crickets when the sound of three horses walking up the street caught his attention. It was pretty dark but he could make out three riders making their way to the saloon.

\* \* \* \* \* \*

"Can't wait to get me a drink, Huxley. You think they got women there?" one of them said in a gravelly voice.

The name sounded familiar to Blake, he knew a man named Huxley back in the war but that was a long time ago and what were the chances it was the same man. Besides, he always rode with a man named Luther Bent and they were nothing but trouble.

"I told you two drinks and no dallying with the doves," the man warned. "You got that, Bent?"

"Aw, shit," Blake muttered to himself.

Blake stood and went inside. He took his gun off the coat-stand by the door and buckled it on. Checking to make sure it was loaded he put on his hat and turned to the door. Caleb had been working on his homework and looked up.

"W-where ya going?" he asked.

"Out for a while," Blake said.

"Is th-there t-ttrouble?"

Blake realized Caleb had seen him put on his gun, which he hadn't worn much lately. He smiled at Caleb. "Naw, just put this on out of habit," he said, patting the handle of his revolver. "You get back to work and make Bonnie proud."

"I-I will," Caleb replied smiling back.

Blake left the house and started walking toward the saloon. Staying in the shadows behind the three riders he quickly caught up to them. He noticed how they all three took a long glance at the bank when they rode by. "What are you up to, boys?" Blake whispered to himself. The trio stopped at the hitching rail in front of the saloon as Blake slipped into a shadow nearby and listened.

"Town is pretty quiet. Maybe we can do this without him," Bent said.

Huxley shot him a harsh look. "When you're the boss, you can call it, until then keep your mouth shut." Bent said something under his breath that Blake couldn't hear. "Two drinks and no trouble, we're just here to find out what kind of lawdog we're dealing with."

The third man Blake didn't recognize said in a low voice, "Once I put a bullet in him, he won't be no trouble."

"You shoot a lawman and we'll have every starpacker in a hundred miles down on us. We wait for Pudney to show and do this so nobody gets hurt. Got it?" Huxley hissed.

"When the hell is he comin'? I'm tired of sleepin' on the trail," carped Bent.

"Two, maybe three days," Huxley whispered. "We don't make a move without him."

"Fine," grumbled the other man. "But I'm gettin' me a bottle for camp, I hates waitin'.'"

The three of them made their way up the steps and through the batwings of the saloon.

Blake wished he could get closer but that would risk Huxley recognizing him. He looked around and spotted Dan LaClare walking out of the hotel toward the Trail's End.

When he got close enough, Blake whispered, "Pssst, Dan, come here."

Dan looked down the alley and Blake stepped out just enough for him to see him. "That you, Blake," he drawled quietly. "Why may I ask are you lurking in the shadows?"

Blake kept his voice low. "Three men just went into the saloon. I know two of them and they are bad to be sure. Go in there and see if you can find out what they are up to."

Dan turned to the saloon and squinted at the doors, "And why on earth would I do that?"

"Because you're bored and could use some excitement."

"Truer words were never spoken, but it is hazardous to meddle in another man's affairs," Dan whispered flatly.

"What if told you you could be a hero?"

"That is a fine epitaph for my gravestone."

"Look, if you don't help me there won't be any money for you to fleece people out of at cards."

"Good heavens," Dan said, "that would be a tragedy. What do you believe are their intentions?"

"Unless I miss my guess, they're going to rob the bank."

"Scoundrels," Dan smiled. "Of course, if I meet with an untimely end, I will be very annoyed with you."

"I'll make sure you get a real nice marker in the cemetery," Blake said with a smart ass smile.

"Hmmm…lovely." Dan sauntered away and entered the saloon.

Blake sat on a wooden crate and waited. Half an hour later Huxley and the other two left the saloon. Bent put two bottles of rotgut in his saddlebags and got mounted. They rode quietly back out of town the way they came in. Blake watched them until they disappeared and turned toward the doors. Dan was standing outside the batwings lighting a cheroot. Blake climbed the stairs and they both went in. He ordered two whiskeys and gave one to Dan.

"Rather an unsociable lot," Dan said, sipping his drink.

"So you didn't hear much?" Blake asked.

"Sometimes it is not what a man says as much as what he doesn't say," Dan mused, as he pointed at his glass for the bartender to refill. When that was done, he continued, "They weren't forthcoming with last names, but I believe there was a Pete, Luther and Frank. Sound familiar?"

"Pete Huxley and Luther Bent are. I don't know Frank."

"They made some inquiries about the local law enforcement, but were rather vague as to why."

"Who is the sheriff, anyway?" Blake asked.

"Are you planning to rob the bank also?"

"Yeah, sure, that's why I bought a house and started a business, so they wouldn't suspect."

"A devious plan indeed," Dan quipped. Blake shot him a frustrated look. Dan smiled. "The sheriff is Iver Johansson, a former

Texas ranger who desired a more sedentary lifestyle. He's very tough and mean as a…" Dan searched for the words, "Sun burnt rattler, as they say. Anyway, he has made peace with the fact that the town pays his wages and he answers to the mayor."

"Who is?" Blake asked.

"Why none other than our illustrious banker. Phineas Weatherby. And, as a side note, Ian MacIntyre would be the bank's largest depositor."

A large piece of the puzzle that is the town of MacIntyre just slipped into place. Blake smiled and shook his head. "Anything else I should know?"

"Our sheriff is quite enamored with his extensive collection of firearms."

"Hmm….lovely," Blake said, raising his glass in a toast. Dan raised his and clinked Blake's.

\* \* \* \* \* \*

Blake had a lot of work to do in the forge the next morning but he figured if he put the sheriff on Huxley's trail he could stop the robbery before it got started. He made his way to the jail, which was a single story stone building that looked like it could withstand an attack by anything. The windows had bars and heavy oak shutters with slots for shooting from and the front door was sturdily built and looked like it could be barred from the inside. Blake entered the front door and found a tall thin man sitting behind the desk polishing a large bore Sharps rifle with a telescopic sight. He could tell the rifle was a showpiece, the way it gleamed.

The man behind the desk glanced up at Blake with suspicious eyes; he looked to be well in his sixties with a strong jaw and light blue eyes. He was the type of man who when he looked at you, you felt you had already done something wrong. He stopped wiping down the rifle and stared at Blake. "Something I can help you with?" he asked gruffly.

"I hope so," Blake said extending his hand. "Name's Blake Thorton."

He let Blake's hand hang there for a few seconds and then dropped the cleaning rag and shook Blake's hand with his gnarled fingers. "State your business, Mr. Thorton."

Blake didn't mind a man being tough, but could not abide rudeness. "I take it you are Iver Johansson, the sheriff?"

"That is the name my mother gave me," he said flatly, "and that man sitting behind you is my deputy, Mike Ventosa."

Blake turned and saw a man sitting with his feet propped up on the pot belly stove. He had been sitting behind the door when Blake came in.

"Howdy," he said.

Blake stepped over and shook his hand. "Pleasure."

"You the man who has been beatin' on the bouncer over at the Trail's End?" he asked grinning.

Blake smiled back. "We've come to an understanding."

"That big bastard has thumped me a couple times," Mike said. "Would've paid money to see him beat on."

"One man is somethin', all right," the sheriff grumbled. "I've come out on top taking two that size."

Mike rolled his eyes so Johansson couldn't see.

Blake turned back to the sheriff. "Mind if I sit?" pointing to a chair in front of the desk.

"I guess so," he said impatiently.

Blake took off his hat and set it on the desk. Sitting down he saw the disapproving look from the sheriff. Blake took his hat off the desk and deftly threw it onto the coat rack near the door. "I'm here as a courtesy, sheriff. I saw three men ride into town last night, and I have a feeling their going to try and rob the bank." Blake heard Mike's feet hit the floor and he walked around to look at Blake. The sheriff didn't move a muscle.

"What makes you think that?" Johansson asked calmly.

"I rode with one of them in the war. He was no good then and I doubt he changed much."

"Which side?" Johansson asked.

The war had been over several years but feelings still ran strong. Blake knew that he had to be truthful and it would probably count against him. "Does it matter?"

"Does to me."

"North." Blake said.

Johansson sucked his teeth and grimaced. "Yankee, huh? Now why would a blue belly come in here and offer to turn in one of his own?"

Blake could feel the anger rise inside him. "Just because we fought on the same side, that doesn't mean I owe him shit. There were good and bad on both sides, and I'm telling he was one of the worst."

"If you say so," the sheriff said in a disbelieving tone.

Ventosa chimed in, "What makes you think they are gonna rob the bank?"

Blake cut his stare from the sheriff to his deputy. "I followed them to the saloon and overheard them talking."

"They said they was going to rob it?"

"Never heard them say that clearly, it's just a hunch."

The sheriff sputtered, "So you come in here with no proof anybody's going to do anything and expect me to do what? Lock 'em up and throw away the key on your say so?"

"No, I don't," Blake said. "Just check them out is all. They're camped outside of town north of here. Their handles are Pete Huxley, Luther Bent and Frank something-or-other; I never got his last name. They are waiting on a man named Pudney. He should be coming in soon."

Mike got up and rifled through some wanted posters on the desk. "What the hell are you doin'?" the sheriff growled.

As he looked through the posters Ventosa muttered, "Huxley and Bent sound familiar but they ain't got no paper on them," he stopped searching and pulled out a wanted poster. Handing it to the sheriff he said, "Thought I recognized the name Pudney, he's wanted for bank and train robbery plus a murder down El Paso way. He's a bad one for sure."

"I imagine there's more than one man with the name of Pudney, I doubt it's him." the sheriff said, throwing the poster on the desk. He leaned back in his chair and gave Blake an arrogant stare.

"I'm wasting my time here," Blake growled and stood up.

Mike held up his hand and said, "Hang on now, don't get all riled. I can send out some telegrams to see if anybody knows these men or what they may be up to."

"Waste of time if you ask me," grumbled the sheriff. "Thorton here is probably in on it."

Blake had enough of the sheriff's bad attitude. He stood and placed his hat firmly on his head and put his two fists on the desk leaning in toward Johansson, "Look, I don't give a rat's ass if you believe me or not. In case you want to check me out, talk to the mayor. I am reopening the blacksmith shop, and I've bought a house in town. I'm putting down roots here and I don't want anybody hurt. I thought I could help by telling your bony ass about what I heard."

The sheriff rose slowly out of his chair and placed his fists on the desk and leaned into Blake, their noses were about four inches apart. He gave him a calculating stare at Blake's unblinking eyes. "You best watch your tone when speaking to me, Yankee," he snarled, "I would suffer no compunction putting a bullet in you."

"Funny thing," Blake growled back.

"What's that?"

"That's exactly what one of them said about you." Blake stood up and opened the door. He looked directly at the deputy and said, "Let me know if I can help you find out anything." Blake left closing the door hard enough to make the windows rattle.

The sheriff eased back in his chair glaring at the door, "Snotty Yankee bastard, I should've kicked his ass."

"Why, because you know he's right?" Mike said leaning against the file cabinet.

"Of course I know he's right," growled Johansson, "I've seen Huxley and Bent on a wanted poster up north of here, and if'n they've teamed up with Bob Pudney they'll be capable of all sorts of hell." He drummed his fingers on the desk, thinking, "Go ask Weatherby about Thorton and see if his story rings true."

"Don't have to," Ventosa said rolling a quirley, "The story is all over town about him. He bought a house and blacksmith shop and took that stuttering kid under his wing. He even got those two knuckleheads, Hap and Avery, cleaned up and got them jobs." Mike scratched a match on the cabinet and lit his cigarette.

BRYAN A. SALISBURY

"Shit. How come this is the first I'm hearin' about all this?"

"Dunno," Mike smirked. "But that rifle sure does shine."

Getting the full drift of Mike's comment, Johansson shot him a dirty look. "Kiss my ass," he growled and pointed his thumb toward the door. "Go send them wires you were talkin' about."

* * * * * *

Mike Ventosa left the jail and headed for the telegraph office. On the way he swung by the blacksmith shop to find a very foul-tempered Blake. "Hey, Thorton," he called while strolling up. Blake turned to him and frowned.

"You come to arrest me for talking straight to your boss?"

The deputy smiled, "No, nothing like that. I think he believes you."

"Strange way of showing it," said Blake.

"Aw, he lost two brothers to the union army and his father lost the ranch to Reconstructionists, I guess he's still plenty pissed. He acts like he's got a weed up his ass most of the time, but he ain't a bad sort when you get to know him."

"So he's going to check them out?"

"Can't do nothing 'til they break the law, right now they're out of our jurisdiction. If we find paper on them we can send for a federal marshal."

"They'll be long gone by then," Blake said scratching his head.

"It's the best we can do till they break a law," Mike said shrugging.

Blake drew a deep breath and let it out slowly. "I guess we'll wait then."

Blake and the deputy shook hands and he went back to work. He and Caleb started making the braces to jack up the roof. Blake calculated that they have to jack it up three times, each time using a longer jack pole. After they jacked up the first one the roof creaked and groaned. Every time there was a loud popping sound Caleb jumped.

"Easy son," Blake smiled, "she's just complaining about being disturbed."

The second time they put the jack on it went up harder because the building rafters had warped and they resisted being straightened. When they had the second jack as high as it would go they tightened up the pulley, spanning the forge to pull the walls back in. Blake inspected everything closely and was pleased with the progress. "Looks good Caleb, one more time and we'll be in business."

The third time was going well until the old brace holding the roof suddenly broke loose and came crashing into the temporary jack brace. Blake had instinctively shoved Caleb clear of the falling timbers but gotten pinned next to the new oak beam. Dust and soot filled the air, choking him. He struggled against the wood bracing but it wouldn't budge. He looked up at the pulley ropes holding the side walls and they starting to quiver under the strain. If those broke the whole building would collapse on top of him. Caleb was frantically trying to get to Blake. Blake yelled, "Go get some help; I'll be all right for a minute."

Caleb disappeared and a few seconds later Joe and Avery were in the doorway. "Damn, Blake, you all right?" Joe called in.

"We need to jack the roof back up," Blake wheezed, "but I'm pinned in here."

"We'll need more men," Joe yelled. "I'll be right back."

"Take your time," Blake grimaced.

"Hey, Thorton," Avery yelled, "if you die, can I have your horse?"

In spite of the pain in his chest Blake laughed, "Sure, you asshole, saddle too, but not until they bury me."

Suddenly, the doorway was filled with men trying to help. Hap, Josh Dooley, Bill Brady, Mike Ventosa, Joe Bergman, Caleb and a bunch of men Blake didn't recognize were trying to get the jack reset. Blake was starting to lose consciousness but could hear them frantically working. A large pair of hands started separating the men forcing his way to the middle. Percival Feathers picked up the first jack pole and placed it in the ridge of the forge, with a deafening yell he lifted up on the pole and the whole building shook. The pressure on Blake's chest left immediately and he drew in a life-saving gulp of air. Hands grabbed him and pulled him out toward the door.

"Get the center brace in," he gasped, "or else it will crash down on him."

Blake had placed the right length beam on top of the main

brace so when the building had been jacked up enough it would hold the roof up. Caleb and Hap scrambled to the top of the brace and stood the beam up.

Hap yelled, "Needs to go higher."

Avery poked Big Man in the side. "Higher, you big dummy," he yelled.

Percival's arms quivered and he groaned as he forced the roof up more. The beam slid in and Hap yelled, "Good!" Big Man slowly let the roof down on the beam. Dropping the jack brace he bent over breathing heavily. The helpers who had arrived cheered and clapped him on the back. Finally, he straightened up and flexed his back turning toward Blake. His hair was cut short and his freshly shaved face revealed a broad grin. Although he was a monstrous man he was quite handsome.

With the help of other men Blake stood and smiled back. "Damn good to see you, Big Man. Thought I was a goner for sure."

"Didn't want to lose my only friend so quick," he laughed.

"Cost me a horse," Avery grumbled.

"Maybe next time." Everyone laughed and started back to their lives.

Blake went into the forge to take a look at the new bracing. His ribs pained him some but nothing seemed broken. It seemed like he had gotten a bear hug from the Big Man. Drawing in a deep breath and letting it out slowly, he smiled, for the man who would have torn him to pieces had just saved his life. Life sure did take some interesting turns sometimes, he thought, you never know how things can turn out. He walked out of the shop still holding his ribs.

"You gonna be all right?" Big Man asked.

"I'll be fine, no worries, thanks to you," Blake replied, "and may I say, damn boy, you clean up pretty good."

Percival rubbed his naked chin and smiled. "Been a long time since I didn't have no whiskers, feels strange."

"Well it looks good, makes you look like a new man."

Caleb who was sitting on the hitch rail in front of the trough snickered, "Y-yeah, you s-sure are p-pretty, P-Percy."

The Big Man smiled broadly at him and stepped closer to Caleb. "Had me a big brother who called me Percy all the time, never liked it." He grabbed Caleb's leg and flipped him backward into the trough.

Caleb came up sputtering, wiping his face and laughing. The three of them laughed so hard that when Caleb tried to stand up he slipped and fell back into the water. Blake was holding his bruised ribs and had to sit on the anvil. It felt good to laugh that hard, regardless of the pain. "Best you go get changed before your school lesson or Bonnie will think you took the morning off and went to the swimming hole first."

Percival helped him out of the water and gave him a gentle shove toward the house. Caleb was leaving a muddy trail as he passed Sadie carrying their lunch, and she gave him a puzzled look as she said, "I's hopin' that ain't all sweat on you boy, you is lookin' a fright." Blake, Caleb and Big Man burst into another round of laughter.

# CHAPTER 11

Two miles out of town, camped in a grove of cottonwoods by a small creek were Pete Huxley, Luther Bent and Frank Wilson. They were sitting around waiting for Bob Pudney.

"I'm gettin' tired of waitin' on him," groused Frank. He was in a bad temper from drinking the night before.

"He'll be along soon," Pete said. "Just be patient."

"Is he really as fast as you say he is?" asked Bent.

Huxley poked the fire with a long stick. "Ain't seen the man who can shade him yet. Seen him shoot two men once at the same time, they never even cleared their holsters. You both better keep in mind; he's as mean as he is quick."

"Shit," grumbled Wilson. "Ain't nobody that fast, I bet I can beat him."

"You're welcome to try," came a voice from behind them. Startled all three jumped to their feet and faced the man who just snuck up on them. Robert Pudney was a medium height man with close cropped red hair. Dressed in a black shirt and pants, he wore a Navy colt on each hip, each shining in the morning sun. His black Stetson hat sat squarely on his head just above two of the coldest eyes they had ever seen.

"Damn, Bob, you scared ten years off me," Huxley said smiling. He stepped up to him and shook his hand. "Let me introduce my pards, Luther Bent and Frank Wilson."

"I hope they're better with those leg irons than they are with their mouths," sneered Pudney.

Grinning broadly, Huxley said, "They're just bored and itchin' to rob them a bank, ain't that right boys?"

"Yeah, sure," Wilson muttered. "Didn't mean no harm."

"See there, Bob, we're going to get along fine," Pete said breaking the tension. "Why don't you fetch your horse and light a spell. I'll lay out the whole plan."

Pudney never took his eyes off Wilson. "Hmm…" he murmured to himself and turned to get his horse. He came back into camp leading a big powerfully built blue roan wearing a black saddle. He picketed him near the other horses and removed his saddle and blanket. Placing them near the fire he sat on an old stump and poured himself a coffee. "So what is it you have in mind, Pete?" he asked blowing the steam from his cup.

Pete Huxley laid out the detailed but simple plan. The morning stage from Mariaville was due into MacIntyre about ten o'clock. They would cut down a tree about ten miles out of town blocking it on the road. Frank Wilson would ride into MacIntyre and tell the sheriff that the stage had been held up and when the sheriff rode out, he, Bent and Pudney would ride into MacIntyre to the bank. Bent would hold their horses while he and Pudney took the bank and Wilson would have their backs from across the street. With the sheriff and his deputy on a wild goose chase, that left no one to protect the bank.

"Should be easy, won't even have to pull a trigger," Huxley said confidently.

"Who's the sheriff? Pudney said, considering the plan.

"Iver Johansson, former Texas Ranger."

"That bastard is still alive? Good idea of yours to get him out of town," Pudney said.

"I say we just shoot the old buzzard and be done with him," growled Wilson. "And that peckerwood deputy, too."

Pudney shook his head and laughed, "Oh sure, kill a lawman, a ranger besides, and give every starpacker a reason to hunt us like dogs. Boy, you must be some special kind of stupid."

Anger flashed on Wilson's face as he leapt to his feet. He was amazed that Pudney had stood up equally fast and his right hand hovered above his pistol. "I ain't stupid, and I'll take no crap from a weasel like you," he said between grit teeth. His hand clawed for his pistol when he felt part of his ear separate from his body. Screaming, he grabbed his ear which was bleeding badly and glowered and Pudney who was holding a smoking and cocked revolver in his hand.

"I call it the way I see it," Pudney said in a tone that was smooth as silk. "Still think you can shade me?"

"You done shot off my ear!" yelled Wilson, grimacing in pain.

"I would have put it in your ugly face if we didn't need you for this job. Get sideways to me again and I will, savvy?"

Pete Huxley stepped between them. "Get his ear fixed up, Luther, I think we're done here. Right, Bob?"

Pudney smiled as he spun his pistol and landed neatly in his holster. "Yup."

They had to wait a full day because the stage only ran every other day. Frank Wilson's mood was uglier than ever because every time he tried to sleep he would roll on his shot up ear and yell out in pain. He tried to nullify the agony with what whiskey they had left but that only made him meaner. The morning of the robbery Huxley and Bent rode out to cut down the tree. When that was done they picked up Pudney and Wilson a mile outside of town. Wilson rode into town at a fast gallop yelling that the stage was being held up. Just as he had planned, the sheriff and two men rode past where they where, riding at fast gallop. The three of them trotted their horses into the town and straight up to the bank. They dismounted and handed Bent the reins. After taking a quick look around, Huxley and Pudney pulled their neckerchiefs over their mouths and entered the bank. To their surprise the bank was empty except for one man sitting with one leg on the desk pointing a twelve gauge shotgun directly at them.

"Hello, Pete, been a long time," he said.

"Son-of-a-bitch," Pete said pulling down his neckerchief. "Blake Thorton."

\* \* \* \* \* \*

Two days prior to the robbery Blake was still angry at the way the sheriff had treated him. He tried to put it out of his mind by working on the forge. Things were quiet in the town but Blake knew they were on borrowed time, waiting for Huxley to make his move. Blake thought about going out to find Huxley and his men, but thought better of it because he had no proof of what they were planning and, once Huxley recognized him, the whole situation would change, and not for the better.

Blake had been assigned to the same unit as Huxley during the war. Blake enlisted almost a year before the war ended, because he had been drifting with no real sense of purpose and a friend of his from back home had talked him into it … a decision he regretted moments after he signed on. Having been living free for so long, he immediately found it to be difficult to obey orders from men he didn't respect and the army was full of that sort. He found himself in the stockade several times for minor infractions and was relieved of stripes more than once. That's where he first met Pete Huxley. Huxley was being held on several charges and was on the road to a court martial someday. As many men do in jail, he was a big talker and tried to get the other men to join him. Most men, including Blake, wanted nothing to do with him because it meant most likely they would hang beside him when they were caught. There were many that thought he had good ideas. Luther Bent was one of them and the two became good friends.

At one hearing Blake had, his friend from home vouched for him to keep him from doing more jail time. He told the board that Blake had been a blacksmith back home and maybe that would be a good place for him. So Blake ended up with the unit blacksmith who was drunk a majority of the time. He was much happier filling his days with work instead of the mindless drilling that the infantry did.

News came down that the war was drawing to a close. The news spread like wild fire through the camp and most of the men were celebrating, except for Major James Campbell. Campbell liked the war; he became morose and nastier as the days progressed. He left the camp to go on a patrol with a small detachment of men, Blake included, to search out any small pockets of rebel soldiers. It was strange that he requested a blacksmith but orders were orders and Blake went with him. A week into the patrol they came across a small band of rebels and quickly took them prisoner. The ten men they captured were dirty, tired and hungry. There were barely six rounds of ammunition between them and two of them had no boots. There was no fight left in them and they surrendered easily. One of the men captured was Lt. James Nolte, he ordered his men to lay down their arms to save their lives.

Campbell ordered his men to tie the prisoners up and forced them onto a small circle with no rations. Blake and some of the other soldiers felt pity for the beaten men but could not help them for fear of reprisal from his commanding officer. They made camp in a small copse of trees and settled in for the night.

The next morning Major Campbell ordered Blake to his tent. "I want you to make some special items for me, Private Thorton," he said handing Blake some drawings. Blake examined the prints and thought they were some of the cruelest devices he had ever seen. Collars with shorts spikes on the inside, manacles that allowed no movement whatsoever and a cage made to fit around a man's head that would cause immeasurable pain.

"I've seen pieces like this before, Major," he said. "They are meant for torture, sir."

"They are aids for interrogating prisoners, Private," the major replied with a sadistic smile. "I need information, and I do not wish to dally about it."

"With all due respect sir, shouldn't we turn these men in and let Command question them?"

The Major stood so quickly that his chair overturned behind him, and placing his hand on the desk he glowered at Blake. "Construct these items or find yourself in chains next to the prisoners."

"Yes sir," Blake said angrily snatching the papers off the desk. The rest of the morning Blake moved very slowly making the torture devices. He knew he couldn't allow them to be used but it would mean he would end up in front of a firing squad for disobeying orders.

A very impatient Major paced back and forth checking on his progress, frequently ordered him to move faster.

A fellow soldier brought Blake a tin cup of water. "What's got a burr under his saddle?"

"Look at what he wants me to make," Blake said quietly when the Major was out of earshot.

"Damn," he said whistling low. "That ain't right."

"Private Winslow," the Major yelled, making the man jump. "Bring me one of the prisoners, I am anxious to get started with the questioning."

Blake grabbed Winslow's arm and shook his head, but Winslow whispered, "Got to boy, or he'll string me up." He turned and went over to the prisoners and cut one loose and escorted him to the Major's tent, past the two guards who had been stationed at the entrance, Huxley and Bent.

Screams and the sounds of breaking bones filled the afternoon as Campbell "questioned" the man. Most of the company went about their business trying to ignore what was happening but Huxley and Bent stood grinning and smirking every time another shriek of agony erupted from the tent. Finally, Campbell emerged covered with blood wiping his hands on a white rag. "Huxley, remove that trash and bring me another," he glared at Blake and yelled, "Are you finished yet, blacksmith?"

"Just about, Major," Blake growled back.

"Incompetent fool," cursed the Major, throwing the rag in the dirt.

Huxley and Bent dragged the lifeless form from the tent and threw it into the bushes. They swaggered past Blake to retrieve another prisoner. "You can't let him do this," Blake said in a low voice as they passed him.

"Shit," said Bent. "I was kinda hopin' he'd let me take a turn on these Rebel bastards." Huxley laughed and they went to get the next man.

It was dark when Campbell finished with the next soldier, who fared no better than the first. Exhausted he washed and retired to his tent after admonishing Blake for not completing any of the tasks he had given him.

Blake waited until it was past midnight and the guard

watching the prisoners was asleep at his post. Crawling as silently as he could, he made his way over to the captives. He pressed his finger to his lips as he cut the ties on the lieutenant's wrists. Quietly they cut the others loose and the prisoners crept into the brush. Lt. Nolte smiled at Blake without saying a word, saluted and disappeared. Blake was trying to figure out what his next move was when lightning erupted in his head and his knees buckled. Winslow stood over him holding the rifle that he had just used to knock Blake unconscious. He was in a tight spot himself. He was the guard on duty watching the prisoners and if they escaped the Major would probably have him shot. He waited three hours until he was just about to be relieved when he clouted himself with his own pistol and fired a shot in the air raising the alarm. Men were up and scrambling about when the Major stomped up to him demanding an explanation.

"I caught Private Thorton here lettin' them rebels go. He done knocked me out and when I woke up I tried to get a shot off but he came at me so I hit him with my rifle butt."

Campbell gave him a suspicious look. "I grow weary of the level of incompetence in this company," he snarled. "I want those men recaptured by breakfast and this traitor placed in chains!" he screamed as he gave Blake a savage kick in the ribs. Four of the troopers grabbed rifles and ran into the brush, while Huxley and Bent chained Blake to a tree near the camp. He woke a short time later to a pounding head. When he tried to move he discovered the chains and winced in pain as a wave of nausea swept through him. Blake watched through bleary eyes as Major Campbell cursed and threw things at the four troopers who had returned empty handed. Campbell raised his hand to strike the nearest man when a small round hole appeared in his forehead followed by a gunshot. The camp erupted into chaos as more shots brought down more of Campbell's company. Huxley and Bent ran for horses and made a quick escape while the other confused men tried to make a stand. The camp was filled with gray uniforms who soon overpowered them. Blake was the only survivor. A large Confederate sergeant walked over to him with a smoking pistol and leveled it at Blake's head. "Looks like you was headed for a firing squad anyway boy, I'll just save 'em the trouble," he said cocking his pistol.

"Hold your fire, Sergeant!" someone behind him yelled. Lt. James Nolte stepped around the big man and looked at Blake. "I will take charge of this man."

"Yes, sir," the sergeant said and holstered his gun.

The young lieutenant bent down and released the chains binding Blake. "Stay close to me," he said in a low voice, "my friends might not understand why I saved your Yankee hide."

"Appreciate it," Blake replied quietly.

"I'll post two of my men on you tonight. There will be a horse saddled with provisions to last for a short while and a pistol. They were with me at your camp and they know how you helped us. Ride fast and stay low. I hear the war is over and we lost so keep out of sight, it'll take some time for everybody to get the word."

"I figure this makes us even," Blake said with a trace of a smile.

"Yup," Nolte replied smiling back.

Later that night, true to their word, the two troopers let Blake go after explaining that when they escaped, they came across a company of Confederates. After hearing about what Major Campbell had done they agreed to return and exact revenge on the murderous bastard. Blake thanked them and shook their hands, then he disappeared into the night.

\* \* \* \* \* \*

"What the hell are you doin' here?" Huxley asked. "I figured you dead for sure."

"Not hardly, Pete," Blake responded in a flat tone. "Been drifting around some and wound up here."

"Well I don't see no star on you. Was you robbin' this bank?" Huxley said smiling, "cause if'n you was, we could throw in together."

Blake noticed Huxley and Pudney's hand staying close to their pistols and Pudney had a concerned look on his face.

"Nope," he said. "I saw you and Bent ride in the other night and figured you were up to no good. Took me a while to guess how you were going to do it. Now why don't you boys drop those pistols and we can end this real peaceable."

"You ain't gonna stop us, Blakey-boy," Huxley said slowly closing his fingers around the grip of his Peacemaker.

"Already have," Blake growled. He was watching Pudney close and noticed a slight twitch in the corner of his mouth. Blake pulled the first trigger on the twelve gauge as Pudney cleared leather and fired a shot harmlessly into the floor. The force of the blast blew him backward out the plate glass window in front of the bank. Huxley had his pistol out and cocked when Blake hit him with the second barrel of buckshot slamming him against the wall, killing him instantly. Shots erupted on the street as Bent mounted his horse and began firing at the deputy who had hidden around the side of the bank and came out when Blake shot Pudney. Ventosa cut Bent out of his saddle with a rifle shot leaving him dead in the street. A man screamed in pain as Blake came out of the bank and saw Big Man holding Wilson by his damaged ear while Dan LaClare relieved him of his pistol.

"Damn," said Deputy Ventosa. "You sure called that one right."

"Lucky guess," Blake said smiling.

Big Man crow hopped Wilson over to them still holding firmly on his mangled ear. Blood dripped from his fingers and down the side of Wilson's neck. "I was trying to help!" he yelled. "Let me go, dammit!"

Dan grinned broadly as he handed Wilson's colt to the deputy. "He had his pistol aimed right at you, constable," he drawled. "I believe helping you was the farthest thing from his tiny mind."

"Weren't you the one who told the sheriff the stage was being robbed?" Ventosa asked.

"What stage?" Wilson winced between grit teeth. Big Man tightened his grip on his ear. "Ow, ow. Yeah I told him," he cried, trying to get free.

"Well when he gets back and says there was no robbery, I guess he'll put the noose around your neck. Until then you can rest in the jail." Big Man started marching Wilson down to the jail being none too careful with his ear.

People started coming out of their shops slowly, unsure if it was safe. "The excitement is over folks," Ventosa yelled. A tall thin man wearing a top hat ambled up to the deputy. "Got three customers for you, Mr. Griswald."

The older man grimaced looking at Wilson's lifeless body. "Shotguns make such a mess," he muttered. "Who's paying the bill, deputy?" Ventosa walked over the corpse and looked in his pockets, finding two hundred dollars he handed fifty over to the undertaker and counted off fifty more.

"I imagine Weatherby will be complaining about the mess and his window, this should cover the damages." He motioned to two men on the street. "Take their horses to the livery and tell Bergman he can sell them and the saddles. He can keep half the money and turn the rest over to the sheriff."

Phineas Weatherby came wheezing up the steps to Ventosa. "I would have never agreed to this if I had known there would such a mess," he blustered. Blake smiled and shook his head.

"They were going to rob the bank one way or another. It might have been you lying there," Ventosa snapped at him handing him the fifty dollars.

Weatherby mopped his head with a handkerchief. "I suppose I should be grateful," he said in a sarcastic tone.

Blake and Mike Ventosa looked at each other and then at the banker. "Yup," they said in unison.

Back in the jail an hour later Blake was enjoying a cup of coffee with Mike when the sheriff came galloping up to the door and dismounted. He threw the door open and brushed the dust from his clothes. "Well?" he growled at Ventosa.

"You're the last piece, sheriff. Was the stage robbed?" Mike asked, pouring a cup of coffee and handing it to Johansson.

The sheriff shot Blake a hard look and growled. "No, there was a tree cut down blocking the road but the driver had it just about cleaned up when we got there."

"Then our Yankee friend called the whole thing straight. A few minutes after you rode out they hit the bank. Huxley, Bent and Pudney are shakin' hands with the devil and Wilson is in the back cooling his heels."

The sheriff sat behind his desk rubbing his forehead. "Tell me again how you figured this all out, Thorton."

Blake sat back in his chair and recounted everything he knew. He wasn't sure when they would try to rob the bank until Wilson came riding into town yelling that the stage was being held up. Blake figured that was how they would get rid of the sheriff without killing him and give them plenty of time to escape. Since he had never seen Wilson until the night he rode in with Huxley and Bent, he took the chance on telling Johansson what he thought they were doing. It had been a big gamble but it paid off, when the sheriff agreed to let Ventosa stay back to guard the bank. The tricky part was getting Weatherby to give Blake the keys and be in the bank by himself. Thankfully, Ventosa bought into his idea and practically had to get the keys at gunpoint. Blake quietly slipped into the back door of the bank while Mike had LaClare watch Wilson from across the street. Apparently LaClare enlisted the help of Big Man and together they subdued Wilson.

"Sounds like something one of those dime novel writers would conjure up," the sheriff muttered.

"Would have worked, too," Blake said sipping his coffee, "that is if I hadn't recognized them."

"There's the matter of the reward money for those men," Ventosa said handing the sheriff three wanted posters. "Huxley and Bent were worth five hundred apiece and Pudney was worth two thousand."

Blake stood and put his hat on. "Why don't we split it three ways, we all played a part in getting them."

"Mighty generous of you, Blake," Mike said smiling.

Blake turned to leave and Mike kicked the bottom of Johansson's chair making the sheriff jump. He looked at his deputy and scowled. "Hey, Thorton," he called.

Blake stopped and turned, "Yeah, sheriff?"

"Thanks, I guess," he grumbled.

"No problem, Johnny Reb," Blake said laughing and he left.

**CHAPTER 12**

IT took a couple weeks for people to stop talking about the holdup. Several of the townsfolk came over to the forge to thank Blake personally, and brought a lot of business. Caleb was doing well with his studies, according to Chrissy, and his skills in the forge improved every day. One thing Blake noticed was how fast Caleb was filling out. He walked with a sense of pride and was developing broad shoulders with a set of strong arms.

Sam finished Sadie's room at the house and she moved in. Every day she made sure Blake knew how comfortable it was and felt like a queen in her palace.

Hap seemed to flourish in the hardware store and Josh Dooley had no problem keeping him on as a clerk. Little Madeline had taken to calling him Uncle Hap, making sure he toed the line.

Avery stayed on at the livery, not because he was such a good worker, but more as a drinking buddy for Joe Bergman. Saturday night would find them staggering back to the livery leaning on each other, laughing and most likely singing a raunchy song.

Big Man found himself work at the lumber yard and astonished everyone in town by presenting Michelle with flowers one night and expressed an interest in courting her. She was very reluctant at first because being a soiled dove was how she supported herself but agreed when Percival, as she called him, told her that she would be able to quit that life when he had saved enough money to make an honest woman of her.

Blake had finally found peace. He hadn't realized how much he missed a settled life and had gotten used to a soft bed and hot meals. He would slip down to the saloon occasionally and play cards with Dan LaClare who had yet to move on. Blake hadn't seen much of Tom MacIntyre because his ranch was rounding up cattle for a drive. Every time they did happen to meet, there was always tension in the air. Once he came in with his two tough friends and joined a poker game with Blake and Dan. After drinking heavily and losing three pots in a row, he accused Dan of being a card sharp and demanded his money back. Blake backed Dan and Tom left the game angry. He came back a few minutes later with the sheriff in tow and tried to get Dan thrown out of town. Johansson would not budge and called the game fair. He told Tom and his two thugs to go sleep it off and suggested they lay off the whiskey when they played cards. Tom left the saloon humiliated and vowed to return things in town back to the way he liked them. The next morning he went to the bank to talk to Weatherby. Entering the bank he walked directly over to the banker's desk and sat down.

Weatherby looked up over his glasses. "How may I help you, Tom?" He was annoyed that Tom had sat down without being invited.

"I need you to call in the loan on the blacksmith shop," Tom said coldly.

"Excuse me?" Weatherby asked confused.

"The blacksmith shop that Thorton is in, I want you to foreclose on it and boot that jackass out," Tom said in a mirthless tone.

"I can't," the banker said flatly.

"Why the hell not?" Tom said raising his voice. "You hold the paper on it, don't you?

"He purchased the property lock, stock and barrel."

"Bullshit," Tom sputtered. "What about the house and that nigger cook?"

"Same," Weatherby said throwing his pen on the desk.

Tom, unsure what to say next, stared at him, then said, "Where'd he get that kind of money?"

"He did not make me privy to that information and even if I did I could not divulge it to you."

"Probably robbed a bank somewhere," Tom said sitting back defeated.

"Why do you want him out of here anyway?" asked Weatherby.

"I don't like him. He walks around here like he's something special."

"He has proven to be an asset to the town," stated the banker. "Many people like him being here."

"Well I don't," sneered Tom. He stood, straightening his gun belt and hat. "From now on you clear any land sales with me or my father."

Weatherby snorted, "Good day, Mr. MacIntyre."

Tom strode out of the bank onto the boardwalk cursing to himself.

"How'd it go boss?" one of his men asked.

"That son-of-a-bitch Thorton owns everything," he grumbled. "Loosen one of the shoes on your horse, it's time we pay the blacksmith a visit."

The two men argued who was going to loosen the shoe until they saw their boss growing impatient. The larger of the two conceded and took his knife out and worked his horses front shoe practically off.

"Let's go," Tom groused.

The three of them rode over to the forge and found Caleb busy with another horse; Blake was nowhere to be seen. Riding up very close to Caleb Tom said, "Hey boy, get yourself over here and fix my friend's shoe. It's come loose."

Caleb recognized Tom and his men. Staring at the ground he said, "B-be w-w-ith i-in a s-s-second."

"Now!" Tom ordered getting off his horse. Caleb kept working on the horse he had started.

The man with the loose shoe dismounted. "I don't think shit-for-brains heard you, boss," and he grabbed Caleb and shoved toward his horse.

"I-I h-hear j-j-just f-fine," Caleb stammered. "W-wait y-your t-turn."

The same tough grabbed him by the front of his shirt bringing his nose an inch from Caleb's. "My boss here don't wait for no one," he sneered.

Blake emerged from the forge carrying a large set of tongs. His face was smudged with coal dust and his body glistened with sweat. "There's easier ways to get your arm broken mister, but right now I can't think of one. Turn him loose," his voice sounded like distant thunder.

The three men turned to face Blake. When they saw the look in his eyes it chilled them to their bones. Letting go of Caleb the one man said, "My horse has a loose shoe and this boy said I has to wait."

"He will tend to your horse at his earliest convenience," Blake said coldly.

"We're in a rush to get back to the ranch," Tom stated.

Locking his eyes on Tom, Blake responded calmly, "A man died who was in a hurry once."

The other man riding with Tom moved his hand closer to the colt on his hip.

Without taking his gaze from Tom, Blake said, "Tell your friend if he makes a grab for that shootin' iron he'll be picking teeth out of his shit."

"Not here," Tom said out of the corner of his mouth, then back at Blake, "We'll be at the saloon. Tell that stuttering fool to come fetch us when he's done."

"Come back in an hour. He's too busy to be chasing around after you," an unwavering Blake replied.

"You'll have to explain why we were late to my father," sneered Tom.

"Looking forward to it."

Later that day when Caleb had gone to the café for school the man returned for his horse and did a considerable amount of complaining. Blake charged him a dollar for fixing his horse's shoe. Blake explained fixing the shoe was two bits and roughing up the boy accounted for the rest. The tough slapped a silver dollar in Blake's hand and mumbled something about "doin' a hell of a lot more than that." Blake smiled as the man rode off and thought to himself, "Damn, my first dissatisfied customer."

\* \* \* \* \* \*

Blake went back to work in the forge. He needed a box of rivets to repair a tool he had just straightened and when he removed it from a high shelf, the box slipped and sent dirt, sawdust and assorted grime cascading down on his head and down the back of his shirt. Trying to clear the dirt from his eyes he made his way out to the horse trough to clean the grime off him. Feeling the sawdust trickle down his back he stripped off his leather apron and shirt. He slapped his shirt on his back and heard a gasp from behind him. Turning he saw Chrissy standing with a man in a long black coat and flat crowned hat. Chrissy had her hand placed over her mouth and her cheeks bore a rosy glow.

"Sorry ma'am, I just dumped a whole bunch of sawdust down the back of my shirt and that'll itch like crazy if I don't clean it off." Blake knew it was not polite to not have a shirt on, but then he remembered his tattoos. He quickly turned and pulled the garment back over his broad back. Tucking the tails into his pants he turned back. "Now what can I do for you?"

Chrissy was still taken aback and could not seem to form words. The man in the black frockcoat waited for her to make the introduction but decided to start. "I am Father Grimm," he said revealing a heavy German accent. "Pastor of Christ's Episcopal Church here in town. Mrs. O'Bryan was kind enough to bring me over to meet you."

"It's a pleasure, Padre," Blake said shaking his hand. "Please forgive my state of undress, I was not expecting you."

"Good heavens, don't give it another thought. You are a working man after all," Grimm said smiling. "Please forgive my staring. I have seen tattoos on men before. Although that was when I was in Virginia fresh out of seminary and assigned to a church in Portsmouth. Many of my congregation were sailors. Were you in the navy?"

"Merchant service mostly, spent some time in the South Pacific."

"You are aware that the church frowns on decorating one's body in this sort of fashion?" the Father asked. Blake was aware how the church felt about tattoos and any other time he would have felt that this priest was looking down on him for it, but this one was different. He had an easy going way about him, and, although he commanded respect, Blake felt he left the judging to God. Blake liked him immediately.

"Well, Padre, I didn't exactly volunteer to get tattooed. An island chief thought I earned them. It's a long story, but once they were put on I figured that he put some stained glass on my temple," Blake said smiling broadly.

"Indeed," the Pastor laughed. "That is a story I would like to hear."

Chrissy had collected herself by now and joined the conversation. "Father Grimm is in need of your service, Mr. Thorton."

"Our bell in the steeple has a broken support and it cannot be rung. Sadly, we have not been able to call for mass for nearly a year," the Padre said.

"I'll be over first thing in the morning with my man, and we'll take a look at it for you, Padre."

"It's quite high in the steeple. Is that a problem?" he asked.

"It can't be any worse than repairing a topsail in gale force winds. We'll be fine."

"Splendid," the priest said, grinning. "I'll see you then." He shook Blake's hand and turned to leave. "Shall we go Mrs. O'Bryan?"

Chrissy leaned toward Blake and whispered, "Stained glass?"

"The cathedrals in New York are full of it," Blake whispered back.

Cocking her eyebrow and smiling she replied, "As are you, Mr. Thorton."

\* \* \* \* \*

The next morning Blake and Caleb were over at the church after stopping by the forge to pick up some measuring tools. They were greeted by Father Grimm and his wife, Gretta, who was of German decent also and spoke with a thick accent. They appeared to be well suited for each other, both middle aged and portly. Gretta had prepared bear claws and coffee, and Blake and Caleb were invited into the kitchen. Gretta seemed quite fond of Caleb and chatted with him like an old friend. Caleb didn't say much but, then again, his mouth was mostly full of the pastry she made. The bear claws were delicious and Blake made Gretta promise to share her recipe with Sadie. The Padre asked Blake about his life and was quite interested in his sea stories. Blake left out the rougher parts out of respect for Gretta.

"Are you a man of God?" she asked in a pleasant manner.

"I was born and raised attending an Episcopal church in Duanesburgh, New York, ma'am," Blake replied sipping his coffee. "After I left, I had traveled some and seen a bunch of things that made my faith wavier. I still believe, and try to live my life right, but it bothers me when people who claim to be Christians do wrong during the week and they think going to church on Sunday makes everything all right."

The Padre considered that and scratched his chin. "The trick is, I think, that to concern yourself with what you can't control is wasted time. Maybe you would become an example for others to follow."

"Maybe, Padre," Blake said. "I don't think I'm all that great of an example, though."

Gretta developed a mischievous grin and in a singsong voice said, "Mrs. O'Bryan thinks you are."

Blake choked on his coffee and his cheeks burned red. "Gretta!" the Padre scolded. "Forgive my wife, Mr. Thorton, she is an eternal matchmaker."

"Ach," she said waving her hand. "Men are always the last to see."

"I think we should get to work," Blake said, changing the subject. "Thank you for the pastry, ma'am."

They got up from the table and the Padre led them to the ladder in the steeple. Once they were up there the problem was immediately apparent. Blake showed Caleb how the bracing for the bell was grossly inadequate and when one side had broken, it cracked the bracket for the bell and the bell had wedged itself in the tower. "They're damn lucky this two hundred pound monster didn't crash down on them," Blake said blowing out a deep breath. "We are going to have to pick up the bell and re-brace the whole thing. We'll need a bunch of stuff from the forge to fix this." He and Caleb descended the ladder and met the waiting Padre.

"So can it be repaired?" he asked.

"Caleb seems to think so," Blake said winking at the Padre. "He recommends we need to go get some tools."

Laughing, he patted a confused Caleb on the back. "Thank you sir, I'm sure we have the right man for the job."

"Y-you're w-w-welcome, I t-t-think," Caleb replied.

An hour later they returned with a horse and wagon they borrowed from Joe Bergman, loaded with tools and supplies. Blake was amazed how well Caleb had learned to read a measuring tape. Lifting the bell was no small project, and Blake needed to construct some temporary braces to support it. He stayed up in the steeple and called down measurements for Caleb to cut the wood and then pulled them up with a rope. Caleb never missed a cut and every board he sent up was perfect. When it came time to lift the bell, Blake brought up pulleys and several chains. Soon, the bell was up and out of the way. Blake showed Caleb how to secure it with some short chains so they could work without worrying about the pulley ropes breaking.

They removed the metal brackets for the bell and lowered them down. When they were back on the ground, they were surprised to find Sadie setting the table under a large tree for lunch. Earlier that morning, Gretta had gone over and invited her to lunch at the church. Just as they were sitting down Satan come romping around the corner. Wagging his tail, he sat patiently waiting for scraps.

"And who is this?" the Padre asked, looking at the dog.

"T-that's S-s-satan," Caleb replied while chewing on a biscuit.

"Pardon me," the padre said in a shocked voice.

Blake smiled and said, "It's a long story, just don't make him mad."

"You gentlemen have a lot of long stories," a skeptical Pastor replied.

"You's has no idea, Father," chimed in Sadie. "They can't tell no short one."

After lunch was finished Blake explained that they would be back tomorrow morning to finish the job because they had to make a new set of brackets for the bell. Blake and Caleb returned to the forge and started laying out the materials. "That was a good job you did cutting those timbers today. You seem to be learning a lot," Blake told Caleb.

"B-Bonnie says I-I'm g-good with n-numbers," he said taking out his pocket watch. "B-better get g-going."

\* \* \* \* \* \*

Blake spent the afternoon making new brackets for the bell. He wished Caleb had been there to work with him because making one of anything was not a problem but making an exact match was far more difficult. Being an experienced blacksmith, Blake didn't have much difficulty with it, but a new blacksmith could have a lot of trouble. Schooling was far more important at this time and Caleb was making great strides. There was no sense in stopping now.

Mike Ventosa appeared in the doorway. "Hey, Blake," he said. "How's it going?"

"Fine, I'm making some new brackets for the church bell," Blake said bringing the four-pound hammer down squarely on the bright orange metal. He checked the piece for straightness and set it next to the fire. "What can I do for you, Mike?"

"My granpappy tried to teach me blacksmithing when I was a yonker," he mused. "The only thing I managed to do was burn off my eyebrows."

"That'll happen for sure," Blake laughed.

"Anyway," Mike began, "the circuit judge is coming into town next week to try Wilson. We'll need you to testify."

"Happy to do it. Is he enjoying his stay with you?"

"He pisses and moans about his ear a lot; Doc Baker tried to sew it back on but infection set in and he had to cut most of it off."

"It'll be hard to wear glasses I expect," Blake laughed.

"Never thought of that," Mike smiled. "I'll be glad to see him gone. He seems to have taken this whole thing right personal. Claims he's gonna kill you, me and the sheriff if'n he gets a chance. He's a mean cuss."

"You never found paper on him?" asked Blake.

"Naw, I don't think the judge will hang him, probably just get prison, seeing as he didn't kill nobody."

"Too bad, I got a feeling if anybody needed killing, it's him," Blake said.

"That's a fact. By the way, all the bounty money cleared for them others. You want Weatherby to put your share in your account at the bank?"

"That'll work," Blake said. "Anything else, because I need to finish these brackets up."

"Just one more thing. Big Man is in the jail, he broke some cowpoke's leg in the saloon for getting too friendly with that dove he's sweet on. He won't pay his fine 'cause he says he's saving to marry her. It was one of MacIntyre's men and the mayor made Johansson give him a fifty dollar fine."

"Damn fool," Blake said. "How long does he have to stay locked up?"

"Old fat Weatherby insisted on thirty days," said Ventosa.

"Shit," exclaimed Blake. "If he loses that job at the lumberyard he'll never save enough."

"Yup," Mike said. "Just thought you'd like to know. I'll be seeing you, Blake."

"Thanks, Mike," Blake called after him.

Blake finished his work and shut down the forge. He cleaned up and headed over to the Trail's End. Being the middle of the afternoon it was practically empty. He stepped up to the bar and ordered a beer. When the barkeep set it down for him, Blake asked, "Is Michelle around?"

"She ain't come down yet, but if you're lookin' for a poke, I can see if she's ready," he said.

"No, I just want to talk."

"Let me go get her," the bartender said. "She ain't been too crazy about her work lately." He stepped around the bar and went upstairs. A moment later he appeared with Michelle following. Her eyes were red from crying and forced a smile when she saw Blake.

She was wearing a provocative blue dress and swayed her voluptuous hips as she came closer. "What can I do for you, handsome?"

"I came to talk about Percival."

Her eyes welled up with tears and she brushed them away. "That big lummox has gone and got himself jailed. I know why he did it but he knows what I do and a girl's got to make a living."

"Would some brandy help your nerves?" asked Blake.

"Normally I don't, but it wouldn't hurt today," she said.

Blake ordered the drink and she took a sip. Suddenly she looked at Blake and said, "Are you the damn fool that told him to clean himself up and try to court me?"

"Courting you was his idea, I just gave him a few ideas how," Blake said staring at his beer.

"Why? So we could both get our hearts broke?" she cried. "In case you haven't noticed I'm a whore, not some prim and proper lady."

"I think you deserve the same chance at happiness as any other woman."

"Fancy talk," she said.

"Do you love him?" Blake asked.

She considered the question carefully. "Yes, I do, God help me. He dotes on me something fierce and is one of the gentlest people I know. You know he even talked about having a passel of kids someday? Imagine me a mother," she laughed.

"Yes, I can," Blake replied. "Is there anything else you're good at?"

"Besides the obvious?" she asked. "I guess I've always been handy with a needle and thread. I make my own dresses when I can."

"What about working for the dressmaker in town?"

"Psst, that old biddy hasn't got a clue what catches a man's eye. A dress can be for working, but that doesn't mean you have to look like a school marm. Now I'm not sayin' you have to show off the twins like this," she said pushing up on her ample breasts. "But a man likes to know that you got them," she giggled.

Blake smiled and sipped his beer. "I agree wholeheartedly."

"Oh hell, it's all a dream thinkin' about that anyway," she said finishing her brandy.

"What about your own shop?"

"Oh sure," she laughed. "I'll just bat my eyes and the banker will give me a shop with pretty lace curtains. Whose gonna buy a dress made by a whore anyway?"

"Ever hear the phrase, build it and they will come?" Blake asked.

"Yeah, but I think they were talkin' about a cathouse," she laughed her bawdy laugh and Blake joined her.

\* \* \* \* \* \*

Blake left the saloon and strolled into the bank. He arranged with Mr. Weatherby to open an account in the name of Mr. and Mrs. Percival Feathers and had him place the thousand dollars from the bounty he earned along with five hundred more as a wedding gift. Weatherby objected because there was technically no Mrs. Feathers, but agreed when a marriage license was produced. Blake asked if it was going to be necessary for him to come in and broker the deal for the new dress shop and Weatherby grumbled that it would not.

Blake met Caleb coming out of the café and told him he could go straight home and get to his studies. He then walked over to the jail and went in. Johansson was doing paperwork at his desk and Ventosa was sweeping the floor. "Howdy, gents," he said smiling.

"Didn't my deputy tell you your money would be in your account at the bank?" the sheriff asked gruffly.

"I thought you southern boys were supposed to be gentlemen," Blake said still grinning.

"We are to other southern boys," Johansson replied. "What do you want?"

"I want to talk to Big Man, if I may."

"About?"

"The jailbreak we're going to do," the still-grinning Blake said. The room went deathly silent and Johansson shot him a hard look. "Oh, for Christ's sake, sheriff, loosen the saber a little," Blake laughed, "I just have a proposition for him."

"Leave your gun on my desk, smartass," the sheriff grumbled.

Blake took off his gun belt and placed it on his desk while Ventosa opened the steel door to the back where the cells were. Wilson stood up and sneered at Blake, "What are you doing here?"

"Looking to see the pretty job the doc did on your ear," Blake said flatly.

"Well, get a good look peckerwood, so's you know it's me when I shoot you," Wilson growled.

Mike Ventosa smacked the bars in front of Wilson's face. "Sit down and shut up, stupid."

"You, too, asshole," he grumbled, waving a finger at Mike.

There were four cells in the jail and Big Man was across and down from Wilson. When he saw Blake he hoisted his enormous frame off the cot and came up to the bars. "Guess I done a bad thing, huh?"

"Well it wasn't the smartest thing," Blake said. "Hear me out. I have an idea if you're agreeable." Blake told him of the money he deposited in the bank under his name and the wedding gift. He explained that he could only get to the money if he showed Weatherby a marriage license. Percival was so shocked he found it hard to speak. Blake told him there should be enough money to get a dress shop started for Michelle and he could keep his job at the lumberyard. Also, being a married man, he had to act respectable and couldn't go around breaking legs whenever he got the urge. He made him promise to behave and to always treat Michelle right.

"What about the fine?" Percival asked.

"I'll take care of that. It's the least I can do for helping with those bank robbers." Blake told him.

"You just made my list, ya big elephant!" Wilson called out.

Big Man looked through the bars toward Wilson, "You say no more broken legs?" he asked Blake quietly.

Blake smiled and said, "There are always exceptions."

# CHAPTER 13

THE next morning Blake and Caleb were busy at work in the church tower. The bracing was finished and all that was left was mounting the brackets for the bell. Suddenly, they heard gunfire coming from the direction of the jail. Blake had a pretty good view of the whole town from up in the steeple and caught a glimpse of Sheriff Johansson working his way around the back of the jail, his colt drawn and his left arm seemed to be bleeding. The Padre came running into the main part of the church to see what the shooting was all about. Blake saw him and called down, "Get back, Padre; there's trouble at the jail." Blake started to climb down and suddenly had a thought. "Hey, Padre, you wouldn't have a rifle would you?"

The priest looked around the corner and yelled up, "I have an old Spencer rifle we had when we made the trip out here. I have never fired it, though."

"Can you fetch it and tie it on the rope?"

"Good heavens," he said, "I'll try." He scurried away toward his house in the back.

"Caleb, go down and help him and be quick, we don't have much time," Blake said earnestly. Caleb made his way down the ladder and ran through the church as fast as his legs would carry him. More shots rang out from the jail. Just as Blake was getting ready to get down again, a breathless Caleb grabbed the rope and tied the rifle to it. Blake hoisted it up and took a close look. It was a large bore Spencer that obviously had little use, but it seemed to be in good shape, probably been stored in the back of a closet. Unfortunately, it only had two rounds loaded in it. Blake thought, "I hope this isn't a long fight." Blake peered over the edge of the rail and saw Wilson cat footing around the building next to the jail trying to make his way to some horses tied out front. He was holding a revolver high, ready to shoot. Iver Johansson was now working his way across the front of the jail, his arm had been bleeding badly and he was unsteady on his feet. In a few seconds Wilson would have the drop on him. Blake lined up the sights and squeezed the trigger. His shot went high and left in back of Wilson and buried itself into the house. Wilson crouched down and tried to figure out where the shot came from. Thorton jacked the other round in the rifle and took aim again compensating this time for the sights. He let out a slow breath and squeezed the trigger once more. Wilson's body slammed up against the house with enough force to knock the pistol from his hand, and he landed face first in the dirt. Blake called down to the sheriff, "I think I got him good, be careful, he could be playin' possum."

Johansson waved his pistol in recognition and eased around the corner. Leaning against the wall he worked his way over to Wilson and used the toe of his boot to roll him over. "Deader than hell," he yelled back.

Caleb and the Padre ran over to Johansson to steady him. "Never mind me," he snapped, "go check my deputy in back of the jail by the privy."

Mike came from inside the jail with blood running down the side of his face and a large egg forming on his head. "I'm alright, that son-of-a-bitch got the drop on me," he said leaning against the post.

Blake had arrived in time to catch him as he started to fall. "Easy there, Mike, you've got quite a knot on your head," he said as he lowered him into the rocking chair.

The town's doctor, Thaddeus Baker, had arrived carrying his bag. He was a small man, graying at the temples and sporting a well-trimmed goatee. He went to the sheriff first and wrapped his bleeding arm tightly to stem the blood flow. Then he moved quickly over to the deputy and examined his head wound. "We need to get these men over to my office where I can tend to them properly. Move them with care, head injuries can be tricky," he said, snapping his bag shut. Some more of the men from the town had arrived to help and they carried Mike over to the doctor's office.

Caleb helped the sheriff by letting him lean on him. Johansson looked at Blake and said, "Nice shot ... although it took you two."

"Wasn't my rifle, I didn't have time to adjust the sights," Blake replied smiling.

"Likely excuse," Johansson said, but this time he was smiling for the first time since Blake met him. Griswold the undertaker came trotting up the street to meet the sheriff. "Got you another customer over by the house next to the jail," he said to the merchant of death.

"Not another shotgun killing is it?" the thin man asked, wrinkling his nose.

"No, but it was a big bore Spencer," said Blake.

"Better than a shotgun, I guess," the thin man replied. "And who will be paying for the burial?"

"Jumpin' Jehoshaphat," growled the sheriff. "I'm bleedin' like a stuck pig and you're frettin' over money. Bury him and send the bill to the mayor."

"I apologize for my lack of sensitivity, sheriff," Griswold said in a singsong voice. "I am only trying to make a living."

"Well go make it then," grumbled Johansson.

Once they had Johansson and Ventosa in the doctor's office, Blake and Caleb went back to the church. "Y-you k-k-killed a lot of m-men h-haven't y-you?" Caleb asked when they got to the top of the steeple.

"I've never killed someone who wasn't in desperate need of it. I'm not proud of it but sometimes a man has to step up and hold others accountable," Blake said.

"I-I d-don't never w-w-want t-to k-kill n-nobody," Caleb said.
"I hope you never have to, son, it stays with a man his whole life."

\* \* \* \* \* \*

They finished mounting the bell and lowered all the tools down. After they loaded the wagon Father Grimm came out and looked up in the steeple. He looked like a man who had a troubled mind. "I understand why you had to shoot that man this morning," he began. "But it weighs heavy on me that I had a part in it."

Blake leaned against the doorway and said, "I pulled the trigger, not you, Padre."

"Yes I know, but still I supplied the instrument of destruction."

"Padre, that was an evil man who died today, pure and simple. He would have killed the sheriff, his deputy, and anyone else he took a notion to. You helped save some lives today; I think God will be agreeable to that."

"Perhaps," Father Grimm replied. "Still it weighs heavy on me."

"Me, too," Blake said. "If it didn't, we wouldn't be any better men than them."

Father Grimm considered that. "Well I guess all we can do is pray that the Lord forgives us," he said smiling slightly. "Is the bell repaired now?"

"We were just about to give it a try," Blake said. "Why don't you give the rope a tug."

"I think Caleb should, it was his job after all," the Padre said, winking at Blake.

"Give it a pull, son," Blake grinned. "Let's see how you did."

Caleb took a firm hold of the rope and pulled. The big bell swung effortlessly and rang with a clear loud tone.

The Padre clapped his hands together and smiled broadly. "What a marvelous thing to hear on a day like today. Splendid job, gentlemen. What does the church owe your wonderful work?"

Caleb looked at Blake for an answer, and Blake smiled and whispered in his ear. "C-c-consider it a d-donation," Caleb said.

The Padre put a hand on each of their shoulders. "God bless the both of you."

They all shook hands and Caleb and Blake got in the wagon. Blake stopped by his house to let Sadie know that she needn't bring lunch today because he wanted to check on the sheriff and Mike. Then they would have lunch at the café. Blake changed his shirt and Caleb went to get cleaned up.

"What was that shootin' about?" Sadie asked.

"That fourth bank robber tried to make a break today."

"Did he gets away?" she asked in a concerned voice.

"He was shot and killed, the undertaker is preparing his dirt nap now," Blake replied.

"I's hopes the Devil is proddin' him good with his pitchfork," she stated.

Blake laughed, "I'm sure he is."

\* \* \* \* \* \*

Sadie was thrilled to have a chance to go visit with her family and accepted a ride with Blake to Sam and Marie's house. After leaving her they returned to the forge, unloaded the wagon and returned it to Joe. Blake and Caleb found the doctor's office and were met by his nurse. She showed them to the back where the doctor was leaning over Mike and a very grumpy Johansson was sitting in another bed with his arm in a sling.

"How is he, Doc?" Blake asked quietly.

"Hard to say," he said concerned. "I don't believe his skull is fractured, but there is always the danger of his brain swelling. He's sleeping now; all we can do is wait."

"Lousy, no account varmint," the sheriff growled. "Should have hung him straight away."

"You ever figure out what happened?" Blake asked Johansson.

"Wilson was bitchin' about havin' to go to the privy because he had the runs. What we didn't know is every time he went out there he was loosin' up a board. When he came out the last time, he cracked Mike on the head with it and stole his pistol. Doc says Mike's lucky to be alive." The sheriff grimaced when he tried to get more comfortable. "Anyway, I heard the ruckus and was comin' out to see what was going on and that bastard

Wilson took a shot at me. Nicked the bone, too, damn that hurts like hell," he groused.

"It's a wonder that bullet could even penetrate your ornery hide," the doctor laughed.

Johansson shot him a dirty look and continued. "I was tryin' to catch him when you plugged him from the steeple. "Why'd you have a rifle up there anyway?"

"I didn't at first, the Preacher loaned it to me," Blake said.

"Who would have thought that bible thumper even owned a gun," said Johansson.

"Glad he did," Blake replied. "Wilson had you dead to rights from what I saw."

"I owe you my life, sure enough. I hope you ain't expectin' a big kiss from me."

"I'll settle for a drink when you're able," Blake said holding up his hands.

"That I will do, Yankee boy. That I will do," laughed the sheriff.


* * * * * *


It took Mike Ventosa the better part of a week to wake up. Blake checked on him every day and had worried about whether he would wake up and when he did if he would be alright. Blake had seen head injuries addle a man for the rest of his life. Blake entered the doctor's office and was greeted by his attractive nurse, Anne. "He's awake, but he's still pretty weak," she said smiling.

"Can I go back and see him?" Blake asked.

"Oh please do, he'll be happy to see you, just not too long; he still needs plenty of rest."

Blake made his way to the back where he found Mike sitting up in bed. "You look like a fella I knew from India with your head wrapped up like that," Blake teased.

"Hey, Blake," Mike smiled, "any chance you can get me out of here? I'm about ready to pick the flowers off this here wallpaper."

"Why don't you pick a nice bunch for that nurse?" Blake laughed.

"She's the only reason I ain't lit a shuck. I like the scenery."

"Sorry to say, pard, she might be right about taking your time getting out of here. Can I get you something to do?" asked Blake.

"Naw, Johansson was kind enough to bring a fat stack of paperwork to wade through," he said pointing at a pile of wanted posters. "He said he wouldn't feel right about payin' me if I didn't do some kinda work."

"He is one generous son-of-a-gun, ain't he?" laughed Blake.

"Word is you saved his bacon with a shot from the church steeple using the Padre's rifle."

"Yeah, I was working on the church bell and saw Wilson trying to escape. Guess I was in the right place at the right time. I got lucky."

"You sure were," Mike laughed. "Heard it took you two shots."

Blake smiled and shook his head. "Kiss my ass." They both laughed and shook hands.

\* \* \* \* \* \*

That day Percival had spent most of the morning cleaning himself up. He took a bath, got a shave and a haircut. He put on a new pair of pants, a clean shirt and even cleaned the dirt from his boots. Stopping by Dooley's store he bought a small bouquet of flowers, drew a deep breath and headed for the Trail's End. The saloon was about half full by the time he got there, mostly cowpunchers playing cards and sipping beer. The entire room stopped what they were doing and stared at him as he walked through the batwing doors. He cleared his throat and said in load clear voice, "I am here to call on Miss Lipton."

The men started looking around and asking each other if they knew a Miss Lipton. Michelle was at the top of the staircase and started down, followed by a cowboy pulling on his vest. She stopped for a second and swallowed hard. "Percival?"

Big Man saw her and smiled broadly. "Yes ma'am, may I have a minute?"

Slightly embarrassed, she continued down while looking around at the unbelieving stares. She came to a stop in front of the huge man. "Perhaps we can go somewhere else to talk," she said sweetly.

The Big Man's face became very firm. "No ma'am, now I know who you are, what you does for a living, and that don't make no difference to me. I want all these here fellas to know that I intend to make you my wife." Then, suddenly he dropped to one knee. "That is if you want to."

She took the flowers he was holding out and placed her hand over her mouth, tears welled up in her eyes and she nodded her head yes.

Percival looked shocked. "Really? Ya mean it?" She nodded her head harder and hugged him tightly. He stood up picking her up as he went and hugged her back.

"I got her all loosened up fer your wedding night," yelled the cowboy who followed her down the stairs and the room erupted in laughter. "Hey, I helped, too!" yelled another.

Big Man slowly set Michelle down and with murder in his eyes he reached for the offending cowboy. Closing his massive hand around his throat he lifted him off the wood floor. The cowboy tried to reach for his pistol and Percival grabbed his wrist hard enough to hear the bones crack. Michelle pulled on his arm and screamed, "Percival, no!!!"

Iver Johansson had been making his rounds in the town and saw the Big Man coming out of Dooley's store with flowers in his hand. The sheriff watched him as he made his way to the saloon. "What is that big lunkhead up to now?" he asked himself. Sensing there was going to be trouble, he started toward the Trail's End. He stood outside the batwings and listened, and when things seemed to be getting out of hand, Johansson pushed through the doors.

A deafening blast filled the room from his Greener shotgun. The place went silent as the sheriff walked up to Big Man choking the cowboy. "Put him down, big fella," as he eared back the hammer on the second barrel. Percival made no motion to drop him so the sheriff said louder, "Now."

"Please, Honey," Michelle sobbed.

Big Man turned his head and looked deeply into her wet, green eyes. He opened both hands and let the cowboy fall into a gasping, choking heap. Michelle wrapped her arms around him and buried her face in his chest.

"Now, I'm from Texas," shouted the sheriff loud enough for all to hear, "and we are raised to treat our womenfolk kindly and any varmint that insults another man's woman is due whatever punishment he is given, short of murder."

"He broke my arm," cried the cowboy Percival manhandled.

"You're God damn lucky you didn't get your fool head pinched off," growled Johansson. "This here woman," he continued, "has accepted this man's proposal and is deserving of respect for changing her ways. If any man here finds that troublesome, he can drop his pistol and hash out his differences with my big friend one-on-one right now." Johansson looked around the room. "Any takers?" No one moved a muscle, so he said, "I consider the matter closed." Then he set his shotgun on his shoulder and turned to the Big Man and Michelle, "Let me be the first to congratulate you both on your upcoming nuptials."

\* \* \* \* \* \*

The following day Percival and Michelle were married. Johansson convinced the circuit court judge to perform the ceremony and to stay another day because there was no need to try Wilson anymore. Because there was no courthouse in town yet, Chrissy closed the café and decorated it for the ceremony. She also made a large cake and other desserts for the people attending. There was Blake, Caleb, Sadie, and Dan LaClare, the bartender from the Trail's End, two other doves who were friends to Michelle, Chrissy, Bonnie, Sheriff Johansson and even Mike Ventosa who was helped over by Anne. Even Caleb's dog Satan lay by the front door happily munching on a ham bone supplied by Chrissy. He was not allowed in because everyone knew his reputation and did not care to upset him. After the marriage was over Percival and Michelle cut the cake and everyone sat around eating and laughing. As was the tradition, Michelle threw her bouquet over her shoulder and it was caught by Anne who blushed and smiled at Mike Ventosa who looked extremely uncomfortable.

When it came time to leave they all stood outside and threw rice at the newlyweds, who were on their way to the hotel for the honeymoon.

"C-c-congratulations, P-Percy," Caleb said shaking his hand. Big Man hung onto Caleb's hand and tossed him in the watering trough.

The Sunday that followed found Blake on his way to the livery to take Bull for a ride. Caleb and Sadie had made a habit of attending church each week and left the house at the same time Blake did. It was a warm beautiful morning and he was looking forward to being alone to cogitate about his life. When he was just turning the corner a voice called out breaking his train of thought. "Mr. Thorton, may I speak to you a moment?" Blake turned and saw Chrissy looking prettier than he had ever seen her. She wore a bright blue dress that hugged her body in a way that made him swallow hard. The color of her dress brought out the blue in her eyes, and sparkled against her rosy cheeks. Bonnie was walking with her, dressed far plainer but her hair was pulled back to expose soft brown eyes. Though her scar was visible somehow it detracted little from her looks.

Blake smiled and removed his hat. "What can I do for such a lovely pair of ladies this fine morning?" he said in overly dramatic voice.

"I was hoping you would be in attendance at church this morning, so you could witness the marvelous job you did repairing the bell." She was standing in front of him and he caught the faint smell of roses from the perfume she was wearing. He had had whiskey that was less intoxicating.

He smiled and said, "I heard it the morning we fixed it and, besides, Caleb deserves the credit, it was his job after all."

"So I heard," she smiled back. "But you played a small part and we would like to thank you, also."

"Well ma'am, my horse gets downright surly if I don't take him out for a ride once a week and I hate to upset him. Perhaps another time."

Chrissy drew a deep breath and let it out slowly. "You're not going to make this easy are you?" she said cocking her trademark eyebrow. "Mr. Thorton, Bonnie and I would like you to accompany us to the service this morning as our guest. I will explain to your horse, if need be, why you were late."

"Damn," Blake thought, "she's got me boxed in." He didn't mind going to church, he had been raised going to service with his family, but the years had weakened his faith and he didn't know if he was ready to accept God back into his life. He tried one last thing. "I'm not dressed for church, ma'am."

"You look presentable enough," she said firmly.

He looked up at the sky and said, "Well, I don't see any storm clouds, so I suppose I could, but if I hear thunder I'm gone." Turning and holding out his elbow he said, "I would be pleased to accompany you."

Chrissy smiled so sweetly, Blake felt his knees almost buckle out from underneath him. She slipped her hand into the crook of his elbow and they started for the church. As the three of them neared the church the bell rang out several times. People who did not know it had been fixed clapped and cheered. Caleb was standing with Sadie and saw them approaching, "H-hey B-B-lake" he called running up to them, "a-are y-y-you c-coming i-in?"

Blake smiled and looked at Chrissy. "Wasn't given much of a choice."

Caleb turned his attention to Bonnie. "Good morning, Miss Bonnie," he said.

"That reminds me, Bonnie," Blake said. "It is truly amazing how much Caleb has learned with you teaching."

"He works very hard and is an excellent student," she replied.

Suddenly a loud booming voice distracted them. It was Percival and his new bride. "If I go in there the whole dad-blamed roof is gonna fall in," he exclaimed.

"No it won't, honeybunch," she pleaded. "Just give it a try, for me, please?"

Blake escorted Chrissy over to the newlyweds. "How's it going, Big Man?"

"Blake, buddy, you has to help me. She's forcin' me to go in there and I'm afraid somethin' bad's gonna happen."

"I told him we are going to be respectable from here on out, and respectable people go to church," Michelle stated with her hands on her hips.

"Mrs. Chrissy ain't forcin' Blake none," Percival said.

Blake coughed and scratched his neck. "Well...I..."

Chrissy chimed in, "I'm sure you love your wife and this is a small thing you can do for her. Jesus loves us all, Percival, you'll be fine."

Sensing defeat he said in a low voice, "I reckon I can try."

"Thanks, honeybunch," Michelle said hugging him tightly.

"Just don't sit under the steeple," Blake said.

"Why's that?" asked Big Man.

"That's where the bell is and when the roof comes down, it might hurt." Chrissy slipped her hand to the inside of his arm and pinched him.

* * * * * *

Father Grimm delivered a powerful sermon that day and struck many chords that Blake related to. The Padre had a way of delivering his message that had the people engrossed and captivated without the hellfire and brimstone that he was accustomed to as a child. Blake could see why he was well-liked. After the service the ladies of the parish laid out some baked goods and lemonade on tables under the trees next to the church. Chrissy stayed by his side most of the time as they talked and laughed with the rest of the congregation. The only time there was any tension was when Ian MacIntyre approached them, with his two daughters and Tom in tow.

"Bonny job on the church bell," he said to Blake with a broad smile. "I did not know you was a church goin' man."

Tom was giving Blake a disapproving stare but Blake ignored it. "Well this fine lady convinced me to attend today," Blake said sipping some lemonade.

"Ah, tis true, you are an angel sent from heaven, ma'am," Ian said gently picking up Chrissy's hand and kissing it. He held her hand a little too long and an uncomfortable Chrissy pulled it away. "I myself have tried to gain the attentions of Mrs. O'Bryan, but alas, they have fallen on deaf ears."

"Work keeps me very busy," she said in her customary cold tone. "Also, caring for Bonnie after her parent's unfortunate accident." She gave Tom a cold hard stare, to which he gave a slight, evil smile.

"'Twas a tragedy, tis true. How is the lass faring?" Ian asked.

"It is a hard thing to recover from," she replied flatly. "But Mr. Thorton has employed her as a teacher to help the young man who works for him. That seems to help a little."

"How is that stuttering nitwit doing anyway?" Tom asked.

Ian shot Tom a menacing look over his shoulder but it did not compare to the one Blake was giving him. "He's doing an excellent job. I'm very proud of all he has accomplished. I'd request you keep a civil tongue when you speak of him."

"Gentlemen," Ian said holding up his hands. "'Tis the Sabbath and it would be no time for harsh words. I am sure my son meant no harm to the lad. Would I be correct, son?" Ian asked in a firm tone of voice.

Tom shrugged his shoulders. "Yeah, sure."

Ian turned back to Blake and smiled. "See there now, no harm done."

Blake could barely keep his anger in check. "Yeah, sure," he said.

"Then we'll be going on our way," Ian said ushering his children toward their carriage. "Good day to you both."

As they got in and Ian snapped the reins to get the horses moving, Chrissy said under her breath, "Asshole."

Blake burst out laughing. "Good heavens, Mrs. O'Bryan, do you kiss your mother with that mouth?"

**CHAPTER 14**

L ATER the next week, Blake and Caleb were making their way to the café for lunch. It had rained the night before, which was a welcome relief to the dry spell they had for a few weeks. It had settled the dust in town and the air was fresh and clean. Blake hadn't talked to Chrissy since last Sunday and, it being Friday, he came up with an excuse to eat lunch in her restaurant. Little did he know the next sequence of events would change things forever in his and Caleb's lives, if not the whole town's.

They were just about to enter the café when four riders came trotting into town headed for the saloon. One of the men seemed to be having a lot of trouble controlling a wild eyed red roan mare. He cursed at it and spurred it mercilessly only to make the mare more agitated. Finally in front of the saloon he lost his seat in the saddle and was sent flying into the rider beside him almost unseating him, also. The angry cowpuncher got to his feet and pulled his revolver from its holster and pointed it at the crazed animal.

"As God is my witness, you worthless nag, I'm going to put a bullet in your sorry skull," he yelled excitedly as he eared back the hammer.

"Do it, Ike," laughed on of his fellow riders. "I'm tired of you not gettin' a handle on her."

"Take yer saddle off first. It's a bitch doing it when they're on the ground," added another.

"Good point," Ike said, putting the gun back and jerked her head around so he could loosen the cinch straps. Pulling on the horse's mouth as hard as he did spooked the horse even more and she lashed out with a hind leg and kicked him in the thigh. The kick didn't break his leg but it hurt like hell and would leave a sizable bruise. "Ah, the hell with it," he cried out and pulled his pistol again.

When Blake saw them ride in, it was evident to him that the horse was in pain. Being a blacksmith in those days also meant you were a farrier and dealt with shoeing horses on a daily basis. He could tell just by watching a horse walk how they needed to be shod, or if they had a lameness problem. Just by the way this horse crow hopped and danced there was no doubt it was hurting bad.

"Hold on there a minute, mister," Blake called out as he approached him.

"What the hell does you want?" Ike said nastily.

"I'll buy that horse from you," Blake said calmly.

"This ornery piece of shit?" asked Ike still pointing the pistol at the mare.

"Yup, I'll give you twenty dollars."

"She just kicked me and that means she gets a bullet," snarled Ike.

"If you shoot her, then you'll have to get rid of the carcass," Blake pointed out. "And you'll have twenty less dollars in your pocket."

"Why does you give a damn anyway?"

"There are kids around that don't need to see you shoot her, and I'm feeling generous."

"It'll teach them life is hard," Ike said earring back the hammer.

"Fifty then," Blake said. Ike paused and looked back at Blake. "Fifty will buy you whiskey, a few hands of poker and maybe a visit with one of the ladies in there."

One of Ike's friends piped up, "Shit, mister I'll sell you my horse, an' he's a good one."

"Nope, I want this one." Blake took fifty dollars out his pocket and held it up. "You get to keep your tack, all I want is your rope so I can lead her back to the barn."

"All right," said Ike putting away his pistol, "but you are a damn fool."

Blake looked at Caleb and said, "Go in the saloon and get me some paper and a pencil, will you?" Caleb hurried in the saloon and returned with paper. Blake started writing out the bill-of-sale.

"What cha' doin?" Ike asked.

"Writing out a bill-of-sale," Blake said, "keeps everybody honest." He finished and handed it to Ike. "Here sign this."

Ike handed to one of his friends. "I can't read too much. Is it right, Bud?"

"Looks right to me," he said.

Ike took the paper back and scrawled his name on it. "Here, let me get my saddle." He removed the saddle and gave Blake his rope. Blake quickly made a halter and held the horse while Ike took off the bridle.

Blake handed Ike the money and said, "Pleasure doing business with you." He turned and started back to the livery. As he walked away he heard Ike yell, "First round's on me, boys!"

\* \* \* \* \* \*

The mare had a natural distrust of people because she had been mistreated so badly. She snorted and tried to pull away but Blake held firm and kept his manner calm. He had to stop three times on the way to the livery and just hold tight on the rope. He didn't hold on up by her head but instead gave six feet of rope between them. He held firm until she stopped straining and the second she stopped he let go of the pressure. Soon, she walked quietly beside him. Caleb gave him a puzzled look and Blake said, "Horses are a fearful animal by nature, they're always afraid something is going to eat them and they don't care much for being trapped, that's when they fight. Most cowboys strong arm them and force them to do what they want but you can do a lot more with them if you let them think they're making the decisions. Just walking right now she decided it's easier not to pull on the rope and walk beside me."

Caleb wrinkled his brow and considered what Blake said, "M-makes s-sense."

"I hope so, because she's yours," Blake said handing Caleb the rope. "You've done a good job with your schooling and the forge, so here's a reward."

Caleb took the rope very timidly and was nervous because he saw how the horse acted earlier.

"She can sense it if you're scared of her," Blake told him. "I have some ideas why she is acting up, she's in pain. So you have to let her know that we're going to try and help. She has to know that you will be a good leader and protect her."

Caleb dug deep and faced his fear head on. For the first time he had the face of a man, strong and controlled. He stood calmly as the mare tossed her head and pawed the ground. He simply held out his hand down low and waited for her to settle down. It took some time before she quieted and stuck her nose to sniff his hand. He brought it up slowly and stroked her head, "Good, girl," he cooed. "I'm going to fix you up." The mare's eyes softened a little and she held her head lower.

"That's a good start, now let's get her to the barn," Blake said. When they got to the livery, Joe came out to meet them.

"Howdy boys," he said. "Whatcha' got?"

"Just bought this mare from a fella who was going to plug her," Blake said softly stroking her neck. "I got a feeling I know what the problem is, but I could use some help. Hang on to her Caleb; I want to check her feet." Caleb stroked her neck and talked softly to her as Blake slowly ran his hand down her leg and gently picked up her hoof. Using his thumb, he began pressing all around the hoof until when he pressed directly on the bottom, the mare's flesh quivered. He set the hoof down and proceeded to check the other three. When he was done he stepped back and scratched the back of his neck.

"You think you found a problem?" asked Joe.

"I haven't seen this since I was a kid, working with my father," Blake said. "I think she has a very thin sole on her feet, some horses are born that way and it's pretty painful for them to walk. Plus, you put the weight of a rider and saddle on them; it makes it a lot worse."

"C-can you h-h-help h-her?" Caleb asked.

"Maybe," Blake considered. "Joe, do you have boots I can borrow?"

Boots for a horse were made out thick leather that could be strapped on a hoof. Usually they were used to mask prints so they couldn't be tracked or to hold medicine on the hoof.

Joe thought for a second and said, "I think I can scrounge some up, let me have a look." And he left for the barn.

"Good, thanks," Blake said. "Caleb run to the store and fetch me some chamomile and devil's claw and about twelve plugs of tobacco."

"T-t-tabacco?" Caleb inquired.

"We're going to pack some in her hoof well and hold it on with the boots from Joe. That will toughen up the soles and allow them to thicken. It's a trick an old Dutch farmer I knew used to do. The chamomile will quiet her down so she can rest and the devil's claw will help with the pain. We'll mix up the herbs in some grain for her."

Caleb handed Blake the rope and took off running for the store. Shortly after Joe came out holding the boots with Avery following him. Avery looked at the mare with a suspicious eye, "Ain't that Ike Smullen's hoss?"

"Was," Blake said. "I just bought her."

Avery cackled, "What the hell fer? That nag ain't no good. Ike played hell with her forever. She ain't right in the head."

"I don't think he spent the time to figure out why she was acting so badly. I'm going to try and help her."

"Waste of your dad-burned time," Avery said waving his hand.

Blake stopped stroking her neck and turned to Avery. "People said the same thing about you."

Avery opened his mouth like he was going to say something but nothing came out. Joe laughed and said, "I do believe he is at a loss for words, I never thought I'd see the day." The expression on Avery's face was priceless and Blake joined in with Joe laughing.

"The both of you can take a sweet bite of my ass, I's got horseshit to pitch," he said as he stomped back to the barn.

Caleb returned with items Blake requested and he fed the mare the herbs while Blake packed the feet and put on the boots. Then they led her to a nice cool dark stall in the back of the barn to let her rest.

\* \* \* \* \* \*

The day was drawing to a close at the MacIntyre ranch. The sky was a light shade of purple with orange streaks from what was left of the setting sun. Ian MacIntyre and his three children were sitting on the front porch of their house. Ian was swabbing out the bore of a Henry rifle and his two daughters were working on cross-stitch doilies. Tom was sitting in a rocking chair with feet up on the railing smoking a cigar. He drew deeply on the cigar and blew out a large cloud of smoke. Being downwind of Tom, the two girls took the brunt of the plume and coughed.

"Move to the other end of the porch with that foul thing," growled Ian. "The smoke is bothersome to your sisters."

"Why can't they move?" Tom said lazily. "I'm right comfortable."

Ian stopped working on the rifle and glared at Tom. "Because a gentleman always moves for a lady, Boyo."

"Whatever," Tom said, dropping his feet hard onto the floor and got up slowly. He moved so his smoke would blow away from his sisters and leaned against a post. Three riders were coming down the road to the ranch toward the bunkhouse. Tom called out to them, "Hey Bud, c'mon over here."

The three veered their horses toward the house and stopped at the hitch rail. "What's up, Boss?" Bud Hanley asked.

"Where the hell is Ike?"

Ian barked, "Language boy, your sisters are present."

Irritated, Tom drew a deep breath. "Where is Ike? Did that fool get himself tossed in jail?"

Leaning on his saddlehorn, Bud said, "Naw, nothing like that, he sold his horse. I'm going to take him another one in the morning."

"Sold his horse," Tom exclaimed. "Why would that d...," Tom stopped and caught himself, "Why did he do that?"

"He was ridin' that crazy roan mare, and she was givin' him fits. Bucked him off right in front of the saloon and he was about to feed her some lead when this feller offered him fifty dollars for her."

"What feller?" Tom asked impatiently.

"I think it was that new blacksmith in town," Bud said looking at the other two to collaborate his story. "Thorton, I think his name is."

Tom threw his cigar in the dirt and said between gritted teeth, "That son-of-a-bitch again." Ian grunted at him for cursing. "Sorry, Pa, but that man is getting to be a burr under my saddle." Tom looked hard at Bud. "You never mind about going to town tomorrow. I'll ride in and get Ike and that confounded horse back."

Bud pursed his lips. "I don't know boss, Thorton paid him more than she was worth and had him sign a bill-of-sale. It was all real legal."

"I'll get it back, if I have to beat it out of him," insisted Tom.

Ian stood up and leaned the rifle against the wall, "You'll do no such thing, Thomas. Bud, take Ike another horse come morning. I want every one of you working on time tomorrow."

Bud touched the brim of his hat. "Sure thing, Mr. MacIntyre," and the three left for the bunkhouse.

Smiling sweetly at his daughters, Ian said, "Sure an' there's not enough light for you to be workin' on your sewing. Why don't you turn in so not to harm your pretty eyes."

"Yes, Papa," they said in unison and started gathering their sewing.

"You, boyo," he said to Tom in an unkind voice. "Come to my study." He snatched the rifle leaning against the wall and walked heavily into the house.

"Tommy's gonna get in trouble," Kate teased as she scooted by a very embarrassed Tom.

"Shut up," he snarled.

Tom took his time getting to the study; he stopped at the heavy door, drew a deep breath and knocked. "Enter," a booming voice said and he went in the room which was magnificent. It was his favorite room in the house. There was a large ornate oak desk with soft leather chairs in front and a larger leather chair in back of it. Many paintings adorned the walls, along with several antique firearms and powder flasks. The walls were solid cherry boards that glistened in the firelight from a large stone fireplace. Ian was sitting behind the desk underneath a pair of longhorns the must have spread seven feet. Tom often snuck in that room and sat at his father's desk and envisioned that someday it would all be his but, for now, he would have to settle for the other side of the desk. He strolled over to the table with several crystal whiskey decanters and pulled the glass stopper and went to pour himself a drink. "You'll not be needin' any of that," Ian said without looking up. "Sit down, lad."

Tom replaced the stopper and strode confidently over to one of the chairs and sat. He was Ian MacIntyre's son and to show anything less than total confidence would be a mistake. Weakness, in any form, would not be tolerated. Having been called to his father's study many times before, he knew better than to speak first. Ian finished making entries in his ledger, closed it and sat back. "Now tell me, what is the problem with this Thorton fellow?"

Tom sat back and crossed his legs and, looking straight into his father's eyes, he began. "He drifted into town a couple months back and has been making a lot of changes. He seems to be flush with money, where he got it I have no idea, probably stole from somewhere and has himself a real smartass attitude. This is our town, Pa, and he thinks he's the big dog around here."

"Our town?" Ian said with a strange light in his eyes. "I named this town when it was a few tents and you were suckling your fair mother's breast, lad. I wouldn't be forgettin' that."

"I know, Pa; I just don't like him trying to take over."

"I'm not thinking buying a blacksmith shop and a house is takin' over."

"It's more than that, a lot more," Tom was already losing ground and knew it. "He's got Weatherby on his side and the sheriff, too, just because he stopped that robbery. He cleaned up those fools Hap and Avery and got them jobs. He took that stuttering kid in and is teachin' him smithing. Plus, that big bastard in the saloon married one of the whores and is gonna open a dress shop … all on the count of him."

"I'm thinking he is sounding like a good man to have around," Ian replied placing his fingers in a steeple in front of him.

Frustrated, Tom started grasping at straws. "Well, I would just like to know where he's getting all this money and why he seemed to know those men who went after the bank. It all sounds pretty fishy to me."

Ian dropped his hands on the desk and leaned forward. "'Tis many a man who is not wantin' someone prying into his past. I canna fault him there. Now tell me why Mr. Weatherby is askin' my permission to sell properties in town."

Tom was showing signs of being nervous, trying to relax he said, "Because I told him to. I don't want Thorton buying the whole town up."

"Are you thinking he has enough to do that?"

"I don't know, Weatherby wouldn't say." Tom felt like he was getting some footing with his father and pressed further. "He's also got that Chrissy O'Bryan woman batting her eyes at him and I know you have always fancied her."

"Aye, I have thought she would be fitting substitute for your mother, God rest her soul."

Tom was gaining ground now. "Remember that girl, Bonnie? The one who said I raped her? Well now she's playing school marm to that stuttering asshole he's got working for him."

Whatever ground Tom thought he had gained he lost tenfold with his last comment. Lightning flashed in his father's eyes, and looked like an earthquake was building inside him. Ian rose from his chair slowly and glared at Tom. Ian knew the truth about what happened to Bonnie. He tried to write it off as a crime of passion and his youthful son had made a terrible mistake. Wanting to protect him, Ian had done his best to cover the whole ordeal up and, in the back of his mind, he knew Tom had murdered Bonnie's parents by setting the fire. It had been a burden that weighed heavy on his mind. To have Tom act like he had not committed this atrocity heaped him far worse.

Ian stepped around the massive desk and Tom rose up out of his chair. He was tempted to run from his father but to show that much cowardice would go far worse on him. Deep in his bowels Tom felt true terror now. His father grabbed him by the front of his shirt and brought his face close to his, Ian's voice sounded like an enraged bear. "I am fully aware of what happened to that poor lass, you sniveling, black hearted bastard. And to say you had no hand in it would be a crime against God."

"She acted like she wanted to, but then she changed her mind. It wasn't right, Pa," Tom said, his voice shaking.

Ian's gigantic hand came crashing down on Tom's face. Fireworks erupted in his head and his knees buckled. His father's other hand held him up as he brought his hand back and delivered another bone crushing blow. Tom fell to the ground and tried regain his footing. Ian was now in a full rage and brought down his fist on Tom's back driving him to the floor. He kept striking Tom as he yelled, "You have brought shame to my house and it tasks me to call you my son. I rue the day your mother birthed you and the sight of you makes me wretch."

As Ian stood back up his massive chest was heaving trying to get enough air. Tears filled his eyes and he began to sob. "I never taught you to defile women, where did learn such a terrible thing?" Tom could not answer because he was barely conscious. Ian stepped over his quivering son and opened the door. "Jethro," he yelled in a commanding voice. A large black man who was a servant in the house came running up the hall. He entered the study and saw Tom lying on the floor. Ian said, "Take my son to his room and tend to him." As Jethro picked him up and left the study Ian poured himself some whiskey and collapsed in his chair, "I donna want to be disturbed."

* * * * * *

Tom woke the next morning feeling like he had been hit by a train. His lower lip was swollen and his right eye had a deep purple bruise. Tom's back also bore deep bruising that his father had given him and some of his ribs felt cracked. He moved slowly getting up and hobbled over to the water pitcher on the dresser, wetting the towel he dabbed the sore areas on his face and examined the damage in the mirror. Tom had been in fights before but, being a rich man's son, before they got too far out of hand someone stepped in and stopped it. As he got older he always had another hand around to do his snake stomping for him. He pressed a particularly sore spot on his face and could feel a rage building inside him. How dare that old man embarrass him in front of his men, let alone his sisters? He was Tom MacIntyre and when his father was old and dying in his bed, Tom would inherit the old man's ranch, drink his whiskey and smoke his cigars. He would run things how he saw fit and if a man like Thorton got in his way, he would be shot down like the dog that he was.

When Tom looked in the mirror he no longer saw Ian MacIntyre's son, he saw a new man, one who would take control of his life and do as he damn well pleased. His anger exploded inside him and he swept the ceramic pitcher and bowl off the dresser against the wall. Grabbing some saddlebags he began stuffing clothes and various other things into them. Getting dressed was painful to him but the surge of adrenaline helped him ignore it. He stomped on his boots and buckled on his gun belt adjusting the fit and tying it down securely to his leg.

Taking the saddlebags, he headed out of his bedroom door and down the hall half hoping to see his father so he could shoot him on the spot. When he reached the bottom of the staircase he glanced at the grandfather clock in the foyer. It was ten o'clock and he knew the house would be empty because everyone else had chores to do. Stopping at the glass faced gun cabinet in the hall he removed one of his father's prized Winchesters and three boxes of shells. Tom slammed open the front door and started for the barn. The two toughs that normally rode with him, Tug Pearson and Jimmy Rocco, saw him and came out of the bunkhouse.

"Christ almighty Tom, what happened to you?" Tug asked.

"I'm ridin' out," Tom said dodging the question. "I'll be gone for a while. If you two want a change of scenery, you're welcome to come."

"Sure thing, boss," Jimmy said. "How long we goin' to be gone?"

"Until I say," Tom replied sharply.

"Hoo wee," Tug said excitedly. "No more chasin' cows. I'm in, boss. Just let me get my gear."

"Me, too," smiled Jimmy.

"Here, take these," Tom said handing them the rifle, shells and saddlebags. "Saddle my horse and get ready to go. I need a couple more things from the house." Tom walked back to the house and made his way back to the kitchen where he found Jethro coming in the back door carrying a couple freshly plucked chickens. "Where's my father?" Tom asked gruffly.

"He done left early for the high pasture," replied Jethro.

"Fill some sacks with enough grub to last three men a couple of weeks, and be quick about it," Tom ordered. Jethro didn't answer as he took some empty sacks and started filling them. Tom turned on his heel and went to his father's study. Behind the desk was a small safe where his father kept money and valuables. Ian was the only person who knew the combination, or so he thought. Tom knelt down and dialed his mother's birthday. Tom had watched his father open the safe enough times to recognize the combination. He gave the handle a turn and it opened easily. Reaching in, he removed his father's money belt that contained five thousand dollars and removed his shirt and wrapped it around his waist. Buttoning his shirt Tom looked around the room; hate was rising up in his chest again. He gathered a large mouthful of spit and phlegm and spat in the middle of the massive desk. "I'll come back for the rest of what's mine, you miserable old bastard," he snarled.

He left slamming the door of the study and stomped his way back to the kitchen and, without a word, snatched up the food and headed for the front door. Tug and Jimmy were waiting holding his horse and Tom handed them each a sack and got painfully into his saddle. Taking one more look around the ranch, he grit his teeth and growled, "Let's make some dust." The three of them spun their horses around and left the ranch at a high gallop.

CHAPTER 15

THE weeks passed slowly around the town of MacIntyre, spring had left and the summer was in full swing with hot sultry days and cool evenings. Blake and Caleb worked in the forge in the mornings and after lunch they trained Caleb's horse, Rosie, as he named her. Her feet had improved greatly and now Caleb worked on gaining her trust. Blake marveled at the way she took to him and in little time he was riding her bareback with just a halter and a single lead rope. When Blake suggested that he might try a saddle, Caleb shrugged his shoulders and said, "W-we d-do fine." He took to riding her to the café for school and people were astounded when he could just ask for her to bow down so he could get on easier, and she did it without hesitation.

Michelle and Percival purchased a two story house on the main street of town and opened a dress shop. Blake always found it funny that he would never see any women go in the front door but several times they were seen leaving out the back and up the alley with packages under their arms.

Blake attended church most Sundays and usually tried to sit next to Chrissy, but being a small town, people started to gossip and that made her uncomfortable.

It was the following week and Blake was in Josh Dooley's store settling his bill and placing orders for more goods. "So tell me, Blake," Josh said as they were finishing up, "have you called on Mrs. O'Bryan yet?"

"What? No. I mean what made you ask that?" Blake asked taken back.

"Well, it's just the whole town is on pins and needles waiting for you to."

"I don't like being the topic of conversation, Josh. Tell them to mind their own business," Blake said flatly.

Josh stared down at the counter. "Sorry, Blake, I was prodded into it."

"Oh, for goodness sakes," said Terry from behind him, "you men are so thick sometimes. Even Maddy thinks you two are right for each other."

"Well be that as it may, I don't think a four-year-old is the proper judge for my life," smiled Blake.

With that, Madeline crawled up on the counter and took hold of one of Blake's fingers. "I am almost five, and you have to stay here," she said in a very determined little girl way.

Blake laughed, "And why would that be, Little Missy?"

"You'll see," she giggled.

Blake looked at Josh who shrugged his shoulders and then at Terry who just smiled like the cat who ate the canary. Just as he was about to say something the bell over the front door tinkled and Chrissy came in. "Hello, Josh, Hap said you needed to ask me something."

Josh looked helplessly at Terry, who poked Madeline, who got up on her knees and whispered something in Blake's ear. "Really," he said smiling at Madeline. She shook her head rapidly. "All right, but if this goes wrong it's your fault." Madeline laughed.

"I should really be getting back," Chrissy said.

"Mrs. O'Bryan I fear that we are victims of a very clever ruse," Blake said.

"What are you talking about?"

"This young lady has made up her mind that I should ask you a question."

"And what question is that?"

"You probably won't accept anyway."

"You won't know unless you ask. Please, Mr. Thorton, I have a business to run."

Blake looked at Madeline again and said, "What was I supposed to ask?"

Josh blurted out, "Ask her, or I'll ask her myself." Terry shot him a disapproving look. "For him, not for me." He laid his head on the counter defeated. "Please Blake, end my hell."

Blake chuckled, "Miss Madeline thinks I should ask you to go for a buggy ride this Sunday."

Chrissy crossed her arms and cocked her eyebrow, "Does she now?"

"Yup, but I told her you would say no."

"I haven't."

"Then you'll go?"

"I didn't say that either."

Blake was confused. "Then what are you saying?"

"I would rather it be your idea, not Madeline's."

"I intended to ask, but I knew you would say no."

"I haven't."

"Then the answer is yes?"

"Are you certain that this is completely your idea?"

"Mother of God, woman, you're going to be the death of me." Blake steadied himself and stood up straightly. "Mrs. O'Bryan, it is my sincerest wish that you would accompany me for a ride in the country this coming Sunday afternoon after church services. What is your reply?"

She made him wait a full thirty seconds before answering. "That would be lovely, Mr. Thorton," she said smiling. "Shall I pack a lunch?"

Blake was stunned by the recent events. Finally, Terry poked his arm and he said, "That would be lovely."

Chrissy dropped her arms and winked at Terry. "I'll see you Sunday, then," and she turned and left the store.

"God Almighty," Josh said, "I think I need a nap after watching that."

\* \* \* \* \* \*

In preparation for the Sunday afternoon carriage ride, Blake purchased a new suit complete with a string tie and matching vest. He tried to clean his trail hat but determined that it was far too worn and bought a new one. He shined his boots to a high luster and even polished his gun belt and colt revolver. Standing in front of the full length mirror in his room he carefully looked at himself. "Well, I guess that's as good as it's gonna get," he thought. Picking up his new hat, he left the room and headed downstairs. As he entered the kitchen Caleb whistled, "N-now a-ain't you p-p-pretty," he laughed.

"You's take yourself a lesson, sonny," Sadie said. "That a man who knows hows to dress fo' courtin'."

"It's just a buggy ride, you two," Blake groused.

Caleb snickered and Sadie smiled at him, "If'n a man came to my door lookin' that fine, I be lookin' fo' a preacher man to marry him, sho nuff."

Caleb looked up at Blake and batted his eyes, "Oh B-Blake w-will you m-marry m-me."

Blake cuffed him lightly on the back of his head, "Finish your breakfast, boy." Putting his hat on, he started for the door.

"I's told yo' he'd have too many butterflies in has stomach to be eatin' my breakfast," Sadie said nudging Caleb, and they both giggled.

Blake snatched two biscuits off the counter and took a bite from one of them. "Keep it up and the both of you will be bunking in the hayloft down at the livery," he said smiling. He left the house and could hear them laughing until he reached the street. The day was warm and promised to be clear, there was not a cloud in the sky. As Blake rounded the corner to the livery he saw Avery cleaning off the horse and buggy Blake had rented from Joe for the day. Avery spit on the wheel hub and wiped off with a dirty rag. "Some people actually use water for that," Blake said disgusted.

"Joe said hisself to spitshine this here buggy for you, so that's what I'm doing. An' I got to say my mouth is getting' purdy dry," Avery said grinning back.

"I think I'm going to puke," Blake said shaking his head.

"Oh, I was just funnin' you is all, I used water for your sweet-heart."

"It's just a buggy ride, for Pete's sake."

"Oh sure it tis, and I am President Ulysses S. Grant," Avery stated proudly hooking his thumbs high on his suspenders.

"You are an ass, is what you are."

"I's has no time to be trifling with the likes of you, I's has me a Congress to address," Avery said cackling, throwing his rag on the ground and marched back into the barn.

Blake stepped up into the carriage and muttered to himself, "I am surrounded by idiots."

He snapped the reins and drove the horse out onto the main street toward the café. Chrissy and Bonnie, who was carrying a large picnic basket, were just leaving and Chrissy turned to lock the door. She turned back to the street just as Blake pulled the buggy to a stop in front of the café. Chrissy was dressed in a bright yellow dress with her blonde hair pulled back in a pretty fashion that accentuated her heart shaped face. She wore a small matching hat with a yellow feather in it, her blue eyes sparkled when she saw him and she smiled sweetly. "My, what a handsome figure you cut in that suit, Mr. Thorton."

Blake tipped his hat. "It pales in comparison to the image of you fine ladies," he said. "I thought perhaps you would like a ride to church today."

"I'm not sure that would be proper," she said pursing her lips.

"Oh, please," Bonnie said. "This basket is heavy."

"If that's our lunch, the least I can do is put it in the buggy," Blake said jumping down and taking it from Bonnie. "Can you drive a buggy, Mrs. O'Bryan?"

"Certainly," Chrissy responded.

"Then why don't you and Bonnie take it to church and I will meet you there?"

"That is truly gallant, but I think…"

"Thank you, Mr. Thorton!" Bonnie said as she hopped in the carriage.

Blake grinned at Chrissy and placed the basket in the back, then he held out his hand to help Chrissy into the seat. "It would appear the decision has been made, ma'am."

"Apparently," Chrissy said entering the carriage. "Thank you."

The service was short and to the point that week. Father Grimm focused on the evils of drink. It had more than one man squirming in his pew. Blake sat with Sadie and Caleb but his eyes were fixed on Chrissy who sat several rows in front of him. After the service was over he waited outside for Chrissy and Bonnie. Ian MacIntyre came out of the church with his daughters behind him; there was a sour look on his face as he passed Blake. "Good morning," Blake said pleasantly.

Ian stopped dead in his tracks and gave Blake a cold stare. "Girls, go to my carriage and wait, I wish to be havin' a word with Mr. Thorton," he said without glancing away.

"Yes, Papa," they said in unison, and hurried to the buggy.

"What can I do for you?" Blake asked. He was somewhat bewildered as to why Ian wanted to speak with him.

"I would like to be knowin' what your quarrel is with my son," Ian said flatly.

The question took Blake off guard, so he kept a calm demeanor. "I don't have a quarrel with him directly."

Ian drew up to full height. "He thinks you are up to no good, and I'm tryin' to discern if it is so."

Blake's voice became even and cold, he did not like being challenged and tried to control his temper. "I will not defend myself to anyone, especially your son. If he has anything to say, I recommend he comes to me personally … as a man would."

"It tis dangerous ground you would be treading on, Mr. Thorton," glared Ian.

"The soles of my boots have seen plenty of it, Mr. MacIntyre."

Ian held his gaze awhile longer. "Aye, of that I'm certain," he said and slowly turned and walked to his carriage.

"What was that all about?" Chrissy asked. She had come up behind Blake and overheard the last of his conversation.

"I'm not sure," Blake replied, and then he smiled. "Are you ready to go?"

"Yes, I am. Caleb is going to escort Bonnie home, so we can leave whenever you like."

Blake held out his elbow for her and she slipped her hand in it. He escorted her to the buggy and helped her in and then they were off.

As they started out he said, "I'm still not real familiar with the surroundings yet. Do you know of any nice places to go?"

"There is a lake south of here that's very pretty, if that sounds good."

"South it is then," he said.

\* \* \* \* \* \*

It was a very pleasant ride to the lake. They talked about their lives and how they got there, but mostly where they wanted to go with them. They circled the lake and found a secluded place to spread the blanket for their picnic. The day had become quite warm so they sat under a large oak tree with a spectacular view of the lake. The lunch tasted wonderful, fried chicken and biscuits with apple pie for dessert. Chrissy brought a bottle of wine and they shared that, too. She had removed her hat and let her golden hair cascade down around her shoulders. Blake lazed on his side holding his head up on his hand and marveled at her beauty. Finally she stood and leaned against the tree looking out onto the lake. There was a melancholy look on her face as she tried to hide wiping a tear away. Blake stood slowly and came up behind her. "Have I done something to upset you?" he asked.

"No," she said softly. "Yes, I mean, I'm not sure." She turned and looked at him with sad eyes. "I don't know what to feel. You are a strange man. One minute you make me mad and then an instant later I feel attracted to you." She placed her hand lightly on his chest. "It has been a long time since I have let myself feel like this, I'm afraid of being hurt."

"I would never try to hurt you, but I'm not perfect. Just know from the second I saw you I knew you were a special woman and I would be the luckiest man alive just to be around you."

"That's very sweet," she said. "But there are some things you don't know, I…."

"Chrissy," Blake interrupted.

"Yes?" she said her lips quivering.

"Hush," he said and leaned down and kissed her. They held the kiss for a long time and she slipped her hand around the back of his neck. Slowly the passion grew and he pulled her tiny waist closely to his own. When the kiss parted he looked deeply into her eyes and she brought a trembling hand down to the end of his string tie, pulling gently she untied it and unbuttoned the top button of his shirt. "It's been so long," she whispered and undid another button. Tears ran down her cheeks as Blake kissed her again, with more urgency. He could taste her salty tears as he slipped his hand behind her and unbuttoned the top of her dress. He moved his mouth down to her neck and softly caressed it with his lips. Her breath came faster as she frantically opened his shirt and pressed herself firmly against him. They brought their mouths back together and started removing each other's clothes. Blake slid her dress and bodice from her shoulders exposing her breasts and pulled her tightly against his naked flesh. When they were both naked he slowly lowered her to the blanket and lay beside her. He glanced down and admired her soft creamy flesh and caressed her with his strong hands. She cupped his face and brought his eyes to hers, "Make love to me," she whispered and brought her lips to his.

When they were finished, they laid side by side holding each other, Blake reached up to brush away one of the curls of her hair that slipped down on her face. Suddenly her mood changed dramatically and she burst into tears. "Damn you," she sobbed.

Blake was shocked. "What the heck did I do?" he asked.

Chrissy rolled away and stood up with her back to him and started getting dressed. "I gave into temptation with you, I'm no better than one of the saloon girls."

Blake was mystified. "I don't see how you can say that. We are two adults that have a strong attraction for each other, that doesn't make this wrong."

"We're not animals," she snapped. "I think a man and woman should be wedded first."

"It's a ring and a piece of paper, that's all," Blake said pulling on his shirt and buttoning it.

"Not in God's eyes it isn't," she stated trying to button the back of her dress. "I don't think I could ever marry a man like you, you'll never settle down."

"Whoa, whoa, whoa, who ever said anything about getting married?" Blake stammered. "I like you a lot, but I don't know if I'm ready for that." The second the words left his mouth he would have given all his money and more to get them back.

Chrissy stared at him and her mouth hung open.

"Damn," Blake said hanging his head. "That came out all wrong." He took both of her arms in his hands and looked deeply in her eyes. "Look, a couple of months ago I didn't know this town existed. All of the sudden I'm opening a blacksmith shop and living in a house. I've taken on a wayward kid and stared creating a life. Ever since I got back from sea I've only taken life a day at a time, not giving much thought of how it would affect people. One part of me is scared out my wits and wants to pack up and skedaddle, while another part wants to stay here and settle down."

Chrissy set her jaw hard and said coldly, "Am I part of what makes you want to skedaddle?" she said mocking him.

Blake searched her eyes for a moment. God, she stirred feelings in him like no woman ever had. "No, Chrissy O'Bryan, you are what makes me want to stay here forever."

She shrugged his hands off her arms and said flatly, "Then, Blake Thorton, I recommend that you make up your mind, because I will not wait long." She bent down and started jamming the picnic dishes in the basket, not being too careful with the dishes because Blake was sure he heard a few break.

Blake felt like he had been kicked in the gut by an angry mule, he searched his mind for the correct words and, once again, chose the wrong ones. "I don't like being pressured," he said immediately regretting it.

"Oh my dear, Mr. Thorton, there is no pressure. I'm just feeling a tad used for your pleasure. I wish to go home now," she said coldly, picked up the basket and marched to the buggy and got in.

Once again, Blake searched for the right words and finally took the most intelligent action he could think of, and he shut up.

\* \* \* \* \* \*

It was undoubtedly the longest ride of his life back to town that day. Chrissy was completely silent except for an occasional sniff when she dabbed her eye with a lace handkerchief. Every time Blake wanted to say something he elected not to because of his track record that day. He became more and more frustrated as the ride went on, until he stopped the carriage in front of the café and let Chrissy off. He tried to get out of the buggy to help her but she jumped out so fast his feet never touched the ground. This was all new territory for Blake Thorton. He had been with several women in his life, although they were whores mostly, and not very often at that. Whores were easy; you paid your money, had a couple laughs, filled your lusty desires and went about your way. Never once had he ever felt so out of sorts as he did with Chrissy. Sure maybe he might have thought about a wife and family someday, but all of the sudden it was staring him in the face. It might as well have been a tornado he was looking at, he had never been so unsure of anything in his life.

He had only loved a woman once in his life enough to marry her, but that was different, he was stranded on an island and it was more of a status thing in the tribe. The marriage was practically arranged and he was presented with little choice. The tribal culture was so different than his situation now. Chrissy was a free woman, able to make her own choices. She was fiercely independent and smart, a true force to be reckoned with, and would take him to task if she felt it necessary. But yet he saw a softer, more vulnerable side to her today and that made him want to be around her all the more, and now he had probably ruined any chance of that forever. That's what pissed him off the worst. He was just living his life one day at a time and failed to consider the long term ramifications of what he was doing. He had killed men before, he had seen the horrors of war, he had witnessed and taken part in some terrible things, but nothing compared to how low he felt when he made her cry.

He returned the carriage without having to see anybody at the barn, which he was grateful for. He decided he needed a drink, or two, enough of them to make him forget the damage he'd done. He headed for the Trail's End and pushed through the batwing doors. Walking straight to the bar he met the bartender. "Whiskey," he growled.

"Coming right up," the barkeep said taking out a bottle of the good stuff he kept under the bar, and pouring the amber liquid into a shot glass.

Blake usually sipped it but tonight he drank the entire shot in one swallow. The burn felt good as it spread through his body and he said, "Again."

The barkeep obediently poured another shot and went to put the bottle back and Blake said, "Leave it," tossing a double eagle on the bar.

Smiling, he picked up the money and went back down the bar to another customer.

Dan LaClare saw Blake enter the bar and took notice of how Blake was drinking whiskey in an unusual manner. Smiling, he strolled slowly over to him and leaned against the bar. "It has been my experience that only two things make a man drink like that," he drawled, "either someone urinated in your oatmeal, or a woman."

Blake downed another shot and refilled his glass. "My oatmeal is untouched." He motioned to a clean glass on the bar and Dan handed it to him. He filled it and slid it over to him.

Dan picked up the glass and took a sip. "Then I am correct about the latter?"

Blake bugged his eyes and blew heavily while staring at his glass. "Where do they get the power to make a man so bat-shit crazy?" he asked.

"Ah," he said taking out a cigar, plus a spare and offered it to Blake. "The female of our species has remained to be a complete mystery to me, my friend," he paused lighting the cigars. "One that is sure to drive a man to madness, should he try to understand their thought processes."

"Amen," Blake said refilling their glasses.

"Am I correct in assuming your carriage ride with the fair Mrs. O'Bryan did not go well?"

"It was great right up until I opened my mouth and it blew up in my face." Blake downed another shot. "It wasn't entirely my fault though, she backed me in a corner."

"How so?"

"She brought up marriage, I never saw it coming."

"Good Lord," Dan laughed, "she should be horsewhipped."

"Shut up, you shithead," Blake laughed back; he was feeling the effects of the whiskey now and started to relax.

Blake had not noticed the cowpuncher sitting near them and listening to their conversation. "Hey, Thorton," he said loudly. "If you're through with that widow woman, can I have a try at her?"

Blake stood straight up and glared at him. Dan paced his hand on his arm and directed his attention to the cowboy. "Sir, I am sure you are trying to be funny, but the wounds are still fresh to my friend here and I would recommend that you keep your comments to yourself."

"Bullshit," he said even louder. "That's one horse I could ride to Californy and back."

"Oh, damn," Dan said as Blake shot around him and landed a solid punch on the cowboy's jaw. He flew backward with his eyes rolling up into their sockets and landed squarely on a table occupied by six men playing poker. The table legs snapped under the pressure and sent the contents of the game spraying across the room. One of the poker players stood dumbfounded and glared at Blake. "You had no call to hit Willie like that. I was winnin' and you owe me money."

"Go to hell," Blake sneered and turned back to the bar.

"Get him, boys," the player yelled and the saloon erupted in a fight. Chairs flew through the air and glass smashed on the floor. Two of the poker players grabbed Blake's arms and held him while another punched him in nose. Dan was busy fending off another to help him much but was doing some damage with his own fists. Now every man in the saloon was hitting someone else, except the bartender who was trying to save the huge mirror in back of the bar by fending off flying objects. Blake managed to shake off one of the men holding him and threw him out a window in the front. He rolled a couple of times and got up jumping back through the same window.

Percival had been in the back when the whole thing started and came out and entered into the melee. Five men jumped on him trying to bring the monster down but he threw his arms apart and they flew in all directions. One man was foolhardy enough to rush headlong at him and the Big Man tossed him easily over his shoulder directly into the precious mirror. The bartender seemed to take the damage personally and grabbed the patron and pulled him across the bar punching him squarely on the jaw. Blake and Dan were now standing back to back swinging at any one within reach. Suddenly an ear-shattering blast erupted in the saloon and everyone stopped to gaze at the sheriff who had just unloaded a barrel of buckshot into the ceiling.

"Everybody just simmer down," he yelled. "Next man to move gets the other barrel."

Dan and Blake looked at each other breathing heavily, Blake's shirt and face were covered in blood because of the punch to his nose, which bled the way noses do, and Dan had one eye swelling shut as he stood there, his fine clothes in tatters. Percival dropped a semi-conscious cowboy on the floor with a sickening thud.

"Just who the hell started this dustup?" asked Johansson in an authoritative voice.

The cowboy who Blake had thrown the first punch at sat rubbing his chin and said, "I can't rightly remember sheriff, I think somebody said somethin' stupid." Blake looked at him and gave a little grin. He turned to Johansson and added, "Yeah, things got a little out hand."

"They sure as hell did." Still wanting answers, he gestured at Dan with his shotgun. "What do you say LaClare?"

"Umm," Dan stalled, "my eye hurts." Someone snorted and it spread through the saloon, soon everyone was laughing except Johansson who stood stone faced.

"Well someone owes the owner damages, and that would be the man who threw the first punch. So who would that be?" Johansson stated firmly.

Blake held up his hand and said, "Sheriff I'm not admitting guilt but I abhor violence and am deeply ashamed of myself for taking part in it. I will pay the damages as long as everyone agrees to act like gentlemen from this day forth."

The sheriff gave him a disapproving look and sucked his teeth. "I don't believe I've ever heard so much bullshit, but if the owner agrees I guess we can consider the matter closed."

"Mirror, too?" the barkeep asked.

"Yup, mirror, too," said Blake.

"Then I'm happy," the bartender said.

"Fine," Johansson growled. "I think it would be best if everyone went home. This here saloon is closed for tonight." He turned around and went back out in the street.

As the men started to file out the offending cowboy stopped beside Blake. "Sorry for what I said, I was just drunk is all."

"So was I," Blake smiled. "No real harm done."

Blake and Dan left together but took opposite sides of the street because the fight had attracted the attention of the townsfolk who were standing on the sidewalks watching, Chrissy and Bonnie among them. If Blake stayed with Dan he would have had to walk right in front of her. He continued down his side without turning his head. Dan on the other hand walked right up to her.

"What happened in there?" she asked him.

"There was a minor disagreement," he said casually.

Chrissy looked concerned at his eye. "Would you like a piece of steak for that eye?"

"Why yes, ma'am, I would like that very much, thank you."

"How's he?" she asked in an indifferent tone, while pointing her chin at Blake.

"Would you referring to Mr. Thorton, ma'am?"

"Uh-huh," she said quietly.

"As I do not know the particulars, I believe any pain he is in now truly pales to the agony he feels over hurting you." She looked at him and he was smiling gently at her.

"Let's see to that eye, Mr. LaClare," she said smiling in a similar way.

# CHAPTER 16

A hundred miles away in a town named Sweetwater, Tom MacIntyre was not fairing all that well. It had had only been a couple of weeks but he was just about out of the money he took from his father's safe. Last bit of what he had, save twenty dollars, laid in a poker pot on the table in front of him. He sat in his usual manner, slouched in his chair and his hat pushed back on his head. He thought a casual position made him look unconcerned as to the outcome of the hand, but nothing was further from the truth. Tom was genuinely worried that if he lost this hand he would be broke and have to return to his father's ranch. A thin trickle of sweat ran down the side of his face as he studied his cards; three kings, a two and a jack stared back at him. The last man to participate in this hand was a professional gambler and was stone faced. It was his move to either fold or call the bet. Placing a twenty dollar chip into the pot he smiled and said, "Call."

Smiling, Tom relaxed and set his cards on the table. "Three kings," he said grinning.

The gambler grinned back and said, "Not bad, a respectable hand to be sure." Tom leaned in to take the pot, but stopped when the other man said, "Unfortunately for you, not respectable enough to beat a full house, my friend." He laid his cards on the green tablecloth, two queens and three fives.

"Damn cheatin' card sharp," Tom muttered under his breath and leaned back in his chair.

Being a professional, the gambler had been called a cheat many times in his life so he was able to retain his composure. "I assure you, sir, there have been times in my life when that may have been a necessity, but here tonight it was the furthest thing from my mind, because of your inferior method of play," he said stacking his chips into orderly piles. He grinned an evil smile at Tom who was concentrating on his eyes, not on his right hand as it slipped under the table.

"Just what the hell does that mean?" Tom gritted his teeth.

"Simply stated, friend, you stink at cards."

Tom stood up suddenly, throwing his chair back with his legs and clawed for his revolver, but stopped before it even cleared leather because a forty-five caliber Peacemaker was pointed directly at his head. The gambler's hand was steady as a rock and Tom knew he was facing death right in the eyes. "Go ahead and finish pulling that hogleg, sir, and I will end your foolish life where you stand," the man said coolly.

Tom knew the man had the drop on him and tried a bluff. "I have friends here and they will gun you if you twitch."

The gambler's face was as rock steady as ever. "Your bluff in life is as bad as your card playing. The two men who came in with you have not even reached for their pistols. So I can confidently say that before they clear leather, I will have killed you and one of them and the third will have lead in him. Now the three of you drop your guns and piss off, as I grow wearisome of your company."

"I ain't leavin' here without a gun."

"Ah, I am certain you will because my dear friend who tends bar here will raise very serious havoc with your insides when he cuts loose with his favorite scattergun," smiled the gambler.

Tom heard the sickening sound of the hammers being pulled back off to his right. Turning his head slowly he saw a stout man holding a coachgun squarely in their direction. Tom swore under his breath and told Jimmy and Tug to drop their gun belts, as he did the same.

"You may pick them up in the morning but know this; if I even get a whiff of you in my vicinity I will assume the worst and shoot you like a skunk in the henhouse. Good night, gentlemen," the gambler said flatly.

Tom left the saloon red faced, with Jimmy and Tug close behind.

\* \* \* \* \* \*

The next morning they returned to pick up their guns and were greeted by the bartender holding his shotgun at the end of the bar. Grinning, he slid the three gun belts one at a time down the bar. The three men snatched them up and put them on. Going outside they mounted their horses and rode slowly out of town.

"Where to now, Boss?" Jimmy asked innocently.

Tom was in a foul mood and grumbled, "We ain't got enough money to get back home, I reckon we'll have to find some."

Tug smiled, "I like the sound of that."

Twenty miles away they sat on top of a rise watching a stagecoach coming their way. "You reckon they is carryin' a strongbox?" Jimmy said to Tom.

"One way to find out," Tom said pulling a neckerchief over his nose. "Just follow my lead and keep an eye on the driver and his sidekick."

He spurred his horse into a gallop and the others followed suit after covering their faces. Tom came to a sliding stop in front of the coach and fired a shot in the air. Reining back hard on the horses the driver managed to get the team under control and stop the coach just in time. Just as Tom was about to speak, two riders came out from the opposite side of the road, both with their faces covered, all five men had their pistols pulled and pointing at one another.

"What the hell are you doin'?" one of them yelled. "We is robbin' this here coach."

Tom couldn't believe his luck and was trying to figure out what to do when out of the corner of his eye he saw the sidekick raise a sawed off shotgun. Tom spun in his saddle and shot him in the chest, the driver went for his pistol and one of the new men shot him.

Tom pulled down his neckerchief and said, "Damn, boys, I guess we're in this together now. What do you say we split the money?"

Pulling down their masks they looked at each other and shrugged their shoulders. "Seems fair, I guess," the fat one said.

Tom turned to his two men. "Jimmy, check up top for a strongbox," he ordered. "Tug, check the coach."

Jimmy leapt off his horse and climbed to the top and Tug got down and opened the door of the coach only to be greeted by a thirty-two caliber slug in the forehead. As Tug fell backward, a well-dressed man leaned out of the coach and aimed for Tom. Jimmy drilled him with a shot from the top of the coach and killed him instantly. Inside the coach a women was screaming as Tom dismounted, running for the door. Inside was a pretty brunette woman who pinned up against the wall, trying to hide. She tried to kick him as he grabbed her by the ankle and roughly yanked her out onto the hard ground. Still screaming she tried to scurry away as Tom brought the barrel of his gun hard down on her head. She laid on the ground moaning softly.

Jimmy jumped down from the top and looked at his friend. "Is Tug dead?" he asked disbelieving.

Tom jammed his pistol in his holster and said, "As a goddamned doornail."

"Sorry about your friend," the taller of the two new men said as he came around the wagon, "Was there any money on here?"

Tom was irritated now, "Well we didn't have much time to check, did we?"

"Suppose not," he said sheepishly. "Let's have us a look around."

After they tore the wagon apart, the grand total of the take was forty-seven dollars and fifty-five cents. Tom was incensed with anger. He started to throw items from the coach cursing the whole time.

"Well that's just way it goes sometimes," the taller man said matter-a-factly, spitting on the ground.

"I lost a good man for forty-seven dollars today," he yelled. "I ain't about to take that lightly." With that the woman lying on the ground began to stir, Tom turned and looked at her and a thought of pure evil came over him. "That bitch is the only thing left. Let's see if she can help ease our losses." He strolled over and grabbed her by the hair, pulling her whimpering face to his he gave an evil grin. "C'mon honey, I need something from you." Dragging her kicking and screaming he found a log next to the trail and began tearing her clothes off. Dropping his gun and pants he ravaged her helpless body. When he was done the others if the gang took turns raping her into unconsciousness.

Tom sat back and watched, smoking a cigarette, the malevolent look on his face was pure wickedness. Jimmy came over buckling up his pants laughing. "We sure made her pay for ol' Tug, didn't we?"

"You know, Jimmy," Tom mused, "my whole life turned to shit because of a splittail, and I'm thinkin' she deserves the same as this one."

Tom rose and stretched. "Except for one thing," he said. "You boys done with her?" he called to the other men. They looked at each other and shook their heads. Tom walked over to the naked form moaning on the ground, pulling his pistol and cocking it. He aimed at her head and shot her. Turning back to Jimmy he said, "Let's go home."

\* \* \* \* \* \*

They all mounted and took off at a fast gallop; occasionally they took measures to cover their tracks in streams and over rocky ground. Night began to fall and when they were satisfied no one was following, Tom decided they should make camp. Leaving their horses saddled in case they had to make a getaway, they loosened the cinch straps. Jimmy built a small fire and cooked their meager dinner and coffee borrowed from the two strangers.

"I never did get your names," Tom said after lighting a cigarette.

The taller of the two spoke up. "I'm Les Palmer and this is my brother Troy."

Tom looked at Troy and nodded his head. "My name is Tom MacIntyre and this is my pard, Jimmy Rocco," he said. "You boys got any prospects in the wind?"

"Naw," Les said spitting into the fire. "Less you count the twenty some odd dollars you owe us."

Tom stood up and took twenty dollars out of his pocket and handed it to Les. "How would you two like to earn a hundred times that much?" Tom asked.

"Two hundred dollars? Hell, yes!" Troy blurted out.

Les shook his head and winced. "My bother ain't no good with cypherin' and such. It's two thousand dollars, Troy."

Troy whistled long and low, "I ain't seen me that much money at one time in my life."

"Where is we gonna get that kind of scratch, friend? And what do we have to do to get ours?" Les asked.

"Ride to MacIntyre and get it from my account. Once we get there I'll get a couple of small jobs for you to do."

"Didn't you just say your name was MacIntyre?" Les asked, the firelight dancing in his eyes. "What the hell is going on here?"

Tom laughed. "Let me explain, the town is named after my father, he owns a pretty big spread there and has a lot of money in the bank that I have access to. Him and me don't see eye to eye on some things, mostly what I'm entitled to. Plus, there's some folks that I need to settle a score with. That's where you come in. You can help them around to my way of thinking."

"Then why was you robbin' a stagecoach if you has all this money?" Les asked frankly.

"Needed a roadstake and I thought I'd give it a try, see what happens," Tom said casually.

"Yeah, well, you got your friend killed along with four other people, that's what happened," Les said gruffly. "You're either stupid or reckless, or both."

"Keep in mind, if I'm paying wages, you ain't gonna speak to me that way," Tom hissed. Their eyes locked and both men were measuring the grit the other had. Finally Les relaxed. "O.K. friend, is there going to be any killin'?"

"If I say so, there is."

"Then the price for us is two thousand apiece."

Tom pursed his lips. "For that kind of money, when I say shit, you squat."

Les smiled, "Sure thing, Boss."

\* \* \* \* \* \*

The days after the fight in the saloon were hard on Blake. He took to leaving the house without stopping for breakfast and went straight to the forge. He just wanted to work through his thoughts and the rhythmic pounding on the anvil helped. By the time Caleb showed up he was hard at work, already dirty and breathing hard. Caleb was respectful of his space and set some biscuits with bacon on the bench near him and went about his own duties.

One of the things that required a lot of pounding was making Damascus steel for knives. It was a method of welding two different types of steel together in the forge and then repeatedly folding the bar over onto itself and re-welding it several times. This method would produce a very strong and flexible blade that could be easily sharpened and take a great deal of punishment. This type of work required a master smith and a great deal of attention. Blake knew his mind wasn't working right when either the welding process would not stick or there were a lot of cracks and coldshuts in the metal. He knew every coldshut was a place where the steel separated and formed gaps. Every time that happened it was a weak spot in the blade causing it to break more easily. There was a pile of ruined steel billets next to the forge where Blake had not worked the metal correctly and started on another. He did manage to make four good ones and created some beautiful large Bowie style blades that exhibited several hundred layers of the different steels. When his arms got so tired it was difficult to lift the hammer he would set about grinding and polishing the blades, then attaching bone handles known for their durability.

Blake spent several days working himself to exhaustion, eating little and sleeping less. It seemed no matter how much he worked he could not get Chrissy out of his head.

Chrissy was not faring much better. Her efforts in the kitchen suffered, burning several pans of biscuits and forgetting what people ordered. She snapped many times at the customers who complained and ended up giving away free meals as an apology. Whenever Caleb came in for school she was polite to him but he reminded her of Blake and she got mad all over again. She wanted desperately to ask him about Blake but she knew it wasn't fair to put him in the middle. One time it was almost two o'clock and she knew he was coming, so she made an excuse to Bonnie and left before he got there. Not knowing where to go she wandered up the street and window shopped. That's when she came across one of the most beautiful dresses she had ever seen. Michelle was in the window placing it on a dress form for display and she waved for Chrissy to come in.

"Mrs. O'Bryan," she said cheerily, "how lovely to see you."

"Please call me Chrissy," she said smiling back. "That is a gorgeous dress."

"I'm kinda proud of that one," Michelle said brushing back an errant curl from her forehead. "I don't mind saying it was a lot of work."

Chrissy stepped closer to it and closely examined it. "I should say so. You have a marvelous talent, very professional."

"How kind of you to say," Michelle said. "I'm trying to get a few more made for the Founder's Day dance coming up."

Chrissy had been so distracted lately she had completely forgotten about the dance. Some time back the town started an annual celebration on the first of August recognizing the naming of the town. It was a big party with food, music and games all day long. They built a large platform for dancing and ended with fireworks. It was a time the whole town looked forward to. "Well I'm sure you will have no problem selling this dress, it's stunning."

"I hope so," Michelle answered. "The women in this town are a little shy about coming in here, given my past reputation."

"They'll come around, it just takes time."

"I was going to pour myself some tea," Michelle said. "Would you like to join me?"

"That would be nice," Chrissy said. "I could use someone to talk to."

"I'll be right back then," and she disappeared in the back, coming out a moment later carrying a tray with a teapot, cups and some cookies. Setting them on a small table with two chairs they sat down and Michelle poured. "So what is it you want to talk about?"

Chrissy sipped her tea and thought for a moment. "You've known a lot of men, right?" Chrissy asked, and then realizing how that sounded she quickly said, "I'm sorry that didn't sound nice, I mean…"

Michelle giggled. "No need to be sorry, I don't hide from my past, and yes, I made the acquaintance of a few."

Chrissy laughed lightly and stared down at her cup. "I'm sorry, this is so embarrassing, but I don't really have any one else to ask."

"Sweetie," she said placing a hand on Chrissy's arm. "There's only you and me and that dress dummy in here. It's all right."

"Well there's a man," Chrissy started.

"Blake Thorton?" Michelle interrupted.

"Yes."

"He seems like one of the good ones, for sure."

"I think he is too, but he makes me mad because it's hard to get a straight answer from him. It always seems like a game with him."

Michelle laughed, "Of course it is. Look, I think there are four types of men. The first are like mice, they are little pipsqueaks who are easy to boss around. The second are wolves, mean and nasty, they'll hurt you both mind and body and won't look back. The third are hounds, like the one a family has, kinda dumb but loyal, good protectors and providers but get fat and lazy."

Chrissy giggled, "I never looked at men that way, but it's true, I know a lot that will fit into those groups."

"In my opinion, all critters to avoid," Michelle grinned.

"What about the last?"

"Those are the special ones," she said. "If they were an animal I guess they would be a wild stallion. Strong, loyal and full of life, galloping around tending the herd. They can be playful and tender, sweet as the day is long, and yet they won't be tamed. If one of them gets cornered they are hell on wheels. I know men like that who will take on the entire Comanche nation singlehanded and walk away. They just have a way about them that makes you safe and secure, like you are wrapped up in a warm quilt. One of the most frustrating things about them is one word that scares the Beejesus out of them and makes them run like a scalded cat."

"Really?" Chrissy asked. "What's that?"

"Marriage."

Chrissy stared at her blankly, her mouth opened slightly.

Michelle's smile slowly disappeared. "Oh, sweetie, did you mention marriage?"

"Yes, I mean no," Chrissy stammered. "I just think a man and woman should be married if they ..." She stopped and put her hand to her mouth.

Michelle smiled knowingly, "Oh please, who am I to judge anybody? Let me guess, he said some pretty stupid things, didn't he?"

"Yes," Chrissy said tears forming in her eyes.

"He didn't leave town then?"

"No, I don't think so," she said dabbing her eyes.

"Whew," said Michelle. "Then he's yours."

"What do you mean?"

"Men like Blake Thorton are where they are because they want to be there," Michelle said assuredly. "He loves you, he just doesn't know it yet, and men like him are slow on the uptake. Time will cure that."

"You think he would have left if he didn't care?" Chrissy said hopefully.

"Like a scalded cat, honey," Michelle laughed. "Like a scalded cat."

They both laughed a long time over that and finally Chrissy asked, "So what word scares Percival? He seems indestructible."

"Actually, children," Michelle giggled. "And unless I miss my guess, he is going to be one scared son-of-gun pretty soon."

Chrissy smiled broadly, "Are you with child?"

"I'm pretty sure; I have to go see the doctor yet."

"That's wonderful news, are you happy?"

"I'm elated," said Michelle. "But I'm a little nervous."

"Why's that?"

"Have you seen the size of that man? He might make a baby the size of a calf!" Again, they laughed and Chrissy looked at the clock on the wall.

"I really must be getting back, thank you so much, I feel better," she said.

"I enjoyed it too," Michelle said. "And thank you for using the front door."

Chrissy opened the door and saw two women coming toward her on the boardwalk, turning back to Michelle, she said loud enough for the women to hear, "Can you make this dress in lavender?"

"Sure," Michelle said back.

"In time for the dance?"

"That shouldn't be a problem."

"Then please do," Chrissy smiled and turned to the ladies on the street. "Have you seen this dress in the window? Isn't it gorgeous?"

"Oh my, it is," one of them said. "And the dance is coming up."

"But she worked at the saloon," the other said in a hushed voice.

Chrissy leaned in close and whispered, "She doesn't work there anymore, she's married now, and besides, who would know better what catches a man's eye?"

"True," the first woman said, thinking. "Veronica Simpson bought a dress here and loves it. I can't have her turning more heads than me. I'm going in."

Chrissy turned to Michelle who was absolutely beaming and gave her a wink. Michelle mouthed back, "Thank you."

\* \* \* \* \* \*

Chrissy started back toward the café and heard the ringing of the anvil in Blake's forge. She hesitated for a moment and turned down the street toward where he was working. Her stomach felt as if a flock of birds was trying escape but she pressed on, drawing a deep breath. Putting on the best smile she could, she approached the forge to find Joe Bergman talking to Blake as he worked an orange hot piece of steel. She stood in the doorway and waited to be noticed when Joe turned and saw her. He tapped Blake on the shoulder and pointed at the door. Blake was still hammering when he glanced up and saw Chrissy. He lost his concentration and struck his thumb with a large hammer. "Ow," he yelled, "shit, that hurts," pulling off his glove and nursing his bruised thumb.

"I'm sorry," Chrissy said concerned. "Did I cause that?"

"No," Blake said wincing. "Just clumsy, I guess. What can I do for you, Mrs. O'Bryan?"

"Well, I was just out for a stroll and heard you working," she stated nervously. "I was wondering if I was going to see you at the Founder's Day dance."

"What dance?" Blake asked confused, then looking at Joe. "There's a dance?"

"Big one," he replied. "Every year on August first."

"I didn't know," Blake stammered, "I mean I guess I'll go, I didn't think you'd want…" he stopped himself. "You said you're going?"

"Oh yes," Chrissy said. "It is always a grand time."

"I don't know, I suppose," Blake looked at Joe helplessly. "What do you think, Joe?"

Before Joe could answer Chrissy asked, "Can you dance, Mr. Thorton?"

"Yup," he said sucking the side of his thumb.

"Then I will save a dance for you, good day gentlemen," Chrissy smiled and turned around heading back down the street.

"What in the name of Christ just happened?" Blake said staring at Joe.

"It appears the widow O'Bryan just proved that she is smarter than you are," chuckled Joe.

Blake blew out a deep breath as he watched Chrissy turning the corner. "I need to soak this thumb," he said, heading for the water trough.

"Try soaking your head, too," Joe shouted.

# CHAPTER 17

As the Founder's Day celebration got closer, the town began to decorate with flags and red, white and blue bunting that hung from every porch and rooftop. A large platform for the dance was being erected, enough to hold thirty couples, along with a charcoal pit to roast a side of beef. People seemed to be in a good mood including Blake, who seemed almost back to normal … except for the one morning Caleb teased him about being in love and quickly apologized when Blake gave him a dark look and left for the forge without him. Sadie gave Caleb a good scolding about poking a bear in a sore spot.

As the morning progressed in the forge Blake's mood lightened and they got along fine. When Sadie brought lunch that day they sat under their customary tree and enjoyed a hearty meal. Blake was just about to get back to work when he noticed four riders coming down the street. Tom MacIntyre was in the lead with Jimmy Rocco and the Palmer Brothers, Les and Troy, close behind. All four of them had the look of being on the trail for weeks. Tom MacIntyre gave Blake a cold stare with an evil sneer as he rode by, and Blake remained stone faced. Satan, who was lying in the shade chewing on a ham bone, gave the Palmer brothers a low sustained growl as he watched them with wolfish eyes. Troy made a mock gun with his fingers and pointed them at the dog, then he blew out a quiet "boom." Both he and Les chuckled quietly to each other and rode up to the livery and dismounted. Blake gave Sadie a look that said 'go home' and she gathered up the dishes and walked up the street as quickly as she could. Blake tapped Caleb and motioned to the forge as he rose and stood near the door, his Winchester in easy reach.

The four men talked to Joe for a few minutes and then led their horses in the livery. They reappeared minutes later carrying their saddlebags, bedrolls and rifles and headed back out the way they came. Blake remained in the doorway until they turned the corner. "Shit," he muttered to himself.

Tom led the three men up the street and stopped in front of the bank and handed Jimmy his gear. "Go wait at the hotel," he said, "I'll be there directly," as he crossed the street and entered the bank. He stood and looked around, deciding what to do when he saw Weatherby eyeing him nervously. Smiling, Tom walked over to his desk and sat down.

"What can I do for you, Tom?" the banker asked.

"I need five thousand dollars," Tom said flatly.

Weatherby took a handkerchief from his pocket and mopped his brow. "I'm afraid I can't do that."

Tom sat up in the chair. "Why the hell not?" he asked loudly.

"Calm down, Tom," Weatherby said quietly. "Your father has left strict instructions that if you came back, I was not to give you any funds."

"Son-of-a-bitch," Tom muttered. "That money is as much mine as it is his."

"Be that as it may, the accounts are in your father's name," Weatherby said standing firm but he felt like he going to wet his pants.

Tom sat drumming his fingers on the arm of the chair; he had to think fast. "That ranch my father bought on the north side of the creek last year, he put it in my name didn't he?"

"Well, yes, he did," Weatherby answered. "But at the most it is worth two thousand."

"I'll take it," Tom said.

The banker pursed his fat lips and thought, "I don't know, your father won't like it."

"When my father is dead all of his holdings will be mine and you'll have to answer to me, you fat bastard," Tom growled. "Now go get the deed and the money, and I'll sign it over."

Weatherby mopped his brow again and rose shakily from his desk. He waddled to the safe and found the deed and counted out the two thousand dollars. Returning he handed Tom the deed. He pointed at the place where Tom had to sign and Tom scrawled his name on the deed. Tom stood quickly and snatched the money off the desk. He turned on his heel and walked heavily out the door, slamming it as he went.

Jimmy, Les and Troy were sitting on a bench in front of the hotel. When Tom got there he stopped and counted out five hundred dollars and handed it to each man. Les thumbed through the stack of bills and said, "This here is a damn sight shy of two thousand."

Tom shot him a hard look. "There will be more when you've done something to earn it."

"That wasn't my understanding, I want the money up front," Les objected.

"So you can ride off with full pockets? I don't think so," Tom snapped back.

Les weighed the look in Tom's eyes and settled. "Fair enough, but don't make us wait too long."

Without saying a word Tom grabbed his belongings and walked in the hotel. The mousey little clerk glanced up with disapproving eyes. "Yes?" he said with a mock smile.

"We need four rooms, all facing the street," Tom ordered.

"Yes, sir, Mr. MacIntyre," said the clerk turning and taking down the keys. "That will be five dollars per room per night. How long will you be staying?"

"Till I say," Tom said firmly and took the keys, handing them out.

"Would you care to pay in advance?" asked the clerk.

"We'll pay up when we leave," Tom snapped back getting irritated.

"That is highly irregular, but suppose because of you father's reputation, I can accept that."

The last thing Tom wanted to be reminded of was his father, and now he was genuinely mad. He snatched his things off the floor and turned toward the stairs.

"Please sign the register, Mr. MacIntyre," the clerk said in a huffy voice while holding out a pen.

Tom dropped his belongings and spun and grabbed the little man by the shirtfront and yanked him forward. "You know who I am, you little turd, sign it yourself," he spat.

"What about the men with you?" the little man squeaked.

"Just put 'friends'," Tom said tightening his grip and shoving him back into the cabinet where the keys hung, knocking several onto the floor. Tom picked his things back up and headed for the stairs with other three in tow. At the top of the stairs Tom unlocked the door for his room and growled at the others, "Get cleaned up and meet me downstairs in the morning." Then he threw his things in the room and slammed the door behind him. The other three shrugged their shoulders and obeyed.

\* \* \* \* \* \*

Tom could swear he could feel his blood boiling. Since he came back he had received none of the respect he had been used to. He stood staring in the mirror at his reflection and a plan started to form in his mind. He needed to get his father out of the way. With him gone he would have the money, ranch and all the respect he wanted. They would all answer to him and he would rule with an iron fist. He splashed some water on his face and was thinking how he could eliminate his father when a knock came on the door.

"Who the hell is it?" he yelled.

"Sheriff Johansson. I need to talk to you."

Tom stomped over to the door and flung it open. "What the hell do you want?"

"Just to talk, Tom. Can I come in?" Johansson said calmly.

Tom stepped back from the door. "All right, but be quick. I'm tired and in no mood for your bullshit."

Johansson drew a deep breath and entered the room. He turned to Tom and crossed his arms over his chest. "When'd you get back?"

"About an hour ago, why?" Tom said impatiently.

"Because in that hour, I've already received two complaints, one from Weatherby and the other from the clerk downstairs. He says you roughed him up pretty good."

"He's a whiny little piss ant that needed to be put in his place."

"I'll give you that, but it still ain't right," said the sheriff. "Who are those other fellas you came in with?"

"I met them on the trail, liked 'em, now they ride with me. Is there a law against that?" Tom stated in an even tone.

"Nope," Johansson said. "They got names?"

"Ask them yourself. I need a bath, shave and a drink. I'm done talkin' to you."

"I'll do just that," Johansson tensed, "and I'll have a bottle sent to your room."

"Are you sayin' I can't go to the saloon?" Tom asked defensively.

"I'm sayin' that you seem to have a burr under your saddle, and going out in public and drinkin' ain't a good idea."

Tom gritted his teeth. "I'll go where I damn well please, old timer, best you keep clear of me."

"As long as you know if there's any trouble, you're the first one I'm going to arrest," Johansson said stone faced.

"Watch yourself, you old has-been. My father started this town and owns it, the bank, the mayor and that means you. He wouldn't take kindly seein' me behind bars."

"From what I understand," the sheriff stated, "he thinks that's just what you need."

Tom's face grew beet red as he tried to control his temper, stomping over to door he opened it and glared at Johansson. "Get your sorry ass outta here."

Johansson headed for the door and stopped. "I got my eye on you, boy, be nice now." He left the room and the door slammed behind him.

\* \* \* \* \* \*

The next morning Tom came downstairs famished. He had gone out the day before and gotten a bath, shave and haircut after he bought some new clothes. He disregarded the sheriff's advice and went to the saloon, but in his present foul temper was not interested in cards or socializing so he bought a bottle and returned to his room and drank almost the whole thing. When he woke up the next morning his head pounded and his stomach churned, rebelling from the rotgut he drank the night before. He waited in the lobby for a few minutes for the others and was angry when he saw them. None of them had cleaned up in any way and all appeared to be hung over. "I thought I told you to get respectable looking," he said shortly.

Troy looked at the two others and said, "You was serious about that?"

"Yeah I was," Tom replied. "Y'all stink."

"Well I got wet on the inside, with some fine whiskey and I's got one part cleaned real good by one of them doves," he laughed winking at Les. "Spit shined, if you know what I mean." The other two broke out laughing with him.

Tom winced and pinched the bridge of his nose. "After breakfast, I want all of you to get acquainted with some soap, your clothes, too. I don't want you drawing attention to yourselves by stinkin'. Got it?"

"Kinda early in the day for bathin', but all right," Les said scratching his chin. "Where we gonna eat?"

"Right next door there's a café run by a stone cold widow," Tom told them. "The food is tolerable."

They walked outside and down to the café. The town was in full swing decorating and Troy was looking around. "What's going on? Some big shindig?"

"Founder's Day," Jimmy said. "It's a big day in MacIntyre, lots going on. There's lotsa food, games and dance later on."

"I'm guessin' your daddy plays a big part in it," Les said to Tom.

Tom stopped and shot him a hard look. "Yeah, and soon it will be for me."

"If you say so," Les smiled, then pointing at Chrissy's. "This the place?"

Tom took his time turning to see where Les was gesturing and said, "Yeah, that's it."

The four men entered the café and saw a table near the wall with four empty chairs. Tom didn't wait to be asked, and he led the men over and sat down. Chrissy came out of the kitchen holding plates of steaming food and saw them. After setting down the plates she approached them. "It's customary for you to wait to be seated," she said in a curt voice.

"There wasn't anybody sittin' here, so it ain't a problem. Bring us coffee and some breakfast," Tom said irritated.

Chrissy placed her hands on her hips. "I see your manners haven't improved since you've been gone. What kind of breakfast do you want?"

"We ain't picky," Tom replied, "just bring us the specials."

Troy piped up, "I'm partial to hotcakes and syrup."

"I'll see what I can do," Chrissy said and left for the kitchen. She returned with a large pot of coffee and cups and set them on the table and turned to go.

"What's your hurry?" Les asked, "ain't you gonna pour the coffee for us?"

"I'm very busy," she answered curtly. "I'm positive you can manage."

Les face turned very serious. "My Pappy had a cure for a woman with a sassy mouth."

Just as Chrissy was about to fire back at him, Mike Ventosa appeared by her side. "Lady said she was busy, please allow me to pour," winking at Chrissy who left for the kitchen. Mike picked up the pot and a cup, filling it and handed it to Tom. "You, I know, and I believe you're Jimmy Rocco," he said handing Jimmy a full cup. "But I don't believe I've met you other two," he said filling each one of their cups.

Les gave Mike a wolfish grin. "I'm Les Palmer and this is my brother Troy. It's nice to see the law in this town has a useful purpose."

"Oh, I help out from time to time. Where do you boys hail from?" Mike said hooking his thumbs in his gun belt.

"South," Les replied smiling.

"South is a big place, can you narrow it down a little?"

"No, not really."

"Well all right. I guess it ain't important. You fellas enjoy your breakfast. I'll be right over at the counter should you need anything else."

Les picked up his cup and drained it. "I could use a refill, tin star," he said, very much amused with himself.

"Sure, hold out your cup," Mike said smiling. Les did and Mike filled his cup till it overflowed, burning Les's hand. Les dropped the cup and yelled in pain. "Damn, I'm sorry," Mike exclaimed. "See, I help out, but I ain't much good at it."

"You did that on purpose," Les yelled.

"Yeah, I'm sorry, I guess I'll stick to arresting assholes," Ventosa said as he sauntered back to the counter.

Les glared at Mike and said to Tom, "Nice friendly town you got here."

After they finished breakfast, the four split up and went their separate ways with the understanding to meet in the saloon later that evening. Tom spent the day brooding and planning how he was going to take over. He made a list in his mind of people that needed to be dealt with. Slowly the plan was taking shape.

\* \* \* \* \* \*

Founder's Day started as a cool morning without a cloud in the sky. People milled about heading here and there, conversing and laughing. Blake ate a good breakfast and changed into his suit and visited with the friends he had made in town. The fire pit had a whole side of beef turning on it as one man spun the spit and two others brushed on a barbecue sauce that filled the air with a delicious aroma. There were several beer kegs out in the open and many of the men carried around mugs. At two o'clock in the afternoon there were rodeo style games down by the stock pens as people gathered around to watch. Most of the games were silly but required a great deal of skill, such as riding a bucking horse with an egg in your mouth or a tug of war on horseback blindfolded. Blake managed to finally spot Chrissy and tried to maneuver closer to her through the crowd. When he managed to get right next to her she turned and smiled at him. "Mr. Thorton, you seem to be enjoying yourself," she said.

He grinned back. "It just got a whole lot better, but I was wondering if you could do me a favor?"

"What would that be?" she asked.

"I would be eternally grateful if we could drop the formality and you would call me Blake."

She turned her head and watched a rider fall from his horse, dropping his egg and she giggled. "I think it sounds better if two people are courting to remain formal," she said without looking at him.

Blake was stunned. "But you said…I mean … you still want to see me?"

"I'm here aren't I?" she said still watching the festivities. "Oh look, it's Caleb," pointing to the center of the corral where Caleb was sitting on top of Rosie.

Mike Ventosa, who was acting as master of ceremonies for the games, picked up his megaphone from the top of the platform he was on and announced, "Ladies and gentlemen, I would like to introduce Caleb and his wonder horse, Rosie, in an exhibition of trick riding for your pleasure."

Caleb smiled and waved to the crowd as he urged Rosie into a circle around the corral.

"What is he doing?" Blake said astonished.

"Just watch," Chrissy said with a twinkle in her eye.

Caleb rode Rosie faster and faster around the ring with no saddle and just a halter and lead rope. At one point he sprung up on her back standing at a full canter, and then he jumped again and stood facing backward without breaking stride. The crowd cheered and clapped as he leapt again facing forward and brought her to the middle of the ring and stopped. Then he dropped down straddling her again and started a slower canter around the ring. Sliding off one side while hanging on to her mane he hit the ground with both feet and sprung over her back and did the same thing from the opposite side landing astride her again. The crowd cheered and clapped even more as he took one leg over her back and rode sidewards for a time and then turned again and was riding backward. Rosie cantered to the center of the ring and slid to a stop and sat down. The intention was for Caleb to slide down her back and land on his feet but instead he lost his balance and landed face first in the dirt. People gasped and stopped clapping as he lay still. Rosie turned and went over to him and shook her head.

Slowly he stood up dusting himself off. Smiling he pointed his finger and she cantered around and as she ran past him he grabbed her mane and started the whole trick over. This time when she stopped he slid down her back and took a deep bow for the audience. He turned and held out his hand to Rosie and she also took a bow by getting down on one of her front knees. The people of the town gave a long standing ovation and Bonnie ran out and threw her arms around Caleb's neck. No one clapped harder than Blake who stood feeling a father's pride. He pushed his way to the front of the crowd and climbed over the fence. Caleb saw him and walked over with his arm around Bonnie leading his horse

"Wasn't he wonderful?" Bonnie said grinning from ear to ear.

"He sure was. When did you learn how to do that?" Blake laughed.

"W-we k-kinda taught e-e-each other," Caleb smiled.

"Damn proud of you, son," Blake said giving him a bear hug.

"Hey, kid," a cowboy from the audience yelled, "Ike wants to buy his horse back." A bunch of them broke out laughing and prodding a sour faced Ike.

Caleb looked at him and said in a firm voice, "Not for sale!"

"Then can you teach Ike to ride?" he yelled back and they all teased a slightly embarrassed Ike some more.

Mike Ventosa picked up the megaphone and announced, "Ladies and gentleman, I just got word that the beef is done and the tables are set. Let's head over and get to the eatin'."

Blake found Chrissy in the crowd and held out his elbow. "May I escort you to the dinner?" he asked.

"Certainly," she replied. They strolled along for a while and Blake steered her under a large tree.

"Let's hold back for a second," he said. "Did you know Caleb was going to do that?"

"Yes, I did," she smiled. "He wanted so much to impress you. He been working very hard and wanted it to be a surprise."

"Well he did and it was," Blake said leaning against the tree. "The day's been full of surprises."

"How so?"

"Well you for one," he started. "Why the change of heart?"

Chrissy gave a little smile and said, "I never really had a change of heart. I'm quite fond of you. I overreacted and said something I shouldn't have."

"That goes both ways," he said.

"I hope you realize I wasn't trying to trap you," she said looking down. "I try to be strong…."

He lifted her chin up so he could look in her eyes. "I wasn't trying to run, and you should speak your heart so there are no misunderstandings."

Her blue eyes sparkled as she gazed at him. "So we can start over?"

"How about after we eat? I'm starved," he said and smiled.

"I don't know, that may be too late," she teased and started for the tables.

"Darn pushy women," Blake laughed as he ran up to her.

\* \* \* \* \* \*

Everyone was seated at the tables as Father Grimm gave a moving blessing from the porch of the hotel, after which Ian MacIntyre came out in his full Scottish regalia complete with kilt and uniform from his days serving the Blackwatch in Scotland. He wore a tartan sash of his family and a highly polished set of bagpipes under his arm. Blake was impressed at the magnificent form before him. "I promise to be keepin' this short, for if I play too long a riot will be formin'." He inflated the pipes and began to play a lively tune from his homeland. The people at the tables clapped in time and seemed to enjoy it very much. Blake almost hated him for being able to play so well. When that was over he played a beautiful rendition of "Amazing Grace" bringing it to a dramatic end. Everyone clapped and whistled as he took a deep bow. Standing up again he shouted, "Let us eat."

No one seemed to notice the figure standing in the window of the second floor of hotel. Tom MacIntyre stood leaning against the sash slowly bringing the bottle of whiskey to his lips and muttered, "This time next year, it'll all be mine."

When dinner was over the women quickly cleared the tables and hurried home to change for the upcoming dance. The men broke down the tables and cleared the street. They stood in the shade sipping whiskey and smoking cigars while the women got ready. Blake stood with Josh Dooley, Mike Ventosa, the sheriff, Joe Bergman and Caleb, they laughed and told stories, but mostly praised Caleb on his riding.

Josh checked his watch and said, "Well boys, I guess we should go escort our women to the dance, they're probably wondering where we are."

The only one left standing was sheriff Johansson who said something about being tied to no one.

Blake and Caleb were waiting outside the café when they saw Percival escorting Michelle down the street like he was carrying a hundred eggs. "Evening Big Man, Michelle," Blake called out, "everything all right?"

Percival looked at Michelle with hopeful eyes and she said, "Go ahead, they're going to know soon enough."

"I'm going to be a Papa!" he blurted out barely able to contain himself.

Blake and Caleb rushed over and shook his hand. "Congratulations, that's great news!" Blake said excited.

"G-good f-for y-you P-Percy," Caleb said grinning.

Percival reached out to grab him but Michelle said, "Please don't, honey, he's dressed so nice."

Big Man gave Caleb a friendly look and tousled his hair. "Well, all right, but I owe you one." He took Michelle gently again, "Tell me if I'm walkin' too fast."

"Good Lord," she huffed, "he thinks I turned to glass."

Just after they left, the door to the café opened and Bonnie and Chrissy came out. Bonnie was wearing a dark blue dress that fit her perfectly and her hair was pulled back and in curls. She smiled at Caleb who was speechless. She walked over to him and gave a little push on his shoulder. "Well say something," she said.

Caleb's jaw worked but nothing came out for a second, then finally he managed a, "W-w-w-ow."

Bonnie giggled and took his arm. "C'mon you silver tongued devil," and they headed for the dance.

Blake had seen Chrissy dressed nice for church and he always admired her but tonight she was a true sight to behold. Her lavender dress brought out every beautiful feature she had. Her hair hung loosely around her shoulders and was pulled back to frame her face, exposing her bright blue eyes and rosy cheeks. The dress fit her like a glove accentuating curves and had a neckline that dipped low enough to show her cleavage while being tasteful. "Well, say something," she said.

Blake turned his head and made sure Caleb was out of ear-shot and then said, "W-w-w-wow."

"Very original," she said taking his arm.

"I like to stick with the classics." Blake chuckled.

\* \* \* \* \* \*

The dance commenced as darkness fell and torches were lit around the dance floor. The band played song after song and people crowded the floor for each one. Blake couldn't help but notice every time he glanced at Ian MacIntyre he was look-ing at Chrissy. Even when they danced his eyes followed her. At one point during a slower waltz Blake saw him approach-ing them. When he spun Chrissy away he felt a tap on his shoulder and found Ian standing there. "I would be likin' to cut in with the lady's permission," he said gentlemanly. Blake turned his face to Chrissy's and she nodded it would be all right. He stepped to the side and left the floor. Ian stepped in and turned Chrissy to the far edge of the floor where it would hard for Blake to see. "I dinnae think I would get a chance to dance with you, m'lady."

"I did arrive with Mr. Thorton," Chrissy replied.

"I have heard that you were not pleased with his company."

"We had a misunderstanding before, but that is forgotten."

"'Tis a tragedy for me then, though you never favored my intentions."

"I would like to go now," she said trying to pull away.

He held her firmly and set his jaw. "Surely you won't be deny-ing me the last of this dance, would you?"

"You're hurting me, please let go," she pleaded.

Suddenly there was disturbance at the other side of the floor, people stopped dancing and watched and Chrissy took the opportunity to pull away. She dashed across the dance floor toward Blake with Ian following behind. When they got there they found Tom holding Bonnie tightly swinging her around the dance floor. She was crying, trying desperately to get away. Tom had her in a viselike grip and showed no signs of letting go. Several men were closing in to stop him when he pulled a pistol and aimed it at them. The music stopped. But Tom kept going spinning around like a broken top.

"Thomas," Ian bellowed, "stop this right now!"

Another scuffle broke out just off the dance floor as Blake struck Troy in the jaw. He had Caleb in a bear hug and was laughing while watching Tom's antics. He collapsed out cold and Caleb ran for the dance floor.

"What's the matter, boy?" Tom said drunkenly, "I'm almost done with her."

"You unhand her NOW!" Ian bellowed again.

Tom stopped dancing and swung the pistol at his father. "You ain't bossin' me no more."

Ian's voice changed to a low growl, "I'll not be havin ..." he stopped when Les Palmer leveled his pistol at him.

"That's far enough, he ain't hurtin' no one," Les said calmly.

Iver Johansson pressed the barrel of his colt against the base of Les's neck, "Put it down boy, I can't miss at this range."

Les smiled and eased the hammer down slowly and let it fall to the ground. "You boys sure get riled around here."

Ian turned his attention back to Tom. "Give over the pistol, Tom, and be done with this, he said calmly.

"Why should I, you hate me," he shouted.

"No, son, you're a wee bit drunk, and your thinkin' is nigh too straight," Ian said closing the gap; he noticed Tom hadn't cocked his pistol.

"I ain't living in your shadow no more," Tom spouted. He closed his eyes hard, trying to keep the emotion in. That's when Ian seized the opportunity to grab the gun and backhanded his son. Tom hit the floor, out cold.

"Lock him in the jail an' keep him there 'til he sobers up," Ian ordered Johansson throwing him Tom's pistol.

"I'm keepin' him three days, with a fine to be paid for disturbin' the peace," Johansson growled.

Ian reached in his pocket and handed the sheriff a wad of bills. "Three days then and here be the fine." Ian reached out and grabbed Les by the shirtfront. "And you boyo, point a pistol at me again and you'll be searchin' for your head." He drew back a massive fist and cold cocked him. Ian then turned and walked off the dance floor with his head held high. As he strode to his carriage his two daughters fell in behind him, their heads hung low.

Iver Johansson bent over and unbuckled the three unconscious men's gun belts and grabbed a bucket of water that was used to put out the torches. Splashing water in each one of their faces, they all came around sputtering and gasping for air. "I need some men to give me a hand escorting this trash to the jail," he said in a loud voice.

Blake was the first to step up. "See to Bonnie," he said to Chrissy. "I'll stop by and check on her." Chrissy nodded her head and helped a very shaken Bonnie off the floor. Caleb was there with his arm around her apologizing for not stopping Tom. Blake turned to the disoriented Tom and yanked him to his feet. "You're pretty tough with a little girl," he snarled. "How are you when it's a man set on beating your ass?"

"Let me go and you'll find out, old man," Tom grimaced as Blake pinned his arm behind his back.

"When you get out of jail, come see me, sonny boy," Blake growled as he marched Tom to the jail. Mike Ventosa had Les in a similar hold as did Josh Dooley with Troy.

Johansson picked up the gun belts and threw them over his shoulder. "Don't let this ruin your good time, folks. There's fireworks comin' up," he called in a loud voice. "Hey, fiddler, how about a tune?"

The band complied with his wishes but their heart wasn't in it and only a few people danced. By the time the sheriff got the three men locked up the fireworks had begun and the crowd turned more festive. Blake left the jail and went to the café.

Inside he found Caleb and Bonnie along with Chrissy pouring coffee for some of the concerned townsfolk. Josh and Terry, Percival and Michelle, Sadie, Hap, Avery, Joe and even Dan LaClare sat talking quietly among themselves.

Blake smiled at them and walked over to Chrissy. "How is she?"

Chrissy bit her lip and said, "Pretty shaken up, but it helps knowing all these people are behind her. She won't let Caleb leave her side."

"Poor kid," Blake said.

"What's going to happen to Tom?"

"Not much unfortunately. He'll cool his heels for a few days in jail, but he'll get out and I don't think this is over yet. I guess we keep a close eye on her, there's no telling what he'll do next," Blake said quietly. "Why don't you take her to her room while I talk to these people?"

Chrissy smiled and patted his hand. "Bonnie, why don't we go upstairs and get some rest?" She went over and stroked her hair. "Things will look better in the morning." Bonnie looked up tearfully and shook her head. After giving Caleb a tight hug she went with Chrissy up the stairs.

When he heard the door close, Blake turned to Caleb, "Go on home, son, you can see her tomorrow." Caleb had a hard look on his face and looked like he wanted to say something but left quietly, his hat in his hand.

When Blake turned around everyone had stopped talking and were looking at him. "What happens now?" Josh said.

Blake sat on one of the stools at the counter and set his hat down. "Well," he began. "Hopefully the sheriff keeps him locked up for three days. After that it's anybody's guess. Personally, I don't think it's over, I think Tom has an ax to grind and will be looking for revenge."

"We're the ones who should be lookin'," Avery said angrily.

"Not the way he sees it. He's lost just about everything he had and he feels slighted," Blake countered. "All we can do is keep an eye on him when he gets out. Follow him and if he starts something, call for help. Also, I don't think Bonnie should ever be alone."

"We'll all help," Terry said and the others agreed.

"One more thing," Blake added. "Those three characters that he's been hanging around with are trouble, too. Don't be a hero and go it alone."

Chrissy came down the stairs and said, "She's resting now, thank you all for coming."

Percival rose to his feet. "Don't you be worryin' none. We'll make sure nothin' happens to her," he said resolutely. "Now I think I should be getting' the miss's home. She's in a delicate way."

"Lordy," Michelle rolled her eyes, "I'm pregnant, not dying."

The room burst into excitement as they congratulated the couple on their good news. Blake leaned against the counter and reveled as he watched the men shake Big Man's hand and slap him on the back. The women looked like hens as they offered help and advice to Michelle. After the evening they had, a little good news went a long way. They all filed out the door chatting among each other and Chrissy gently held Blake's arm preventing him from going. "May I have a word?" she asked.

"Certainly," he said closing the door.

"I hope you're not mad at me for dancing with Ian MacIntyre tonight," she said sincerely. "I didn't want to be rude."

Blake smiled. "Can't say I liked it much, but no harm done."

"Thank you for understanding."

Blake squinted his eyes a little. "I never took my eyes off you until the trouble started, but it looked like you wanted to get away and he wouldn't let you go. Did he get out of line?"

Chrissy hesitated and then said, "Maybe a little, but when Tom started his nonsense, he stopped."

Blake searched her face to see if she was holding something back. "I think he's as much trouble as his son. You'll let me know if he is a bother."

"I will, I promise." She reached up and gently placed her arms around his neck. "You're a good man Blake Thorton," then she kissed him tenderly on the lips.

When the kiss ended they hugged for a moment and Blake reached for his hat, placing it on his head he said, "Good night, Mrs. O'Bryan," and opened the door.

"Good night, Blake," she replied sweetly.

# CHAPTER 18

THE sheriff had a tough time holding the men for the three days, not because of them but because of the mayor's insistence that they had paid for their crimes and should be let go sooner. Out of spite, Johansson held them until the morning of the fourth day. He unlocked the cells and stepped back allowing the men to enter the office. He took their gun belts out of a drawer and threw them on his desk. "You boys ain't got no friends in this town, so I suggest you gather your things and vamoose."

"I'll leave when it suits me," Tom said, spinning the cylinder of his pistol and shoving it in his holster.

"Cause any trouble, and I'll pepper your ass with buckshot," the sheriff shot back.

"You're welcome to try," Tom sniped clamping his hat firmly on his head. "Let's go, boys." All three of them walked out into the bright sunshine.

Mike Ventosa was sitting in a chair on the porch of the jail with his feet on the rail. After the three men left, Johansson walked out and watched them. "Follow them and make sure they stay out of trouble," he said to Mike.

"How long?" Mike asked standing and adjusting his hat.

"See if they leave town and if they do, which way they go."

"You got it, Boss," Mike said as he walked off the porch.

He followed them to the hotel and watched them go to their rooms, collect their things along with Jimmy Rocco, pay their bill and walk down to the livery. They saddled their horses and rode at a high gallop east out of town.

Satisfied, Mike headed back for the jail. He walked in and poured himself a cup of coffee. "Well that didn't take long," the sheriff said, "what happened?"

Mike blew on his coffee and sat down. "Not much really, they got their bedrolls and lit a shuck out of town to the east."

"Well it don't sound like he's going back to his Pappy's," Johansson said sucking his teeth. "We'll double the patrols for a while."

"Sounds good," Mike said.

\* \* \* \* \* \*

That night Blake was working in the forge to fill an important order for a customer. He insisted that Caleb stay home to study and brought some fried chicken with him for dinner. Darkness fell as he worked. Concentrating on finishing and getting home, he didn't see the four figures creep up to the livery and waylay Joe Bergman on the back of his head. A shadowy figure kept in the dark as he worked his way toward the front door of the forge. The mysterious man placed a hand over his mouth and yelled, "Fire in the livery!" By doing that it made it sound far away. Blake snapped his head around and threw the hot metal in the slack tub and ran for the door. As he entered the livery he saw Joe lying face first on the ground. Suddenly, fireworks erupted in his head as a pistol barrel hit him from behind. Falling to his knees dazed, he was greeted by several pairs of boots lashing out at him. Blake was a strong man in good condition but the constant pounding was starting to take its toll and he could feel himself slipping away. He thought he heard a rebel yell and a loud crash but he couldn't be sure. As the pounding continued he could see Caleb's dog Satan sneaking into the barn. As sudden as it began the kicking stopped and one of the men yelled, "God almighty," and gagged. The rest of the men started choking and making retching sounds. "I can't stand it," one yelled and ran for the door. Another coughed and said, "C'mon, he's done." The men clamored for the door and Blake heard horses galloping away. In spite of the pain racking his body he smiled. "Saved by a dog's fart," he muttered and his world went dark.

\* \* \* \* \* \*

Two days later Blake dreamt he was in a long tunnel. He could see the end but it was such an effort to move. He stumbled and clawed his way toward the opening. His forehead was cool and wet and it felt like a spider was crawling across his ribs. He tried to open his eyes but it seemed only one would work and that was sticky and blurry. He blinked a couple times and he saw Chrissy sitting in a chair next to him slowly tracing the outline of his tattoos on his exposed chest with her finger. "That kinda tickles," he said weakly.

She stopped and looked up quickly, gently stroking his face, tears flowing down her cheeks. "It took you long enough to come back," she smiled.

"Well, a man died who was in a hurry once," his lips hurt when he tried to smile. "What happened?" he asked, trying to rise up, but his body screamed its objections and he laid back down.

"You lay right there now," she ordered. "I think I can still catch Doc Baker."

"If you insist," Blake murmured as he closed his one good eye.

He heard footsteps and the door open and close. He could feel a cool breeze blowing across his body, sounds of the town in the background. He heard more footsteps and the door opening again. He slowly turned his head and could see Chrissy and another man standing there.

The man set his bag on the bed and took out a stethoscope. Placing it in his ears and the cool disc on Blake's chest he said, "Mr. Thorton, you have the constitution of an ox."

"I feel like one has been dancing on me," Blake managed to reply.

"That's understandable considering the beating you took," the doctor said putting the stethoscope back and removing a small brown bottle. Pouring the thick liquid in a spoon, he held it out for Blake. "Here, drink this, it will ease the pain some."

Blake opened his mouth and took the medicine. Wincing he smacked his lips, "I think that ox did something else in my mouth."

"It's laudanum," he said handing Chrissy the bottle. "Give him a teaspoon every so often, but not too much, it can be habit forming."

She nodded her head and slipped the bottle into her dress pocket. The doctor snapped his bag shut and put on his hat. "I'll check on him tomorrow. What he needs now is sleep and plenty of it."

"Thank you very much," she said and followed him to the door. When he left she came back over to Blake's side and sat down.

"Where am I?" Blake asked as he looked around. He didn't recognize the room.

"It's my room above the café," she said.

Blake furrowed his brow. "Why your room? Why not my house?"

"We all thought it might be safer for you here."

"Safer?" Blake said stronger, "What the hell is going on?" he could feel the effects of the laudanum and the room started to spin slowly.

"You sleep now," she cooed softly, "I'll tell you all about it tomorrow."

Blake relaxed and was feeling a little drunk-like. "Fine," he said. He closed his eye and could feel her fingers touching his face. "Chrissy?" he said weakly.

"Yes, darling,"

"Tell me a story."

She gave him a confused look. "What story?"

"Any story," he murmured, "but if there's a prince, can it be Prince Blake?" he smiled a weak smile.

"Go to sleep, you big idiot," she giggled as he drifted off.

\* \* \* \* \* \*

The next morning Blake woke and his one eye was still swollen shut. He managed to work himself into almost a sitting position. Every muscle in his body protested but the more he moved the better it felt. Exhausted from his efforts, he laid back and drew in lungfuls of the cool morning air. The door cracked slightly and Chrissy peaked in. "What do you think you're doing?" she asked.

Blake winced as he tried to get more comfortable. "I thought I would go for a quick run this morning."

"Oh I can see you're not going to be an easy patient," she said sitting on the bed and feeling his forehead. "Can I get you anything?"

"I could eat something, if it isn't too much trouble."

"It's no trouble but you have to stay in bed."

"Yes, mother," he said lying back on the soft pillow. She got up to leave and he continued. "Aren't you going to tell me what happened?"

"Let's get you some food first. Sheriff Johansson wanted to talk to you if you're up to it," she said as she reached the door.

"Tell him all right but not to take too long, I still want to go running."

Shaking her head she closed the door. Blake managed to get some more pillows behind his back and was admiring the room when she came back carrying a tray. Setting it on the dresser she took out the small bottle of laudanum and filled a spoon. "Here you go," she said holding the spoon out.

"I don't need that," Blake objected.

Standing up straight she cocked her eyebrow and placed her other hand on her hip. "If you want breakfast, you'll take it."

"It tastes like crap."

"Fine," she said, "then you can come downstairs to eat."

"That's all right with me," Blake tried to sit up and swing his legs out of bed but immediately realized that he wasn't going too far. Collapsing back onto the pillows he said breathlessly. "You win, you surly woman."

Giggling, she fed him the medicine. "Now there's a big boy," she teased in a mocking tone. She got up and brought over the tray with a bowl that contained clear broth, dipping a spoon in it she brought to his lips and said in a singsong voice, "Open wide."

Blake furrowed his forehead. "You're really enjoying this, aren't you?" he said taking the broth.

"Yes, I really am," she laughed holding up another spoonful.

"How's the patient?" Johansson said from the doorway.

Blake looked around Chrissy and said, "I am feeling a might abused."

"Yeah, you look it," Johansson chuckled. "Hello, Mrs. O'Bryan. If he gives you too much trouble I can take him down to the jail. We have real comfortable cots."

"I can handle him, sheriff, but thanks for the offer," she smiled, feeding Blake some more broth.

"So is anybody going to tell me what happened?" Blake asked.

Taking off his hat, Johansson pulled up a chair and sat down. "Near as we can figure," he began, "Tom MacIntyre is the one who paid you a visit. He and those other criminals he rides with snuck into the livery and knocked Joe out."

"Is he all right?" Blake asked.

"He's fine. They put a good sized knot on his head, though. Anyway, they must have lured you in the barn and cold cocked you. Then they proceeded to a do a Mexican hat dance on you."

"I remember somebody yelled fire," Blake added.

"Makes sense, I was wondering why you went in the livery," Johansson said. "While they were takin' the boots to you, Avery was up in the loft and saw the whole thing. To hear him tell it, he saved your life by swingin' down on a rope into them fellas. Damn fool stunt if you ask me. He says he knocked all four out the door and they high tailed it."

It hurt to laugh, but Blake couldn't help himself, "I remember a rebel yell and a crash, but I'm pretty sure Satan helped the most."

"Come again?" the sheriff asked.

"Caleb's dog, he snuck in and does what he does best."

"What does he do, bite them?" Chrissy asked.

"Nope," Blake laughed, "he farts. It's the worst God awful thing you ever smelled. It would make a buzzard gag."

"You're joshin' me," Johansson said disbelieving.

"It's true, I swear," Blake said holding up a bruised hand. "Ask Joe, or Hap, or Sadie, they all know."

"I'll be damned," Johansson said shaking his head.

The laudanum was starting to work and Blake felt dizzy, Chrissy saw it on his face. "All right you two, that's enough talking. He needs some rest."

"I still don't know why I'm here in your room," Blake said sleepily.

"Mrs. O'Bryan thought it would be best if we put you someplace that would make it hard for MacIntyre to find you, should he come back," Johansson said standing and putting on his hat. "My deputy has been searchin' for him, but he up and disappeared."

Blake was drifting off to sleep. "Caleb and Sadie, he might go after them."

"We took care of them," Chrissy said. "Go to sleep now."

The next couple of days Blake received a lot of visitors; it seemed to him like he had made a lot more friends than he thought. He hadn't been part of a community since he was young back in New York and, as people came and went, he was filled with a sense of warmth. It was hard to explain but he liked it. He was getting restless though, he wanted to get outside and breathe the air and feel the sun on his face. Six days after he was jumped, he sat up and slowly got dressed. He was barely able to pull his boots on and thought about laying back down. Bracing one more time he stood and walked across the room and down the stairs. As he entered the dining room, Chrissy came out of the kitchen with some plates of food. "Of all the foolish…" she exclaimed. Setting the plates down, she rushing to his side. "You get back up in bed, this instant."

"I'm fine," Blake groused, "I'm going crazy up there."

"You are an impossible man," she groused back. "Are you hungry?"

"Famished," he said easing into a chair.

# CHAPTER 19

"I'm tired of being cooped up in this here shack," grumbled Troy.

"All's we had to eat is beans. Some whiskey wouldn't hurt none." He threw a card on the table and stared at the cards he had left.

Tom's gang was using a line shack on the northern corner of his father's property. It was rarely used except in the winter when two or three hands would hold up in it to watch the herd and shoot wolves. Only a few of the older hands knew about it. They were also a full day's ride out of town which made it too far to search for. Tom left with meager provisions so on the way there they waited outside a farmer's house for him to leave. When the farmer and his family all loaded in the wagon for a trip into town, Tom's group raided the kitchen for food only to find that the farmer was going to town to restock his own shelves. Not much could be taken. Les and Troy were angry and wanted to burn the house, but Tom stopped them with the promise of more money. Reluctantly, they agreed to leave but now they were getting agitated because of the lack of food and entertainment.

"Quit bellyachin'," Tom barked at him. "I figure it's just about time to go back to town."

"Suits me," grumbled Les. "You think that fella we stomped is dead?"

"I doubt it, he seems pretty tough," Tom said leaning in the doorway looking outside. "He'll be laid up for a couple weeks. We won't have no trouble from him."

"So, what's next, boss?" Jimmy asked scratching his chin.

Tom got an evil grin on his face. "I figure on payin' that little girl a visit."

Troy giggled. "Like that stagecoach woman? That was fun, but I ain't goin' last again. She didn't fight much when I got to her."

"She's just for me," Tom sneered. "She needs to pay for all the trouble she's caused me."

"Well now that ain't fair," Troy complained. "I want me a turn."

"You can have that blonde bitch in the café," Tom growled. "Get everything ready to go, we leave in the morning," he said as he walked to the corral.

"Hoo wee," Troy whooped. "She's a good one."

"After me," Les grinned.

"Damn," Troy pouted.

* * * * * *

In the morning they rode out, keeping to valleys so they wouldn't be spotted. Tom talked very little; his thoughts were on Bonnie and what he was going to do. Several times he adjusted himself in the saddle because of his excitement. They waited a mile out of town until darkness fell. The moon had not risen yet and the stars cast little light. The last quarter mile they all dismounted and walked to the back of the café. Although it was closed, the lamps were still lit in the kitchen where Chrissy and Bonnie cleaned up from the day's business.

"What are we waitin' for?" Troy said in a whisper. "They's right there."

Tom shot him a hard look. "We take our time and do this right. Troy and Les, you go to the front of the alley and keep an eye out.

Jimmy, go see if she's locked the front door. If she hasn't, sneak in and wait. I'll come in the back and we'll have them trapped."

Jimmy and the other two crept into their positions. Jimmy tried the front door and found it unlocked, he waved to Troy and went in silently. He crept up to the counter and knelt down.

"I need to use the privy," Bonnie said.

"All right dear, I'll wait by the door," Chrissy replied.

"I'm fine," said Bonnie.

"We still need to be careful, I'll wait."

Bonnie stepped out to the outhouse under the light of a lantern held by Chrissy in the doorway.

"Hello, little lady," Jimmy said leering at her and holding a pistol. "You stay quiet and come in here." Chrissy was paralyzed with fear, she stood wide eyed and shaking. "Why don't you close that door," Jimmy said in a low menacing voice. Chrissy stepped in and closed the door.

Outside Bonnie could no longer see the light from the lantern and called out, "Chrissy?" Suddenly the door flew open and strong hands grabbed the front of her dress and threw her out on the ground.

Tom loomed over her as she tried to scramble away. "Nice of you to have your bloomers down for me," he menaced. Grabbing her hair, he picked her up and clamped a hand over her mouth. Dragging her into the shadows of the alley he began tearing at her clothes.

Inside the café Jimmy was closing on Chrissy. She jumped to the right and he countered. Then she ran to the left and he grabbed her by the waist and threw her against the counter. Reaching in back of her she felt the handle of a large skillet. Grasping it firmly she swung it with all her might and hit him high on the shoulder. Jimmy lost his balance a fell against a large stack of plates causing them to crash to the floor. Tom stopped for a moment and looked around, but his lust overcame him and he started to unbuckle his pants.

Percival Feathers was walking toward the saloon and heard the crash in the café. When he looked in that direction he saw Les Palmer peek around the corner. "Son-of-a-bitch," he yelled and barreled for the alley. Josh Dooley poked his head out the upstairs window. "What's going on?" he yelled to the Big Man. "Get the sheriff, they're in the café!" Percival yelled now, almost to the alley. Les fired a shot at the Big Man, tagging him in the shoulder but it was as though the Big Man was a freight train. Troy shot at him hitting him in the side. "Let's get out of here," he yelled and ran down the alley. When Tom heard the shooting he backhanded Bonnie and ran buckling his pants. Jimmy came flying out the back door with Chrissy chasing him shooting his own pistol at him; when he fell in the kitchen he dropped it. When the shooting started he ran for the door and Chrissy picked it up. As the four men fled for their horses Les and Troy fired back into the alley and scored three more hits on the Big Man. He had seen Bonnie's feet sticking out and stopped to cover her from the flying lead.

The entire town was awake now and lanterns flooded the street. Men tried to get Percival away from Bonnie but he refused to let go. Finally, as his strength was fading they managed to get her up and into the café. It took six men to lift Percival and get him inside. Doc Baker heard the shots and was already running to the scene. The sheriff and his deputy came as fast as their legs would carry them. Blake and Caleb had just finished a game of chess and heard the commotion. Blake had returned home the night before and was still in a great deal of pain. Every step he ran was agony, but he ignored it.

By the time he made it to the café the whole place was chaotic. The doctor had Percival stretched out between three tables and worked feverishly on his wounds, five in all. The Big Man was covered in blood. Everyone was shouting and asking questions. Blake bulled his way through and found Chrissy and Bonnie kneeling on the floor, sobbing and holding each other.

Johansson stood on a chair and bellowed at the top of his lungs. "Everybody simmer down, if you ain't got no business in here, leave, while we sort this out."

The crowd went silent and started to file out, Blake and Caleb stayed with the women and the doctor and his nurse Anne stayed working on Percival along with two others holding pressure on his wounds. Michelle burst through the doors and ran to her husband sobbing.

Caleb was incensed, and he stood over Bonnie pointing at the sheriff. "Y-you l-l-l-let th-th-is happen!" he yelled almost screaming.

Blake grabbed him by the shoulders and spun around to face him. "Caleb," he said firmly, "No one let this happen; calm down, Bonnie needs you now."

"I-if t-that s-son of a bitch w-won't k-k-kill h-him, I-I w-will," he yelled spit flying from his lips.

"Settle down, son," Blake said firmly

"B-b-but he's g-g-getting away," Caleb cried.

"He ain't going far," Mike Ventosa said as entered the café. "We found his tracks headed due west, straight to his Daddy's ranch."

"Good," said the sheriff, "tomorrow we'll follow the tracks to be sure, but my money says that's where he's headed."

"Ian isn't going to give him up easily," warned Blake.

"We ride at first light," Johansson said firmly. "Any man wantin' to come along is welcome." He walked boldly to the door and left.

Blake knelt down and put his hand on Chrissy's shoulder. "Are you two all right? I mean did they…"

Chrissy looked up and shook her head no. "It's my fault, I wasn't careful enough. If Percival hadn't come along, who knows what…" She broke down in tears and hugged Blake tightly.

He kissed the top of her head and said, "And if I had stayed one more night maybe I could have stopped it, too. No one is to blame, I'm just glad you're safe."

Caleb looked up at Blake. "W-w-we kn-kn-know where he is. L-l-let's g-go g-gg-get him n-n-now," he said, tears streaming down his cheeks.

"Tomorrow," Blake said firmly.

"Y-y-ou're a-a-a c-c-coward," Caleb spat at Blake.

The night's events finally caught up to Blake, he was sore and tired. What almost happened to Chrissy scared him to death. His own anger was building inside him and he saw red. "Coward? You ungrateful little shit. What are you going to do? Charge out there without a gun and get yourself killed? You best think like a man and pull yourself together. You stay with the women tomorrow. You'll just be in the way," he shouted.

Caleb stood at full height and tried not to cry; finally he broke into a run out of the café and was gone.

"Damn it all to hell," Blake said hanging his head.

"Everybody is angry," Chrissy said calmly, "Caleb will be all right." She took Blake's face in her hands. "You're the bravest man I know. Would you please help me get Bonnie upstairs?" Blake nodded his head and tenderly picked up Bonnie in his arms and carried her up the stairs.

\* \* \* \* \* \*

Tom and the other three in his gang rode at a break neck speed up the road. Finally Les yelled, "We are going to wreck if we keep up like this, slow down." Tom slowed the pace to a walk and finally stopped, letting the horses blow. He had no idea what to do next, nothing was going his way.

Troy was the first to speak, "Damn, that was some big bastard that was acommin' fer us."

"He is the bouncer at the saloon," Jimmy said.

"Well all I knowed is I tagged him twice and Troy got him once and he kept comin'," Les said shaking his head.

"Shot three times? He's dead." Tom said coolly.

"I don't know, boss," Jimmy said doubtfully. "Man like that takes a lot of killin'."

"I said he's dead," Tom snapped back.

"Sure boss, anything you say." Jimmy scratched the back of his neck. "Where is we goin' now?"

Tom pursed his lips and thought. "Come morning, they'll come after us. We need to fort up, and I know where. C'mon." Tom spurred his horse and the others followed, straight to his father's ranch.

Tom stopped them on top of the hill overlooking the ranch. He gave each man instructions before heading down.

"I ain't so sure this is gonna work," Les said plainly. "Mostly your plans don't go so well."

"Take your chances with the posse then," Tom growled.

"Shit," Les muttered, "I'm guessin' we're in."

"Let's get to it then," Tom said and trotted down the hill.

\* \* \* \* \* \*

Ian MacIntyre had many sleepless nights after the dance. He spent most of his time closed in his study, rarely coming out except to eat or drink. That night he had fallen asleep in his chair behind the desk while pouring over paperwork. He bolted upright in his chair when Tom crashed through the door holding a gun followed by Les and Troy. Blinking his eyes it took him a second to assess the situation. "Thomas," he stammered. "What are you doin' here?"

"Had a little trouble in town," Tom began. "I need your help."

Ian collected himself and asked, "Why would you be pointin' a gun at me then?"

"Because you're going to listen to everything I say, no interruptions."

"Tell me your tale, son," Ian said placing his hands on the arm of his chair.

Tom motioned with his pistol. "Sit on this side, where I can see your hands. If you try to stop me, my two friends will shoot you." Ian slowly stood up and walked around the desk as Tom maneuvered over to his chair. They both sat at the same time and Tom put his pistol back in the holster. "This is nice over here. Feels mighty powerful," he said smiling.

"Your story, Thomas," Ian requested with an impatient tone.

Tom told his father his account of what happened in town. Lie after lie he spun. Basically, he told his father that he saw Percival molesting Bonnie and they tried to help her by shooting him, but the townspeople were pinning the blame on him. Tom thought the story he told his father was very believable, but the look on Ian's face said otherwise.

Ian sat for a time drumming his fingers on the arm of the chair. "That's quite a story, son."

"It's all true, swear to God," Tom replied. "These men will back me up."

Ian glanced over his shoulder and gave Les and Troy a skeptical look. "You are my only son, Thomas. I've been hard on you, to be sure, but I'm not thinkin' the entire truth has been told here," he said quietly turning back to Tom.

"It's the story a judge will hear."

"Then why not let a judge hear it?"

"Because, the whole town is against me," Tom said nervously. "They'll lynch me before I even get close to a jail."

"I cannea' let that happen, son. You will turn yourself in after we employ a lawyer, and we will be clearin' our name in court. Agreed?"

"Sure Pa, sounds good to me," Tom smiled.

"Do you think they will be sendin' a posse?" Ian said thinking.

"I'd bet my life on it. We had to flee for our lives."

"And what would your plan be?" Ian asked.

"Well, hold up here and wait them out."

"No, son, it be a fight they're lookin' for. We have to make them turn back or all will be lost. I have some suggestions, if you're not mindin'."

"Yeah, sure, Pa," Tom said uncertain. He knew his father had military training and fought many battles. "What do we do?"

Ian stood up and straightened his vest, "Come with me and learn." Ian turned to the door and was stopped by Les. "You'll be gettin' out of my way now," he growled.

Les glanced at Tom who nodded his head affirmatively. Les slowly let Ian pass and all three followed him into the house. Ian marched through the house like a commanding general. When he bellowed the whole house seemed to shake. His twin girls appeared at the top of the stairs confused. He ordered them to pack their things and get ready for travel. His houseman Jethro came out pulling up his suspenders and Ian told him to get quickly packed and then to get the best team of horses on the ranch hooked up to his carriage. Maids came out of their rooms and he told them to help the girls and then to ready bandages and beds for wounded men. The house came alive as people scurried making preparations. He then marched out of the house over to the bunkhouse and, slamming open the door, he barked orders as the sleepy men got up, lit lanterns, and started pulling their clothes on. "What's going on, boss?" one of them asked as he pulled on his boots.

"The sheriff is comin' with a posse to take my son. We will see that doesn't happen," he commanded.

"We are going to shoot lawmen? That don't sit right with me," another said.

"You men ride for the MacIntyre brand. My son says he is innocent. Any man who lacks the bravery to defend this ranch, may collect his wages and be gone from my sight. Those who remain will be collecting a one hundred dollar bonus from me. Make your decisions for time is short."

The twelve men stood staring at one another, muttering among themselves. "We'll stick, boss," the lead man said loudly.

"Good for ye, lads," Ian grinned. "Now arm yourselves and meet in front of the house." Ian turned on his heel and marched back to the main house. Inside his daughters stood in the front hall dressed and packed. Ian walked past them and into his study and to his safe. He opened it and removed a large sum of money. Placing it in a leather wallet he stood to find Les smiling.

"You can leave that open so's me and Troy can get the pay Tom promised," he said looking at the large stacks of bills.

Ian slammed the safe closed and spun the dial. "Any arrangements my son made with the likes of you will be settled by him. Now move from my sight." Les's face darkened as he stepped aside slowly. Ian pushed past him and stopped to glare at Tom. "The combination has been changed," he growled. "It would seem that somebody pilfered from me." Tom met his gaze and didn't flinch. Ian snorted and went to the front door where Jethro was standing next to the girls. Ian handed him the wallet. "You are my most trusted servant; I want you to take my daughters to a hotel in Sweetwater. Stay there until I send for you." Then Ian turned to the men standing out front. "I need a loyal man to escort my daughters and stay with them."

"I'll go," one man called out, "they'll be safe with me, boss."

"Good, good," he replied. "Jethro, girls, you best be on your way now." The two girls ran up and hugged their father tightly.

"Don't make us go, Papa," Mary cried.

"There's a good lass," he said as he stroked their hair. "It's for a short time to be sure. Soon you will be sleepin' in your own beds again."

"Promise?" Kate said her head buried in his massive chest.

"Aye, now it's time for you to be going," he said ushering them to the carriage. As they loaded in he kissed them both tenderly on the cheek. They held his hands as long as they could before the carriage disappeared into the night. Ian stood staring into the darkness when the sound of hoof beats filled the air.

A man came running from the barn yelling, "Joe, Little Bob, Pete and Juan just rode off," he said breathing hard. "Said they wasn't about to get shot for Tom."

Ian grit his teeth and hissed, "Damnable cowards." That left him with twelve men by his count. Depending on how many the posse had would be critical. "The rest of you men take as much ammunition as ye can carry," he barked. "I want a good rifleman on the water tower and in the lofts of the barns. The rest find safe places to shoot from. No man sleeps and no one fires without my order."

He stood on the front steps of the house and watched the men disperse. He turned to go back in the house and heard a rider coming fast. Turning back he squinted toward the sound. Tom came out on the porch to see who was approaching. The lights of the house cast an eerie image onto the rider. Caleb slid Rosie to a stop in front of the house and leapt off.

"Tom MacIntyre, I've come to kill you," he yelled not stuttering one bit. He ran straight at Tom and leapt through the air crashing into him and started pummeling him with his fists. Tom was taken off guard and shielded his face from the blows. Les and Troy grabbed Caleb by the arms and pulled him off. Caleb struggled but they were too strong. Ian stepped in and backhanded Caleb, knocking him senseless.

"And who would this be?" he asked Tom who had gotten to his feet, dusting himself off.

"That's the kid who the blacksmith took on. He's sweet on the girl who was attacked tonight," Tom said innocently.

"He is seemin' to think you did it," Ian said.

"They all do, Pa, like I told you."

Blowing out a deep breath Ian said, "Bind his hands and hang him from the porch rail.

Caleb started to come around as they stretched his hands high over his head. His feet barely touched the ground. Ian walked over and turned him so he could see his face. "How many men would be comin' lad?" he asked.

Caleb struggled and kicked but Ian held him firm. He glared at Tom, "You go to hell," he spat.

"You lost your stutter boy," Tom grinned back.

"I ain't afraid of you no m-m-more," Caleb grimaced under the pain.

"Oops," Tom laughed, "there's a little left."

Ian wrenched Caleb's face back to his own. "How many, lad? I won't be askin' again." Caleb hung there, stone faced his lips tight. "Well now," Ian said calmly, "he'll answer under the lash."

# CHAPTER 20

**B**ACK in the sheriff's office Johansson and his deputy were making preparations for daybreak. Iver had several of his finest collection of guns laid out on the desk with boxes of shells stacked neatly next to them. The door opened and they both drew their pistols. The mayor came in wearing a coat over his pajamas looking disheveled.

"Good, Lord," he squeaked holding up his hands. "Bad idea not to knock, Mayor," Johansson said putting his pistol away. "What is it that brings you out at this early hour?"

"You know full well why I'm here," Weatherby said mopping his brow. "I want you to stop this nonsense of arresting Tom MacIntyre."

"Do you now," Johansson said matter-of-factly.

"Yes I do," blustered Weatherby. "From what I understand, there is not one shred of proof he is guilty."

"What about an eye witness?" Johansson replied calmly.

"Bah," he said waving his hand, "a hysterical young lady claims it was him. How could she be certain in the dark?"

Mike Ventosa reached his breaking point. He kicked a chair out of his way and stood in front of the mayor yelling, "You fat sack of horseshit. You know he did it and I'm tired of turning a blind eye. You might have the sheriff here bamboozled, but not me. I'm going after that worthless son-of-a-bitch in the morning. You got that?"

Weatherby blinked several times and snorted. "You insolent pup. You're fired!" he demanded.

"Fine by me, you pig faced bastard," Mike snarled taking his badge off and throwing it at him.

"Gentleman, please," Johansson smiled gently placing a hand on Mike's shoulder and moving him so he could face the mayor. "As my deputy so eloquently stated, we have enough proof to bring in Thomas MacIntyre on charges of assault, attempted rape and murder." Johansson sat on the corner of his desk and continued. "Oh, now, I understand that you will fire me after this but I will keep this here badge on long enough to see it through, after which if I find myself lacking employment, I will, in good conscience, have no choice but to notify the Federal Marshals of my findings here. They'll come down and investigate to be sure, and when they find out you're the banker and your principal client is the aforementioned's father, I believe they will request federal auditors to arrive and go through your records with a fine-toothed comb."

"You wouldn't," choked the mayor.

"It would be my civic duty," smiled Johansson. "Now why don't you go home and rest easy knowing that justice is in good hands?"

Weatherby blinked and coughed. He turned his head quickly, with his jowls quivering, between Mike and the sheriff. Finally, he looked like he was on the verge of tears. He hung his head low and left the jail quietly.

Johansson leaned down and picked up the badge Mike had thrown, turning it over in his fingers he said, "As for you, it would be my hope that the next time you get riled up, you would give me first crack at sayin' what you're thinking." He grinned broadly and tossed the badge back to Mike.

Ventosa pinned it back on his chest and chuckled, "Federal auditors?"

Johansson laughed. "Thought of that on the fly. You think they exist?"

\* \* \* \* \* \*

Blake dozed uncomfortably in a rocking chair in Chrissy's room. He had stayed after she had put Bonnie in her bed. Chrissy sat in a chair lying partially on the bed holding Bonnie's hand. Blake took out his watch and checked it. He stood quietly as he could and crept to the door. A sleepy voice whispered, "Is it time?"

He nodded yes and opened the door. Chrissy slipped her hand out of Bonnie's and followed him. At the top of the stairs she stopped him and hugged him tightly. "Would it do any good to say you're in no shape to go out there today?" she asked with watery eyes.

"Nope" he answered.

"I'm so scared, Blake, I don't want to lose you."

"I can't die," he said. "You and I have unfinished business."

"What do you mean?"

"I have to get going," he smiled. "I love you, Chrissy." He kissed her deeply and started down the stairs.

She stayed at the top of the stairs and watched him go. "I love you more," she whispered.

At the bottom of the stairs Blake saw the doctor sleeping in a chair, Percival was laying on the tables his huge chest rising and falling slightly. Blake went over and shook the doctor's shoulder gently. He woke with a start a sat up. "How's he doing, Doc?"

The doctor pursed his lips and said, "He has no right to be alive. Five gunshot wounds and losing that much blood would kill anybody."

"He ain't just anybody, Doc."

"If he survives the night, he is going to take away your award for being the toughest man on earth."

"He's earned it," Blake said patting the doctor on the shoulder. "Take care now." Blake stepped out in the cool night air and walked to the jail. Every step he took, the pain from the beating deepened his resolve even more. Six months ago he never thought he would be here. He could have just ridden on and not complicated his life so badly. He had no intentions of putting down roots or being tied to anyone. He finally decided it was his horse's fault and he would be giving Bull a stern talking to.

\* \* \* \* \* \*

The door to the jail was open and crowded with men. Johansson was handing out badges, firearms and ammo and told everyone who was armed and sworn in to wait outside. Josh Dooley came out first, carrying a Winchester followed by Joe Bergman and Avery. Hap came out adjusting his gun belt and smiled at Blake. The next to come out was Al Conner, the owner of the sawmill and Sam who were both carrying rifles. The bartender Clyde appeared checking his Spencer rifle to see if it was loaded. The last of the volunteers was Dan LaClare smoking a cheroot. "Well, Blake Thorton," he smiled. "it brings my heart joy to see you up and around."

"Dan," Blake said shaking his hand. "I thought you weren't the hero type."

"I am most certainly not," he smirked. "I have placed a wager on the outcome of this endeavor."

"Really? What are the odds?"

"Three to one it will fail. I stand to make a great deal of money should it succeed."

"Little underhanded helping out, isn't it?" Blake asked.

"Not at all, my assistance was implied," he laughed.

With that Caleb's horse galloped into town dragging the lead rope. She was lathered up and breathing hard from running so far. "Damn, damn, damn," Blake said running to her.

"You think Caleb went out there?" Joe Bergman asked as he caught up to Blake.

"Yup, I do," Blake said. "We have to go now."

"Any man that needs a horse, follow me," Joe yelled. "I'll saddle Bull for you, Blake." All the men ran for the livery while Blake went to the jail.

"I think Caleb rode out there tonight," Blake said bursting through the door.

"Damn it to hell," Johansson said. "That's going to change things. Let's go." He snatched up his rifles and they all made for the barn.

The livery was alive with men saddling horses and preparing to ride. Bull pawed impatiently at the ground as Blake approached. Blake's head pounded and his body objected to the recent exertion he was placing on it. He stopped and leaned against Bull to brace himself. His skin looked pale because of the bruising which had turned a sickly yellow-green color. Johansson strolled over and looked concerned. "You really look like buffalo shit."

Blake inhaled deeply and blew it out. "Good, I hate to give off any false impressions."

"Nobody would fault you for stayin' behind."

Blake drew himself up to full height and turned his head to Johansson, the expression on his face left no doubt in the sheriff's mind that staying back was not an option. In fact, they would all probably be behind him.

"You got sand, Thorton," the sheriff admired. "Let's go get this peckerwood."

\* \* \* \* \* \*

Blake checked his watch, it was quarter to four, he figured about two hours to sunrise. They wanted to get there under cover of darkness and get a plan in place. Time was running short. The posse got mounted and followed Johansson at a fast gallop out of town.

"I'm takin' a gamble he's at his daddy's ranch. No time to follow tracks," he yelled to Blake.

"Works for me," Blake called back. The horses thundered along, each with a man whose face was set with determination. The posse covered the distance quickly and Johansson brought them all to a halt and let the horses blow. "If I'm right, they'll have a man waitin' at the turn to warn them that we're comin'. I'll go ahead on foot and take him out, the rest of you come up slowly and don't make no noise," Johansson ordered.

"Beggin' your pardon, suh," Sam said. "I's can sneaks up on him quicker than you. I's needs to borra a knife, please."

"I can do it," Johansson said. "I've had to kill more than one Comanche in my time."

"Yes, suh, but I's snuck up on a fox who was killin' my chickens just yesterday. Kilt him dead, too," Sam said quietly.

"Damn that's good, son. All right, the job's yours."

Blake took out a ten-inch razor sharp bowie knife from his sheath and handed it to Sam. "Don't kill him unless you have to."

Taking the knife Sam said, "Yes, suh." He cat footed away at a quick trot not making a sound, it was as though the night swallowed him up.

"Spooky son-of-a-gun ain't he," Johansson said. "The rest of you follow me and no talkin'."

They followed silently at a walk to give Sam the time he needed. Sam padded along the trail, keeping low and moving fast. The road took a turn and he crouched down listening carefully. Up ahead he saw movement in the bushes and could see the faint glow of a quirley that the guard was smoking. Sam moved slowly and closed the gap on his prey. A rabbit hopped out onto the trail and sat munching on some grass. The guard was startled and chuckled to himself when he saw what made the noise. Sitting back he sighed heavily. It felt like a breeze in the back of his neck when Sam whispered, "You jest sits real quiet now." He could feel the edge of a knife pressing against his throat. He started to say something and Sam whispered, "Hush now." The guard nodded his head and, like a blur, Sam brought the hilt of the knife crashing down on the back of his head knocking him out cold. He dragged him back in the bushes and quickly bound his hands and feet. Sam removed the man's neckerchief and gagged him. Stepping out on the road he waited for the posse to get there. Ten minutes later he heard them approaching and padded back up the trail. Keeping in the shadows he stepped out and said, "I knocked him out, suh."

He startled Johansson who hissed, "Jumpin' Jehoshaphat. Next time whistle or somethin'."

Sam grinned and handed Blake his knife back. "They's good places to hide up ahead, we is real close."

* * * * * *

"We'll walk the rest of the way," Johansson said in a hushed voice. Quietly as they could, the men dismounted and crept up to the bend. Blake took a pair of field glasses out of his saddlebags and Johansson got his spyglass. When they rounded the bend the ranch came into view. Blake figured they still had a half hour till sunrise. Propping himself on a large boulder he surveyed the area. The main house had several lanterns lit and two on the front porch. Blake saw Caleb's body hanging by his hands, his shirt was torn off and Blake could see welts on his back from being whipped. He watched for a while and saw Caleb shift his weight trying to relieve the strain on his arms. "He's alive," Blake said quietly gritting his teeth. "Looks like they whipped him some."

Johansson peered through his spyglass. "I think I see one on the water tower and the bunkhouse is lit up." He felt a tap on his shoulder and Hap said, "Let me have a look."

Johansson handed him the spyglass and Hap whispered, "One on the tower and one in each of the lofts in the barns. I see there be a bunch more scattered around them wagons and such. If'n I had to guess, they about twelve or thirteen down there, and they is forted up nice."

"How do you want to play this, Sheriff?" Blake asked.

"I've brought my buffalo rifle, but need to get closer," he replied weighing the options. "That's seven hundred yards from here."

"What caliber?" Hap asked.

"Forty-five ninety. Why?"

"Vernier sights?"

"Yeah."

"It's eight hundred twenty yards I reckon, I can make from right here," Hap said confidently.

"You can make an eight-hundred-yard shot?" the sheriff asked disbelieving.

"If the wind is right, I can widen your peehole," Hap smirked. "I did me some sniper shootin' in the war. Knocked a Yankee general right out of his saddle once at fifteen hundred yards. No offense, Mr. Thorton."

"None taken," Blake said. "Sheriff, I have an idea if you want to hear it." Johansson nodded his head and continued to stare at Hap. "If we can, we'll get some men to sneak around and take out the men in the lofts. Hap can take out the one on the water tower and maybe in the yard. You and I will ride down and see if Tom will come peaceably. I'll tie a white flag on the barrel of my rifle, if I drop it, we commence shootin'."

The men stood around refining the plan a little and then split up. Sam, Al Conner, Joe, and Avery went with Mike Ventosa and made a wide loop to the back of the barns. Dan, Josh and the bartender circled around the other side to the back of the house and bunkhouse. Blake and Johansson waited with Hap, trying to give the men as much time as they could to get into position. The sky had the gray streaks of morning starting to show and soon the orange arc of the sun came up behind the ranch. Blake sat the whole time watching Caleb, his stomach tightened every time he moved. Blake wanted to get moving but he knew he had to wait. Finally Johansson stood closing his spyglass. "The men are in position. Let's get this over with."

Blake stood and walked over to Bull. "If I make it out of this, you and I are going to have a long, serious talk." Bull shook his head and tried to nip Blake's leg.

"You talk to your horse?" Johansson asked as he got mounted.

"Yup, I blame him for all this trouble," Blake replied

"Someday you'll have to explain that to me," the sheriff said clucking to his roan. He stopped next to Hap and said, "Are you sure you can make that shot? Our lives depend on it you know."

Hal picked up a handful of sand and let it slip from his fingers. Adjusting the sight a little, he said, "Yup."

Blake looked at Johansson who just smiled. Without a word they started down to the ranch.

# CHAPTER 21

IN the house Troy burst into the study. "They's comin'," he yelled. Ian got up from his chair and picked up a shotgun. He calmly checked the loads and walked confidently to the front door with Tom close behind. Les and Troy were already on the porch at either ends. Troy was closest to Caleb with a shotgun pointed at him. When Ian saw only two riders he grew concerned, he expected many more.

In the nearest barn, Sam was busy tying up the ranch hand in the loft as Joe used the butt of his rifle to knock out the man hiding below. In the barn farthest away Avery threw a rope around the neck of the man hiding up there and, pulling back sharply, he pulled from the mow to the floor below. Al Conner had slipped when he went to grab his man and they were wrestling on the floor. Avery picked up an axe handle and tried to hit him but they rolled over too soon and he knocked out Al instead. Realizing his mistake he swung again and cold cocked the right one. He grabbed a bucket of water and threw it on Al. "Good thing I came along," Avery whispered, "he almost had ya."

Al sat up with Avery's help and rubbed his head, "Thanks, Pard."

Blake and the sheriff trotted up to the house. Blake was holding his Winchester rifle resting on his leg with the barrel pointed straight up in the air. A white rag was tied on it and waved gently in the breeze.

Ian stood on the porch like a statue, legs apart, hand on his hip and the other holding his shotgun over his shoulder. His face looked like it was chiseled from stone. Tom leaned against the doorway with a cocky grin on his face. Caleb weakly spun towards Blake with the slightest trace of a smile. Johansson spoke first. "Ain't no use dancin' around it," he said plainly. "I'm here to take Tom in on charges of assault, attempted rape and murder."

"Aye," Ian replied, "my son has told me the tale, but he won't be leavin' till he has a lawyer."

"He will get a fair trial, but he's coming with us. I can't take the chance of him runnin' off."

"He has given his word that he will stay," Ian said firmly.

"His word means shit," Blake growled. "You can't protect him anymore."

"He is my only son, I will do what is necessary to makes sure he comes to no harm," Ian growled back. "Be on your way."

"Last chance, MacIntyre," Johansson said firmly.

"No."

Blake smiled casually and lowered his rifle barrel. A second later Troy Palmer lurched back, smashing against the house and fell dead face first on the porch. The boom of the buffalo rifle was heard a second later. Ian started to bring down his shotgun so Johansson drew and fired, hitting him high in the shoulder. Blake brought his rifle up and snapped a quick shot at Tom who was diving inside the door. Both Blake and Johansson dived from their horses as Les Palmer leveled his pistol and took aim at the sheriff. A forty five caliber slug from the buffalo rifle smashed into the post spraying splinters in his face causing him to jerk the trigger. The slug burned across Johansson's thigh. Les stood disoriented and stepped away from the post and a second later his head exploded. Gun fire erupted around the ranch. Lead was buzzing around like angry bees.

Blake jumped up, drew his knife and, leaping up the steps, he cut the rope holding Caleb, lowering him to the ground. Johansson pushed him away. "Go get Tom!" he yelled," I got the boy." The man on the water tower screamed as another slug from Hap bored its way into his chest. He fell from the tower dead.

Josh Dooley nodded to Dan as he made his way to a window of the bunkhouse. He ripped open the shutter and shot one of the ranch hands in the upper arm while Dan kicked in the front door leveling his pistol. The two remaining men turned and Dan said, "I wouldn't if I were you." They dropped their guns and held up their hands.

Gun fire became more sporadic and Mike Ventosa yelled from the loft, "Any man who doesn't want any part of this can leave, just chuck your guns out and show yourselves." The men who were alive threw out their guns and came out slowly. Three of them were wounded and being helped by the others.

Johansson had pushed Caleb under the porch and hobbled up the steps to help Blake. Caleb reached down and pulled the knife Blake had given him and stuck in a wood post blade up. He began sawing at the ropes holding his wrists. Inside Blake was moving cautiously through the house. Johansson came in and worked his way from room to room. Blake stopped and called out, "You see them?"

"Nope," said Iver darting into another room. As he poked his head around the corner he saw Ian with a crazed look in his eyes. Ducking back, Johansson yelled, "It's over Ian, c'mon out."

"He's my boy," Ian yelled back, "you'll not have him." He fired a shotgun blast into the wall where Johansson had been standing. Johansson fell into the door way and shot at Ian, hitting a kerosene lamp on the table. Fire erupted from the spraying oil and onto Ian's clothes. Ian screamed loudly and Johansson shot him again, finishing him. Back in the kitchen Tom hid as Blake poked his head around the doorway. Tom snapped a quick shot at him and ran for the backdoor. Bits of plaster stung Blake's eyes and he tried to clear them as he made his way to the door. Tom ran down the side of the house and spotted Caleb crawling out from under the porch. Tom grabbed a handful of his hair and stood him up. Jamming the barrel under his chin he yelled, "I got the boy, I'll kill him!"

The members of the posse gathered around all pointing guns at him. Tom backed up against the burning house. Smoke poured from the windows and the fire raged inside. Blake came around the corner holding his pistol and Johansson came out the front door. "Nowhere to go, Tom," he said calmly. "Turn the boy loose."

"I want a horse, or I'll blow his brains out," he cried.

Tom was too busy watching all the guns on him to see Caleb pull his knife. With all the strength he could muster he buried it deep in Tom's thigh and pulled up sharply. Tom dropped his pistol and grabbed his leg. Caleb jerked himself free and dove to one side. Bullets from nine guns slammed into him. The scales of justice tipped in favor of the righteous once more.

* * * * * *

Blake helped Caleb off the ground and examined his back. "We need to get the Doc to take a look at you."

Caleb shook his head and stared at the ground. "I'm sorry for w-what I said."

Blake patted him gently on the shoulder. "Aw, hell boy, you're talkin' to the king of saying stupid things."

They all moved away from the house because the heat was getting intense. Hap rode down the hill leading a couple of the horses. He handed Johansson back his rifle. "Shoots a little left," he said smiling.

"Damn, Hap, why didn' you tell me you shoot like that?" Avery blurted out.

"You was so busy bein' the boss, you never asked."

Johansson looked around. "Is anybody hurt, besides me that is?"

Al Conner rubbed the back of his head, "I got a knot on my head from the fella I was wrestlin' with. Lucky for me, Avery was there. He hit him with an axe handle when we were rollin' around."

Josh looked confused, "If you were rolling around, how did he score a good enough hit to knock you out?"

"Well that's how Avery said it happened," Al said thinking about it, "Hey what really happened, Avery?"

All eyes turned to Avery and he turned beet red. "Are you gonna worry 'bout nitpickin' details? I likes to think of end results," he blustered.

"You hit me, didn't you?" Al said as he started toward Avery.

"Now, Al," Avery said backing up. "You was rollin' 'round an…" He gave up and just ran.

They all laughed as they watched Al chase Avery around the barn and back again. Suddenly, the roof of the house caved in and sent ashes into the air.

Johansson wrapped his neckerchief around his thigh, stood and looked at the remaining ranch hands. "Well, I might as well get this over with." He limped over to where they were standing and said, "You men were defending your brand and I admire that, I'm truly sorry about your dead pards, but it had to be done. The only one I want is Jimmy Rocco; he needs to answer for his crimes."

"He was on the water tower when he got shot," the oldest of the bunch claimed.

"Blake, you knew what he looked like right?" the sheriff asked.

"Yup, I'll check him out," Blake said and headed for where the man fell.

"The rest of you can stay, if you want. I'll send the doc out to tend to your wounded. I'm guessin' the ranch falls to MacIntyre's daughters. Where are they?" Johansson asked.

"He sent them to Sweetwater last night," the older man replied.

"Send word to them and tell 'em what occurred," Johansson said with remorse. "I don't know what will happen, it's up to them."

Blake came back red faced. "It wasn't him."

Johansson glared at the man who lied to him. "Where is he, you lying bastard?"

The man hung his head. "He went to Sweetwater with the girls. We rode together; I don't want to see him swing."

"If I catch you lying to me again, you'll both swing," Johansson said in a deadly voice. He turned to his posse. "Go get the rest of the horses, and let's go home."

# CHAPTER 22

THREE weeks after the assault at the ranch, Blake was in his room getting ready for church. Any bruising he had was gone and he felt strong and healthy once again. Things had been quiet around town and he could hear freight wagons trundling up the street and the sounds of people going about their day.

Bonnie wasn't injured the night Tom attacked her. She seemed mostly back to normal, but she would still wake some nights screaming from nightmares. The doctor said they should pass with time. Blake hoped they would because she had been through so much.

Caleb suffered no lasting effects from his torture at the ranch. He was turning out to be a fine young man. His skills grew every day in the forge and he had developed strong arms and a broad back. His stutter all but disappeared that night, and now he carried himself like a man. Combine that with his natural good looks, blonde hair and sparkling blue eyes, he attracted many of the young ladies in town. Unfortunately for them, his heart belonged to Bonnie and hers to him.

Johansson's leg wound healed and he stayed on as sheriff of MacIntyre, along with Mike Ventosa as his deputy. The banker

Weatherby could see no reason to fire him, even though he defied him. Now that Tom MacIntyre was gone, his job was much less stressful. Johansson had the Federal Marshals issue a warrant for Jimmy Rocco's arrest, but he disappeared in Sweetwater and was headed toward Mexico, with money given to him by the MacIntyre twins, or so they heard.

Mary and Kate MacIntyre, upon hearing of their father and brother's deaths, disappeared with their servant, Jethro. The last anyone heard of them was a wire transfer of money to a bank in Baltimore. Weatherby would not elaborate on the details, but soon after, the ranch was being surveyed and sold off into smaller parcels. The herd and stock were sold and the ranch hands dispersed after being paid the hundred dollar bonus they were promised.

Percival Feathers robbed Blake of his award by the doctor for being the toughest man alive. Four of the five bullet wounds he suffered from that night did not do any serious damage. One of the bullets was lodged near his hip and caused him to walk with a limp using a sturdy cane. The doctor could not remove the bullet. He would carry it with him for the rest of his life. Percival hated using a cane, but Doc Baker assured him it would be temporary. While he recuperated, his disposition was grumpy and he snarled at every one who tried to help him ... except for his beloved Michelle, who doted on him fiercely. He had yet to return to the lumberyard or saloon, but her dress shop business was booming. With that, and some extra money from Blake that he quietly deposited in their account, he could fully heal before having to work again. Percival made good on his promise of tossing Caleb in the water trough, but Caleb taught his horse Rosie a new trick. When he sloshed his way out of the water he whistled and Rosie spun her hind quarters into the Big Man, returning the favor. That was the last time he dunked Caleb.

Blake made his way down the stairs and out the front door. The air had a faint snap to it as autumn was approaching. The day was clear and bright, with a comfortable breeze. Blake tipped his hat and greeted people as he passed them on the street. He felt the best he had in a long time. Taking out his watch, he checked the time and quickened his pace. Walking up the steps of the church he opened the door and walked up the aisle. Everyone he knew in town was there. When he strolled by Avery he was picking his nose and Hap slapped him. Blake smiled and, as he passed Josh and his family, he handed him his hat. He stepped up onto the altar next to Caleb and turned to Chrissy who was holding a bouquet of flowers. Her eyes shined under her veil and she smiled sweetly. "I'm glad to see you could make it," she said softly.

Father Grimm began their wedding ceremony.

Blake looked at her and winked, "A man died who was in a hurry once."

*THE END*

# ABOUT THE AUTHOR

**B**RYAN SALISBURY grew up in rural upstate New York. Yearning for a more adventurous life after high school, he joined the Navy, vowing never to return to the farm. Years later, after his Navy days, Bryan met his wife, Andrea. She had always dreamed of owning horses, and the craving for open spaces had been tugging at Bryan. He found himself returning to what he knew best … a life in the country. They worked hard together, along with their children, and their dream came to fruition.

The need to repair farm equipment inspired Bryan to take up blacksmithing, and he derived great joy from it. His skill eventually turned into a successful business (*www.forgeriesblacksmithing.com*). Having always been an avid reader with a particular fondness for Westerns, Bryan decided to draw on his life experiences which became the basis for writing this book.